Money Can't Buy Love

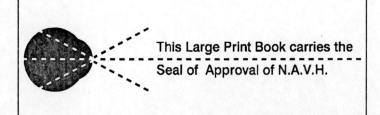

This Large Print Book carries the
Seal of Approval of N.A.V.H.

MONEY CAN'T BUY LOVE

CONNIE BRISCOE

THORNDIKE PRESS
A part of Gale, Cengage Learning

GALE
CENGAGE Learning˙

Detroit • New York • San Francisco • New Haven, Conn • Waterville, Maine • London

GALE
CENGAGE Learning

LIBRARY OF CONGRESS CATALOGING-IN-PUBLICATION DATA

Briscoe, Connie.
    Money cant buy love / by Connie Briscoe.
      p. cm. — (Thorndike Press large print African-American)
    ISBN-13: 978-1-4104-4184-3 (hardcover)
    ISBN-10: 1-4104-4184-9 (hardcover)
    1. Lottery winners—Fiction. 2. African American women—Fiction.
    3. African Americans—Fiction. 4. Man-woman relationships—Fiction.
    5. Large type books. I. Title. II. Title: Money cannot buy love.
    PS3552.R4894M66 2011b
    813'.54—dc22   2011031339

Published in 2011 by arrangement with Grand Central, a division of Hachette Book Group, Inc.

Printed in Mexico
1 2 3 4 5 6 7 15 14 13 12 11

MONEY CAN'T
BUY LOVE

PROLOGUE

Lenora stood above the polished chrome faucet in her master bathroom, razor blade held firmly in one hand, and thought of slashing her wrist. She had just stumbled through the most turbulent year of her life, filled with highs and lows, ups and downs. And now she was at the bottom of the pit. Her fiancé had dumped her, her girlfriends had deserted her, and her brand-new BMW had been repossessed. Last month she had to give up her prized photography studio because she could no longer pay the mortgage.

And just now she got the news she dreaded most of all. The bank was going to foreclose on her beautiful five-thousand-square-foot, million-dollar dream house. After months of receiving default notices and frantic calls to the lender begging for time and patience, she had been served with the papers that morning. Every time she thought her rotten life couldn't possibly get any nastier, it did.

Lenora's eyes shifted back and forth between the sharp edge of the blade and her bare brown wrist. *Go on, you pitiful bitch. Go on and end the misery right now. You're beyond feeling pain anyway at this point.*

She squinted and touched the blade to her skin. The sharp prick jolted her eyes open. She grimaced. Maybe this isn't the answer to my troubles after all, she thought. As bad as things had become, taking her life was something she could not bring herself to do. She was afraid to go on living, but she was terrified of death.

She lowered her arm and placed the razor blade on the countertop just as the front doorbell rang. "Shit!" she muttered as she pushed her dark unkempt shoulder-length hair back off her face and stared at her puffy eyes in the mirror. Who else would disturb her at 9:30 a.m. on a weekday morning? She had no job, no friends, no man. They had taken her car and her house. So now what the hell?

The bell chimed again, and Lenora dragged her bare feet across the ceramic tile floor to the carpeted master bedroom suite. Paws, her white-haired Lhasa apso, scurried from her doggy cot near the fireplace and bounded down the stairs as Lenora grabbed a dingy terry-cloth robe from the foot of her unmade bed.

Downstairs in the foyer, she peered through the glass on the double front doors to see a petite blond woman standing on the threshold. The woman's hair and jacket were damp from a steady, unrelenting rain that had been falling all morning, and she had an anxious expression on her thin face. Lenora knew instantly that this was another pesky reporter, and she was tempted to turn around and flee back up the stairs. But the woman had already seen Lenora, and her eyes pleaded to be allowed inside.

Lenora cracked the door open.

"Hi. Are you Lenora Stone?" came the woman's voice beneath the patter of rain on the pavement.

"Who's asking?"

"My name is Donna Blackburn. I'm a reporter with the *Baltimore View.* We're doing a roundup of people who won a million dollars or more in the Maryland Lottery over the past few years. A feature with the theme 'Where are they now?' " Donna held a business card in her outstretched hand.

"So I figured," Lenora said with impatience, pushing the card away. "You're the umpteenth reporter wanting to talk to me

9

since I won last year. Most of them had the decency to call first."

"Sorry, but I couldn't get through to you. I don't have your landline number and your cell is, um, discontinued."

That's when Lenora remembered that her cell phone service was disconnected a few days earlier; she hadn't paid that bill either. Still, she didn't feel like talking to any damn reporters. She was a photographer herself and had worked around a ton of them. She knew how persistent they could be. How they would dig into your personal stuff if you let your guard down for even a minute. Then they would go out and blab your business to the entire world.

"I've said all I have to say," Lenora said. "Go away."

"I won't take up much of your time," Donna pleaded. "You won five million dollars in the Maryland Lottery almost a year ago, and I've heard about some of your recent misfortunes."

"You and everyone else," Lenora said sarcastically.

"It would give you a chance to air things out if we talk."

"Sorry, I'm all fucking aired out." Lenora stepped back and reached for the doorknob.

"Sure you don't have just a few minutes?"

Donna asked as her eyes darted around the room behind Lenora. Lenora could tell that the reporter had noticed that the large foyer and living room were practically bare, with no furniture, no lamps, no memorabilia. Lenora had sold all of that in a futile attempt to stay afloat. The reporter's expression had changed from mild curiosity to eagerness as she suddenly sensed a much bigger story than the one she imagined when she knocked on the door.

"Yes, I'm sure," Lenora responded and hastily began to shut the door.

Donna stuck a damp shoe in the crack, and Lenora glared at her, ready to punch this interloper smack in the mouth. How dare she intrude so brazenly! Lenora knew that she might be about to lose the house, but right now it was still hers. "Bitch, who the hell do you think you are coming in —"

"I'll treat you to dinner," Donna blurted out. "Steak, seafood, pasta. The restaurant of your choice."

Lenora paused at the mention of free food at a real restaurant, not a quickie meal at McDonald's or a bag of stale chips in her bed. Lenora considered herself a bit of a foodie, so this was like promising drugs to a junkie. Lenora had a sneaking suspicion that the reporter somehow knew this, that she had discovered this tidbit in her research. She pulled her robe tighter around her bulging waistline and cracked the door wider.

"Legal Seafood in Baltimore," Lenora said, thinking of one of her favorite seafood restaurants. She could already taste the steamed littleneck clams.

"You got it," Donna said. "But you have to be open with me. Answer all my questions. We do the interview here first, then go to dinner later this evening."

Lenora glanced down at her bare feet on the cold slate floor of the foyer, the place where an antique Oriental carpet once lay, until she sold it on eBay last month. She was still tempted to turn the reporter down. Even a nice seafood dinner in Baltimore might not be enough to compensate for having to relive the most traumatic months of her thirty-eight-year life. She wanted to forget everything that had happened, not rehash it. She wanted to banish the lottery, Gerald, Ray, Alise, the house, and the studio from her mind forever. But the thought of staying alone inside these half-empty rooms just after getting a foreclosure notice was even more depressing.

Lenora opened the door. "Come on in. Find a chair and give me a minute to get decent." She needed to shower, something she had not done for a few days. There had been no need since she had not left the house or seen anyone.

"No problem," Donna said as she stepped eagerly through the doorway.

Fifteen minutes later, Lenora and Donna were seated across from each other in the kitchen, the dream kitchen Lenora knew she was going to lose soon. It had everything — travertine flooring and granite countertops, a Viking range and two sinks. They sat at the kitchen table, the only piece of furniture Lenora had left besides her bed, and nursed two mugs of hot instant coffee. A couple of months ago, Lenora sold her nine-hundred-dollar coffee and espresso machine on eBay for a fraction of what she'd paid for it, and she had learned to tolerate the microwave variety of coffee.

Lenora now saw the extravagant coffee-maker as one in a long series of greedy, foolish decisions that she had made over the past year after winning the lottery. Her ex-fiancé Gerald had warned her to slow down. "Five million dollars won't last forever with you spending like this," he said repeatedly. Lenora now wished she had listened to him about the money and a whole lot more.

"So, tell me what's happened with you since you won five million dollars in the lot-

13

tery," Donna said.

Lenora sighed. "Long story short, I fucked up everything, that's what happened." She twisted her lips. "But you don't want the short version. You want the whole sad story."

CHAPTER 1

One Year Earlier

Lenora's eyes opened and shot toward the clock. "Oh, no!" she yelled, springing up from the bed. She had done it again, slept straight through the alarm going off at seven a.m. on a workday. What was wrong with her?

Paws, the one-year-old Lhasa apso she had rescued from the dog pound a few months earlier, ran to the bed and wagged her tail in anticipation as Lenora tossed the covers aside. She gave Paws a quick pat, stuck her feet into slippers, and raced across the floor of her two-room condominium. Her boss was going to kill her for being late to work again, she thought as she entered the bathroom and sat on the toilet. Why was she having so much trouble getting out of bed these days? Late-night drinks with her boyfriend Gerald were no excuse.

She grabbed her toothbrush from the

holder and quickly applied toothpaste. There was a time when she would never have stayed out until *two* a.m. on a week-night. Her job had been too important to her to allow that. But she was starting to get supremely frustrated with work, especially with Dawna Delaney, the new managing editor at the *Baltimore Scene* magazine, and a woman whose middle name should be "evil."

So she found herself needing more time to wind down in the evening, more time to chill with her boyfriend or hang out with her girlfriends. Still, she had a mortgage on the condo and a gazillion other bills to pay. She definitely could not afford to do idiotic things like making her boss angry by repeatedly being tardy for work.

She slipped in and out of the shower in two minutes. She had no time for makeup other than a dash of lipstick. That was just as well. She hated putting the stuff on anyway. It was only because she was thirty-seven years old and starting to see a few lines around her mouth that she bothered at all. Some women craved jewelry; others makeup, shoes, or clothes. Her thing was freedom from all of that nonsense.

And food, she thought as she quickly grabbed a pair of baggy cargo pants from the closet, one of only a few pairs that still fit. She muttered obscenities as she squeezed them over her hips. One of these days she was going to admit to herself that her five foot, four inch frame was no longer a size six or even an eight and buy clothes that fit properly, she thought as she tugged at the zipper and squeezed the snap. This was why she avoided shopping as much as possible. She hated looking at her short, roundish figure in a mirror. People often told her she had a cute face but rarely commented on anything below the neck, unless it was to suggest that she needed to lose a few pounds.

Slacks or jeans were customary for her, and not just because of her weight. As a photographer for a city magazine, she needed the freedom to bend over, climb, kneel, or do whatever a photo shoot demanded without snagging some nice designer fabric on a nail or having to worry about anyone's trying to sneak a peek up her skirt.

Today she added a loose-fitting berry-colored top to disguise her bulges. Then she glanced at her watch and muttered more obscenities at the late hour as she grabbed her black camera bag off the chair near the small desk in the living area. Her morning

17

commute into Baltimore was at least a forty-minute drive during rush hour. She didn't have time for breakfast, not even a glass of juice, which was just as well, she thought, given that she should be on a diet anyway.

She ran to the door and was about to open it when she looked down and saw Paws staring up at her with those big brown puppy-dog eyes. "Dammit!" she said aloud. She had to walk the poor dog or Paws would pee all over the condo. Lenora dropped her camera bag on the couch and quickly put the leash on her dog. "C'mon, sweetie," she said as she opened the door. Paws followed happily as Lenora ran down the back stairs of the two-story building and across the parking lot to a grassy field.

"Hurry and do your thing, girl. You want me to be able to buy your dog food, don't you? That means I gotta get to work." Paws seemed to understand and quickly carried out her business. Then they both ran back up the stairs. Lenora dashed into the kitchen, filled Paws's water bowl and scooped some dry dog food into her dish, patted the pooch on her furry little head, and ran back out. In the parking lot, she slipped behind the wheel of her ten-year-old Honda just as her cell phone rang. She dug into the side pocket of her camera bag, pulled out the phone, and saw from the number that it was Dawna.

She agonized over whether to answer for a second, then tossed the phone onto the passenger seat next to the bag. She knew what Dawna wanted — to know why the hell she was already more than an hour late for work. Again. And frankly, Lenora didn't want to hear all the snapping and cussing, which for Dawna went with having her morning cup of coffee.

Lenora would take her licks when she got to the office. Dawna wouldn't fire her — at least Lenora didn't think so. Good photographers were hard to come by, and Dawna, who started at the *Baltimore Scene* only six months ago, was eager to make her mark at the magazine. Lenora had been there for seven years now and Dawna needed her. Yet Lenora realized that she couldn't continue to press her luck.

She turned the key in the ignition and the worst thing possible happened. The crappy car didn't start. It made some strange noises, sputtered pitifully, and then died. Lenora held her breath and tried again. Same thing. She smacked the steering wheel. She couldn't believe this was happening to her. One of these days she was going to win the lottery. Or get that boy-friend of hers to marry her. With two incomes, she wouldn't have to freak out about losing her job and her only source of income.

The cell phone rang, and Lenora could see that it was the boss calling again. It took every ounce of her willpower not to grab the blasted phone and fling it out the window. Instead, Lenora closed her eyes, took a deep breath, and turned the key again.

CHAPTER 2

"Yes!" Lenora yelled when the engine turned over. One day real soon she wasn't going to be so lucky. Her commute between Columbia, Maryland, and Baltimore was over twenty miles each way. The clunker was more than ten years old, and she had already cranked out a hundred thousand miles on it. But there wasn't a whole lot she could afford to do about that right now. The payment on the adjustable rate mortgage for her condo had recently increased, and the last thing Lenora wanted was to lose her very first home after living in it for barely four years.

The condo wasn't all that much, just one large living area with a separate kitchen and bathroom. But it was hers. The minute she saw the units going up near the mall, Lenora knew she had to have one. She barely qualified, but with a little creativity, the loan officer had managed to set her up with an adjustable rate mortgage that she could afford.

Then the monthly payments shot up, the economy crashed, and reality came knocking at the door. The magazine was struggling to hold on, and Lenora didn't get the raises she had expected over the past couple of years. It was a struggle to make her monthly payments. The worst was that she couldn't sell. Because of the recent crash in the housing market, she now owed more on the condo than its current value.

She pulled onto the highway, headed for the office in downtown Baltimore, and ran through possible stories for Dawna. By the time she pulled up in front of her building, she still hadn't come up with a decent reason for being so late. She had already used every excuse known to womankind, some of which were really creative. Like Paws vomiting all over her clothes just as she was about to walk out the door or waking up to discover that her boyfriend had accidentally taken her car keys home with him the night before.

She grabbed her camera bag and phone and ran into the building. She tapped her foot impatiently while waiting for the slowpoke elevator. "C'mon, c'mon," she muttered. The thing finally appeared, and she hopped on and pressed the button for the fourth floor, praying that it would not stop before it got there. No such luck. It ground to a halt at the second floor, and a silver-haired woman using a walker smiled and stepped in slowly. Naturally, Lenora thought, gritting her teeth and rolling her eyes upward. It never failed. Whenever she was rushing about, a slower driver got in front of her on the road or an elderly person dragged his or her feet onto the elevator.

Then Lenora mentally shook her head at herself. Why was she acting like such a bitch? Her tardiness certainly wasn't this woman's fault. Lenora put her hand out to hold the doors open as the woman settled in. "What floor?" Lenora asked.

"Third," the woman said, smiling in appreciation.

Lenora smiled back and pressed three. When the elevator stopped, Lenora patiently held the doors open as the woman got off. Then Lenora took a deep breath as the doors shut and the elevator climbed to the fourth floor. As soon as the doors opened again, she darted across the foyer and through the double glass doors of the entry to the *Baltimore Scene.* She was about to turn down the hallway toward her office when Jenna, the orange-haired, multi-tattooed receptionist sitting in the foyer, looked up from her paperback horror novel and beckoned with a black-polished fingernail.

"Dawna is looking for you," Jenna said. "She wants to see you, like, yesterday."

Lenora nodded and backtracked. She licked her forefinger and held it in the air, a signal that much of the staff used to get a reading of the boss's mood from Jenna.

"Hot," was all Jenna said before she jumped back into her novel. Lenora squared her shoulders and walked down the hallway toward Dawna's office. She had a good idea what was coming and it was going to be ugly.

Lenora approached the office, and Dawna looked up from her big glass desk, a scowl on her face. Lenora froze in the doorway. She was always amazed at how such a gorgeous woman — with a flawless tan complexion, beautiful hazel eyes, long dark hair, and a tall, slender size six figure — could make herself look so mean. Dawna reminded Lenora of Wilhelmina Slater and Cruella de Vil wrapped into one terrifying being.

"Sorry to be late," Lenora said as she inched toward the desk.

"Don't be fucking sorry," Dawna snapped.

"Just be on time. We've got a magazine to get out here. I can't have my key staff late all the damn time. Where the hell have you been?"

Lenora stood stiffly in front of the desk and swallowed hard. All the lies she had prepared were stuck in her throat. "Uh, my alarm never went off. Last night I had to go —"

Lenora paused as Dawna held up a hand adorned with thick gold rings. "Save the drama for your mama," Dawna said. "I'm running a business here. Do you think I care about your fucking alarm and what you did last night?"

Lenora swallowed harder.

"Whatever is going on in your personal life, I don't give a damn," Dawna continued. "Just come in here on time. That's all I ask. Do you think you can manage that?"

"Yes," Lenora said. "I can manage that." Sometimes she thought her single, over-worked boss just needed to get laid. Or to have some other kind of fun. All the woman did was work and yell at everybody all day long.

"I damn sure hope so, Lenora," Dawna said firmly. "This lateness has gone on too long. Don't make me have to fire your ass. I will, you know. If you weren't so damn good at what you do, I would have fired you a long time ago."

Lenora bit her bottom lip and broke out into a sweat. That was the first time Dawna had used the word "fire," and it made Lenora nervous. "It . . . it won't happen again. I'll make —"

"Here, take this," Dawna snapped before Lenora could finish. Lenora eased her camera bag onto the floor and took the slips of paper from Dawna.

"The address is for a park-like setting in front of a new luxury condo on the waterfront. You're going to see Raymond Shearer, a young hot landscaper in the area. We're planning to run a feature on his work in the August issue. The other slip is the shot list. We want him and his crew getting in and out of their pickup trucks, digging holes, trimming trees. All that good stuff. Now hurry. He was expecting you at the site an hour ago, and I need those shots tomorrow morning for the layout. We go to print next week."

Lenora knew this meant she would likely be working late tonight reviewing and organizing the photographs on her computer. And that meant she'd have to cancel her dinner date with Gerald. She had planned to shop and cook a big meal for him, one that she saw prepared on her favorite cooking show, *Down Home with the Neelys,* on the Food Network. Spicy crab cakes, gazpacho salad, and ice cream with an orange liqueur flambé. This menu wasn't exactly diet food, but the way Gerald had smacked his lips in anticipation when she cited the menu had convinced her to skip the diet for one night. Now he was going to have to wait and her diet was back on. Frustrating, but what could she do?

She placed the paper in a side pocket of her camera bag. "Should I focus on the landscaper and his crew or the grounds around the project he's working on? I ask because if it's a new building —"

"Didn't I just say he was a hot young landscaper? Of course it's about him. But get photos of the grounds, too. And the crew! All of it! Now, scram! Go do your job and get the hell out of my office. I have a million things to do." Dawna shooed Lenora out the door. Lenora bent down and quickly grabbed her camera bag, all too happy to oblige.

She went to her office to retrieve a couple of extra lenses and filters that were good for close-ups of flowers and plants then headed back down to the parking lot. She hated rushing about, preferring to talk to the writer of the piece and to plan her shots before going on location. But that wasn't how it worked with this new managing editor, although she was partly to blame for being late.

Lenora just hoped her lousy car would be kind to her. Her job likely depended on its cooperation. She hopped in and hugged the steering wheel for a second, crossed herself and said a silent prayer, and turned the key in the ignition. The engine started right up. "Yes!" she said aloud, pumping her fist in the air. She pulled away from the building and headed toward the waterfront.

CHAPTER 3

It was impossible to find the luxury condominium on the waterfront, even using the
trusty portable GPS sitting on the dashboard. Lenora drove around and around
until she realized that Dawna had likely
given her the wrong address. She finally
pulled into a filling station and asked for
directions.

An hour after leaving the office, she pulled
into a parking lot on the side of the condominium and spotted a crew working on a
magnificently landscaped hillside. They
were smoothing mulch around the shrubbery and flower beds near a fountain. A few
guys toted tools and wheelbarrows back to
pickup trucks. As Lenora stood for moment
taking the scene in, she suddenly realized
with horror that the crew was actually wrapping things up.

She dashed around to the passenger side
of her car, removed her Nikon from the

camera bag, and draped it around her neck. Then she gathered the bag from the seat, slung it over her shoulder, and scanned the scene looking for Raymond Shearer. She saw some jeans-clad men loading gear into trucks and tried to figure out which one was Raymond. She had imagined that someone with the name Raymond Shearer would be white, but most of these men were Hispanic.

She was about to head toward the fountain when she spotted a black man, probably in his late twenties, crossing the parking lot. He was lugging a sack of mulch and wearing blue jeans and work boots. He signaled for one of the workers near the trucks to get another sack from the base of the fountain and follow him to the truck.

Maybe that's Raymond, Lenora thought, and she walked toward the trucks. A couple of the guys stared at her as she approached, and you would have thought the space shuttle had just landed in the parking lot. Evidently a woman in their midst was unusual. Lenora shrugged it off. Such attention was an occupational hazard when she was out taking photos for her job. Guys on construction sites would stop and stare at anything with boobs, even a woman as casual and undone up as she was at that moment.

"Excuse me," she said to one of the guys. "Which one of you is Raymond Shearer?"

He pointed to the black man dumping a sack onto the truck bed. Lenora approached. "Hi," she said, holding out her business card. "I'm Lenora Stone from the *Baltimore Scene* magazine. I'm here to get a few shots of you all while you work, for the feature we're doing on you."

Raymond didn't even bother to look at her. He continued to stack bags of mulch on the truck bed as his workers brought them to him. Even from the side, Lenora could see that the expression on the young man's face was none too pleased.

"I'm afraid you blew it, Miss Stone," he said icily. "You were supposed to be here two hours ago. We have to move on to the next job now."

"Oh, gosh," she said. "My boss gave me the wrong address. That's why I'm so late." Partly true at least, Lenora thought.

He paused and turned to stare directly at Lenora and her stomach flipped. Dawna had described Raymond as a hot young landscaper, meaning much in demand for his work. Now Lenora could see that the "hot" could also apply to his looks. Raymond was heart-stoppingly handsome, with chiseled chocolate features and a perfect build — not too bulky, not too thin. It was a physique borne of hard outdoor work, not from spending a lot of time with machines in a gym.

"You trying to tell me that you been wandering around looking for us for more than two hours?" Raymond's voice was so full of agitation and doubt that Lenora quickly forgot how attractive he was. All she could think of was defending herself and getting some shots for the magazine.

"You're right, not exactly," she said. "I got a late start. But, um, can you give me maybe twenty minutes of your time? All I need to get is —"

Raymond shook his head adamantly. "That's not happening," he said, interrupting her. "We can't just run back over to the fountain and pose for you. We'd have to lug all this equipment back up there. No way, sweetheart."

"I'm not your sweetheart," Lenora muttered, ticked off at his stubbornness.

"Excuse me?" he asked.

"Nothing." She decided to keep her thoughts to herself. She was already on his bad side. Her pride would have to take a backseat for now, in the interests of her job. "You don't have to take all of your things back over there, just —"

Raymond held a hand up in her face. "Sorry. Maybe you didn't hear me right the first time so I'll repeat. Not happening. I'm a busy man. I don't have that kinda time."

What an arrogant prick, Lenora thought as she lowered the camera bag from her shoulder to the pavement in agonizing defeat. He might be drop-dead gorgeous, but he was also an asshole. "Do you have to be so damn difficult?" she countered as she placed her hands on her hips. "You ought to be glad someone wants to feature you and your work."

"Come again?" he said, blinking with surprise at her sudden change of tone.

Lenora shifted heavily from one foot to the other. Now where the hell did that outburst come from? Was she trying to ruin any smidgen of a chance she might have with him? Had she forgotten that her boss had threatened to fire her if she kept screwing up?

"Sorry," she said, tightening her lips. "It's been a rough morning."

"Tell me about it," he said curtly as he opened the door to his truck.

"Do you mind telling me where you're headed next?" she asked timidly.

He shook his head at her in disbelief. "You don't take no for an answer, do you, Ms.

Stone?" She could see him turning her question over in his mind. "The Moss Building over by Johns Hopkins," he finally said. "It's not a nice location on the waterfront like this one here, but they need some landscaping out in back of the building."

Lenora nodded. It didn't sound nearly as attractive a site as this, but she didn't have much choice at this point. She had to get some images of Raymond and his crew on this camera. "I'll find it. Mind if I meet you there and get a few shots? I promise not to take long and I'll stay out of your way."

Raymond smiled reluctantly. "Normally I'd say no. But I'm starting to take pity on you, you seem so desperate. Meet us over there and we'll see if the owners will give you the okay, but I can't promise you nothing."

Lenora cleared her throat and resisted the urge to say something sarcastic. She didn't need a lecture or pity. But she had screwed up badly with him, not to mention her boss. "I appreciate it."

Raymond nodded. "Sure thing. Just don't get too excited. You got to get permission, and there's a good chance they won't give it to you on such short notice."

She wanted to tell him that she realized all of that. She had done this kind of thing countless times before. Instead, she quietly made her way back to her car.

As fine as Raymond was, he was annoying as hell. Like a lot of real attractive men, he was not only arrogant but cocky as well. Thank goodness her boyfriend Gerald was more the intellectual type. Some would consider him geeky. Gerald wasn't strikingly handsome like Raymond, but he was pleasing enough to the eye and clean-cut, preferring suits and open-collared shirts.

She picked her cell phone out of the side pocket of her camera bag and dialed Gerald's number. She needed to let him know that she would not be able to cook for him that evening since she would likely have to work late. She and Gerald had dated now for nearly three years, and Lenora was more than ready to take the relationship to the next level. She just needed to convince Gerald that it was time. She hadn't pressed him to commit up to now. But the big four-zero was on the horizon, and she was starting to think that she needed to insist that it was time for them to jump the broom.

Almost all of her girlfriends were hitched or at least had been at one time. Her close college girlfriend Alise was married to a dentist and had children in high school. And even though her old college roommate

Monica was single now, she had been married once. Lenora was one of the few who had never walked down the aisle.

Alise kept telling Lenora not to waste another year with Gerald. If he wasn't ready to get married after all this time, Lenora needed to move on. But Lenora didn't want to give up on Gerald. She loved him and knew that he loved her. He had a little commitment phobia, but Lenora was sure it was temporary. He worked as an accountant at a public relations firm that he started with two partners. The firm had been doing very well, with clients in Maryland and Washington, D.C., until the recent economic downturn. Now it was struggling, and Gerald and his partners had to put in more and more hours to keep the business afloat. He said he wanted to wait until the business was more secure before taking their relationship to the next level, and Lenora believed him.

Besides, she would have a hard time finding anyone better than Gerald. A man as good-looking or exciting as Raymond, for example, would never look at her romantically. She wasn't beautiful or rich or famous. What she lacked in looks she thought she made up for in personality, but she wasn't going to kid herself that she was a super catch. She figured she was lucky to have Gerald, and she intended to hold on to him.

As soon as she pulled up into the rear parking lot of the Moss Building, Lenora knew she was in trouble. It was in a rough neighborhood of Baltimore and not nearly as photogenic as the fountains and gardens near the waterfront. In fact, the place looked downright depressing, with overgrown shrubbery, grass nearly a foot tall, and weeds sprouting everywhere. Still, she exited the car, her Nikon poised and ready to shoot as Raymond and his crew began to climb out of their trucks. The minute she put the viewfinder up to her eye, Raymond lifted a hand and walked toward her.

"Hold up," he said impatiently. "I think you need to get permission first." Lenora lowered the camera. "And good to see you again, too, Raymond," she said sarcastically. "Nice day, isn't it?"

"I just want to be sure we do this right." He paused in front of her and placed his hands firmly on his hips, daring her to take a shot.

"You don't have to freak out," she said. "I'm going to get permission in a minute. I'm just taking some test shots first to get a feel for the lighting."

She put the camera back up to her eye, and he reached up and covered the lens with his palm. "Test shot or whatever. You still need to get permission first. I don't want to jeopardize my work around here."

The nerve of this guy, Lenora thought as she lowered the camera once again. She stared at him angrily.

"Look, we do this the right way or we don't do it at all," he said.

"I think I know how to do my job," she snapped.

"I'm beginning to wonder," he snarled.

She abruptly threw her camera over her shoulder with the strap. What a complete asshole, she thought. But the last thing she wanted was to get into a full-blown argument with a subject, especially one she had already messed up badly with. "Fine," she said. "Where do I go to get permission? Who do I talk to?"

"The building manager," he said. "Dude named Steve Odell. He's in Room 199 right off the back entrance there."

"Be right back." She marched off in the direction he'd indicated.

"Sure. And I need to see something in writing from him before you start," Raymond shouted after her as he and his work crew began to remove tools and equipment from the trucks.

"Pompous bastard," Lenora cursed under her breath and made her way up the path toward the building's rear entrance. As she approached the back door, a balding, middle-aged man in slacks and a wrinkled cotton shirt exited a side door and walked toward Raymond. Lenora paused, wondering if that could be the building manager. She looked toward Raymond and noticed that he was signaling for her to return to the parking lot.

As she approached the men, Steve handed Raymond a paper to sign, and then Raymond introduced her to Steve. They shook hands and Lenora handed him her business card and explained why she was there. "It shouldn't take much time to get what I need," she said. "Thirty minutes to an hour at the most. I want to . . ."

Lenora paused in midsentence when Steve started to shake his head vehemently. "Out of the question," Steve said. "I doubt the new owners would want anyone taking pictures of the grounds in this deplorable state. In fact I'm sure they wouldn't."

"Let me explain how this would work," Lenora said. "I can take before shots now and return later for the after shots. So there will also be some photographs of the grounds after Raymond's work is completed. We'll show how Raymond transforms the property."

Steve was still shaking his head. "Doesn't matter. I have to get permission from the owners first."

"How soon can you do that?" Lenora asked.

Steve sputtered. "Not now, that's for sure. I'm busy with other things."

Lenora took out her cell phone. "If you give me the name and number of the owner, I can call."

Raymond folded his arms and watched in fascination. Lenora knew she was acting desperate, but now she *was* desperate.

"He's a busy man, too," Steve protested.

"Oh, I'm sure he is, but it's worth a try," she said. "We might all be surprised by the outcome. What harm can come of it?"

"She doesn't take no for an answer," Raymond explained to the building manager.

"Not when I really want something," Lenora added.

"Well, I'm afraid you're gonna have to take no this time," Steve said. "The owner's out of the country traveling around Europe with his family, so he isn't easy to reach. And I'm not willing to bother him for this." With that, Steve waved at Raymond and walked back toward the building.

"But can I just get a few close-ups today?" Lenora pleaded, following Steve. "We won't use them unless you get permission first. And I promise that you won't see much of the grounds, only . . ."

Steve waved her off, entered the building, and closed the door firmly behind him.

Lenora stamped her foot. So aggravating! It was obviously time to give up. She hated to do that, but this was like trying to ram through a brick wall. She turned back toward Raymond and the parking lot.

"Guess I know when I'm licked," she said with disappointment in her voice.

Raymond smiled thinly at her as he pulled a couple of shovels off the truck. "Them's the breaks some days," he said, his voice sounding genuinely sympathetic for the first time that morning. "You gave it your best shot."

Lenora was so bitter she could barely speak. She marched toward her car, opened the passenger-side door, and tossed her camera equipment inside. Then she made her way to the driver's side.

"I admire your tenacity," Raymond called after her. "For what it's worth."

Lenora was a bit startled to hear him use a word like "tenacity." He was obviously no dummy, even if he worked with his hands, and she shouldn't have been so quick to judge him otherwise. But her thoughts were already far away from Raymond and his crew as she climbed into the car, started the engine, and pulled off. How the hell was she going to explain this fiasco to her boss?

CHAPTER 4

"What the hell did you just say?"

Lenora cleared her throat as she stood in front of Dawna's desk. Was Dawna going to make her tell the humiliating story all over again?

"I wasn't able to get any photographs," Lenora repeated firmly. She was not going to let this woman scare her. Not much anyway.

"Fuck!" Dawna jumped up from her executive chair, revealing a beautiful designer suit, and banged a stack of papers on her desk with her fist. Her gold bracelets jingled in fury.

Lenora shifted her weight from one foot to the other. "By the time I pulled up to the condo unit, Raymond Shearer and his crew were leaving." She didn't think this was the time to mention that it was partly Dawna's fault for giving her the wrong address. Dawna would still find a way to place the blame on Lenora.

"Fuck!" the boss repeated. "Did he say where his next job was?"

"I followed them to the next job over near Johns Hopkins, but the manager wouldn't allow me to photograph the site without permission from the owner, who he claimed was out of the country. It's probably just as well, the site was in terrible shape, nothing like the location near the waterfront. We would have to do a before-and-after piece, which I know you weren't planning on."

Dawna flopped back down in her chair and rested her head in both hands. Then she glowered up at Lenora. "You do realize that this means I'll probably have to hold the story and use some lame filler for August instead?"

Lenora squirmed. "I know."

"If you weren't my best fucking photographer I would fire your ass right this minute," Dawna said between clenched teeth. "If this kind of crap ever happens again, I swear I will. You hear me?"

Lenora nodded with understanding. She knew when to keep her mouth shut.

"Now get the hell out of my office."

Lenora left, ignoring the looks of pity from Jenna and the secretaries who sat outside Dawna's office. They had obviously overheard every loud word of the exchange. It served her right for being late to work, Lenora thought, head lowered as she made her way to her own office. She deserved to be chewed out.

Several hours later, Lenora sat on a stool, nursing a glass of red wine and nibbling on some nuts at the sports bar on the ground floor of the building where the *Baltimore Scene* was located, a few blocks from Baltimore's Inner Harbor. The only good thing to come out of her horrible workday was that she didn't have to work late and could hook up with Gerald after work. She was too depressed to shop and cook as they originally planned. So they decided to meet at the sports bar and then go somewhere else for dinner.

She lifted her head to see above the crowd of twenty-, thirty-, and forty-somethings and scanned the area near the entrance to see if Gerald had arrived. Her man had much going for him. Smart and ambitious, he owned his own business. But sometimes he could be downright inconsiderate. Like now, keeping her waiting for more than twenty minutes. Especially on a day like this, when it felt as if she'd been dragged through the coals.

Recently he seemed to be late more and more often. Or worse, he had to postpone altogether. That was why she often offered to cook. Besides the fact that she really got her kicks out of it, when she cooked at her place it didn't matter as much if Gerald was late. She could read or watch television while she waited and kept the food warm. She realized that Gerald and his partners were trying to grow a business, which took a lot of time and hard work. She tried to be patient and understanding. Still, she wished he would put her first more often.

She tapped her fingers on the bar for a few seconds, then decided to go to the restroom to reapply her lipstick. She needed to do something besides warm a bar stool with her butt. She picked up her glass of wine and entered the ladies' room. She leaned toward the mirror and applied a rose shade to her lips, then rubbed them together. She was trying to decide if the lipstick was too heavy when a statuesque woman wearing a formfitting black dress came out of a stall and stopped to wash her hands. The woman carefully studied her reflection in the mirror, tugged at her clothes, primped her long dark hair, and left.

Lenora shook her head with disbelief. She could never figure out why pretty women fussed so much with their looks. That woman's hair was silky smooth, her skin flawless, and her shape to die for. She sort of reminded Lenora of Dawna. Lenora would give anything to look like that instead of always trying to lose thirty or so pounds while her clothing size got bigger and bigger.

She yanked her berry-colored top down over her hips and frowned at her reflection in the mirror. The top had felt a little more snug than usual when she put it on this morning, and that always made her antsy. She had been chubby as a child. In her mid-twenties, she managed to drop several pounds and get down to a size six, only to put even more weight back on. She later lost and gained weight again. At her heaviest, she was more than fifty pounds over-weight.

Just before she met Gerald, she had dropped about twenty pounds. Gerald hadn't known her when she weighed the most, but whenever he came across a photo-graph of her from that period, he pleaded with her never to let that happen again. He said he liked his women full figured but not obese. She was lucky Gerald didn't mind a few extra pounds, but if she wasn't careful about her weight, even he would come to think she was too fat.

She resolved to step up her diet immediately. Absolutely no pasta, no bread, no rice. Nothing white for a few weeks or until this berry-colored top fit her better. And no excuses.

She left the bathroom and walked quickly back toward the bar. She didn't want Gerald to come in and think she wasn't there. He was so busy with work these days, she wasn't sure how long he would wait around for her.

She immediately spotted him near the entrance, glancing around the room. She waved, and when he looked in her direction she pointed toward the bar area. They met at a small round table with two stools, and he kissed her gently on the lips. She loved the way his thick mustache tickled her mouth. They were about the same height, which was one reason why Lenora almost never wore heels.

He removed his suit jacket to reveal a crisp white cotton shirt that had become a little wrinkled from the day's work. He draped the jacket across the back of the stool. "I see you've already started to partake," he said, eying her glass of wine through his round spectacles. "Need a refill?"

"No, this is plenty," Lenora said. "You go

ahead and get something for yourself." She smiled as Gerald walked off toward the bartender. She was lucky to have him. Many women her age had no man at all, since by the time a woman hit her late thirties, almost all the good brothers were taken, gay, or playas who didn't want to settle down.

He came back shortly, placed his beer and glass on the table, and sat down. "Sorry to be so late getting here. Got held up at the office with a new client. And traffic was a bear."

She nodded with a smile, even though it was the same tune she'd heard many times before. His tardiness used to really upset her, but she had learned to let it go. There was no point getting all worked up since he wasn't going to change. His work was important to him, would always be so. If she wanted him by her side, she had to accept that and at least pretend to understand.

"How's work going?" she asked.

He pushed his dark glasses up on his caramel-toned nose. "Times are still very rough with this economy. I don't need to tell you that. People are hurting, and they're always looking to save a buck and trying to get you to lower your fees. The quandary is that if you lower your fees too much, it becomes impossible to make ends meet and stay afloat. It's a tough situation all around, unfortunately."

"You can't blame clients for wanting to save money," Lenora said, shrugging. "There are probably plenty of people who will do the work for less now."

"You sound like my partner," Gerald said. "He wants us to cut our fees, but I'm dead set against it. I look at the finances all day long." He held his hand out and rubbed his thumb across his fingers. "I know what we're worth."

"Could you lower them temporarily, until the economy comes back?"

Gerald shook his head. "You get what you pay for even in this dire economy. Anyone who cuts their fees now is also cutting back on their services. You can count on it. Or else they're losing money and won't be in business for long. I'm not in this business to lose money or to provide substandard service."

Lenora nodded. It was hard to disagree with Gerald when he was talking about his firm — his baby. "I hear you."

"Anyway, I didn't come to talk business with you." Gerald smiled at her. "I want to get away from all that when I'm with my lady. How are things going with you?"

"Where do I start?" Lenora said with a half smile. "I overslept this morning and was late for work."

"Not again. Don't tell me. Dawna cursed you out till your ears felt like they would come off. Right?"

Lenora nodded. "Of course. And I missed an important photo shoot with a new local landscaper. When I go in tomorrow, she wants to see me first thing. Probably to curse me out again."

"I'm feeling kind of guilty for keeping you up listening to jazz and drinking so late last night."

"Don't," Lenora said. "It's nobody's fault but my own. You got in bed later than I did 'cause you had to drive home after you dropped me off at my condo. And you got to work on time."

He nodded. "You can't really blame Dawna. I'd be pissed too if an employee of mine was late to work and missed an assignment."

"I agree, but she doesn't have to be so nasty about it. Her mouth is disgusting. Fortunately, I'm good at what I do. She needs me."

"That you are."

"I swear, one of these days I'm going to find another job. I'm tired of all the abuse she dishes out."

He chuckled. "You always say that, yet you stay."

"I know. I like working for the magazine. I just hate my boss. And it's not like I can afford to quit until I find something else, with a mortgage and all the bills I have."

"Whatever you do, don't quit your job before you find another one," Gerald warned her. "It could be months or years before you find anything else. Consider yourself lucky to be employed in this economy."

"I'll drink to that," she said and they clanked their glasses together. "Now like you, I don't care to spend another minute discussing my job. I need to relax, and talking about Cruella makes me tense."

He patted her knee. "I'm here for you whenever you want to talk, you know that."

She smiled and nodded her thanks.

"How's the pooch doing?" he asked. "Have you gotten used to getting up earlier to walk her every morning yet?"

Lenora smiled at the thought of Paws. "I'll probably never get completely used to it, but it's worth it. She's cute as a button. But she needs a lot of attention. I almost forgot to walk her this morning when I was late. I was hoping we could get dinner in Columbia tonight, somewhere near my place instead of out here in Baltimore, so I can stop and feed her."

"Actually, dinner will have to wait for another day," he said.

"What? Come on, Gerald. We have plans."

"I know. But I have to get back to the office in a few. We're meeting a client for dinner." Lenora's shoulders slumped. "Oh, Gerald."

"It can't be helped. The economy has been murder on the business. When funds are low, businesses are less likely to want a big ad campaign or to spend top dollar on one. That means we get to spend a lot more time wooing clients."

She sighed with regret. Now it looked like she would have to eat alone.

"We can hook up Friday after work for dinner," Gerald added, seeing the look of disappointment on her face. "Maybe even catch a movie. It's been a while since we did that."

Whenever he broke their plans like this, it was hard not to think back to the affair he'd had with a former coworker two years ago, even though she knew that was long past. "I hear you. I'm still disappointed."

"But one of the things that attracted you to me was my ambition, right? I'm just try-

53

ing to get paid around here. I'll make it up to you Friday night, promise. This is important or I wouldn't change our dinner plans. You know that."

She forced a smile. If she was going to be with this man, she had to trust and support him. "Is this a big client?"

He nodded. "Big enough. He's trying to back out of our oral deal just before signing. We have to persuade him that it's still worth his time and money."

"I hope you work things out with him."

"Thanks," he said, squeezing her hand over the table. "That's what I like to hear."

She smiled at him coyly. "Maybe if you close this deal, we can set a date." She sipped her wine and glanced at him out the corner of her eye.

"Date?" he said teasingly. He took a big gulp of his beer. "What date is that?"

She slugged him playfully on the upper arm. "You know what I'm talking about. You're always saying you need to make more money before we can get married. You need more clients, more this, more that."

"Uh-huh."

"So make sure y'all work hard tonight and get that deal in writing," she said. "So we can set a wedding date."

"Well, I'm not so positive that —"

54

"C'mon, Gerald. We've been dating for three years now. Most people get married way before that. You love me, right?"

"You know I do," he said. "And I want to get married — you know that, too. But marriage is a huge step. I want to be sure the business is on solid ground before we take that step. We should be close to being able to buy a house before we get married. You know how high prices are in this area. They're still kind of high, even after the crash."

"You could move into my condo for now, and you'd be closer to work, too. The drive from Columbia to Baltimore is much shorter than the drive from Silver Spring to Baltimore."

He shook his head. "Your place is small. We would get on each other's nerves living there seven days a week."

"If we wait much longer, I won't be able to have children," Lenora said pointedly. "Do you ever think about that?"

"Of course," he said. "You remind me constantly."

"We can save together if we live together. That's what couples do, you know?"

"It will all happen in good time." He stood and kissed her lightly on the forehead. "I've got to go."

"Yeah, yeah. You always have to run off when we talk about this."

"Yep, I'm making my escape before you drown me in this marriage thing," he teased.

Marriage thing? Lenora didn't like the sound of that but figured she had pushed him enough for one day. She didn't want to scare him off.

She smiled. "I understand how important your work is to you. Really, I do."

"Good," he said. He kissed her again, on the cheek this time, and she smiled at the touch of his mustache brushing against her skin. "Don't forget to make reservations someplace nice for Friday night," he continued. "And pick out a movie. I'll call you tonight when I get home."

"I'll be waiting." She paused. "But you already knew that." She took one more sip of her wine as she watched him head toward the exit. She hoped he would turn and wave once more before he walked out the door, but he didn't.

Sometimes she thought she shouldn't be so willing to wait on this man.

CHAPTER 5

Lenora decided to stop at a convenience store on the way home from work and pick up a lottery ticket or two. Maybe she'd have better luck gambling than she was having with her love life. Or her life, period, for that matter, since she'd had a terrible day at the office as well.

She had been playing the Maryland Lottery off and on for years now and had tried everything from the Mega Millions to Multi-Match and Scratch-Offs, but had yet to win more than a few bucks. She knew she had little hope of ever winning big money in one of these things. She'd be thrilled to win just a few thousand to help with the mortgage and other bills.

And she could use a few extra bucks to buy herself a new car, she thought as she stepped out of her Honda at the store. Several weeks ago the mechanic had told her that the car needed work she couldn't afford. Transmission, battery, belts. One of these days the thing was going to refuse to start at all. Lenora just hoped she wasn't trying to reach a big assignment and under threat of getting canned by Dawna when it died on her.

Gerald thought the tickets were a foolish waste of her hard-earned money. Whenever she mentioned buying one, he cited the minute odds of winning and rattled off a bunch of arcane figures to her. That was to be expected, she figured. He was an accountant and watched every penny he spent carefully. Accountants also thought everything in life could be explained by numbers. She realized that the chances of winning big were slim to none, but they were nonexistent if you didn't bother to play at all.

Today she decided to play Pick 3 and Pick 4 and asked the cashier for Quick Pick, to allow the lottery computer to select numbers randomly for her. She never bet more than a few dollars. That way in her mind she wasn't blowing a ton of money, yet was still giving herself a chance to win.

Once back at home, she dumped the tickets and the mail on her desk. She didn't even bother to look through the mail. Most of it was overdue bills, and she wasn't in the mood to torture herself.

Paws was yapping and hopping around her feet, wanting to go out, but she noticed the message light flashing on the kitchen wall phone and pressed the button to flip through the caller ID. "And why did I do that?" she asked herself as the name and number showed up. Just as she had dreaded, the bill collector who was nagging her about her three-thousand-dollar Macy's credit card bill had called twice about payment for the furniture and clothing she had charged.

Lenora knew she should call him back to let him know that she finally dropped a check in the mail on Saturday morning. Although it wasn't nearly as much as he wanted her to send, it was something. But she hated talking to the man. He always made her feel so guilty no matter what she told him she was doing to try to make ends meet. He didn't care that she had to juggle her payments to make sure her mortgage and utilities got paid every month. So he could just wait until she got back from walking Paws. Besides, she had noticed that the later she called him, the less likely he was to answer his phone and she could simply leave a message.

She took Paws out for a quick trip around the grounds of the building, then returned and fed her. She picked up the phone and dialed the bill collector's number, hoping that his machine would come on and she would not have to talk to him directly. For the first time that day, luck was on her side. She left a brief message explaining that he should have a payment from her in a day or two.

Mindful of her diet promises to herself, instead of a Neely meal, she took the time to chop up the ingredients for an elaborate tossed salad with lettuce, tomato, green peppers, and spring onion. She tossed in some black olives and a few slices of chicken from a previous dinner. Finally she added a couple of tablespoons of her homemade low-fat salad dressing.

She poured herself a cup of green tea and sat down with her salad in front of the tube to watch a recording of one of her favorite travel shows, *Anthony Bourdain: No Reservations.* She loved the varied destinations that the chef traveled to, from Baltimore to Bangkok, and the exotic food and cultures featured. Tony was controversial, and people seemed to love him or hate him. Lenora got a kick out of his irreverent comments and his wit. He was the perfect companion when she was at home alone and in a funky mood.

After she finished eating she patted the couch, and Paws hopped up and sat beside her. She was so glad she had gotten her from the shelter. Paws took some of the sting off her lonely nights.

At seven-thirty, she changed into cotton pajamas, slid beneath the bedcovers with a big red apple, plumped the pillow beneath her head, and flipped on the television to wait for the evening lottery drawings.

Gerald hadn't called yet, even though he said that he would phone when he got off from work. She thought about attempting to reach him, but she was trying hard not to pester him or to act possessive. That was the deal they had reached shortly after he cheated on her two years ago. He had promised to be honest with her if he ever thought of straying, and she had promised to make every effort not to crowd him. They had both agreed that it was the only way the relationship would work.

Fifteen minutes later, she was tearing up her losing lottery picks and tossing them into the wastebasket. And wondering why Gerald still hadn't called. She yanked the phone up from the nightstand and dialed his cell phone number. It rang and rang until the answering machine came on. She hung up in frustration without leaving a message. What was the big deal? All he had to do was pick up the phone and talk to her for a few minutes. What was he doing that he couldn't find a few minutes to spare?

She walked to the kitchen in her bare feet and opened the freezer door. She stared at the half-gallon container of Edy's Grand Real Strawberry ice cream for a few seconds, then grabbed it and slammed the freezer door shut. She poured a generous amount of Baileys Irish Cream over the ice cream. This would help her sleep. A salad and an apple were no solution to an empty life.

Ten minutes later she tossed the empty ice cream container into the trash and climbed back into her bed. She turned off the lamp and pulled the covers high up over her shoulders. One of these days her luck with men and money was going to change for the better. She just hoped it happened before she became a fat, gray-haired lady on the brink of death.

CHAPTER 6

When the alarm went off that morning, Lenora realized that Gerald had never bothered to call the night before as promised. For three nights in a row, the same thing. No call. He would probably phone around noon from work and apologize, as usual, but it was still annoying as hell to wait around all evening for a call that never came. He should just say up front if he wasn't going to call.

She sat up in bed and petted Paws while debating whether to call Gerald before getting dressed for work but finally decided against it. She didn't want to risk being late to the office again, not after her tardiness earlier this week had cost the magazine a feature with a landscaper and probably nearly cost her her job.

By the time she pulled into the parking lot at the *Baltimore Scene,* she had changed her mind. During the long drive between

Columbia and Baltimore, she worked herself into a mini-frenzy, wondering why Gerald had become so undependable. Promising to call and not following through had become a pattern with him of late, and Lenora didn't like it one bit. She was going to call him and insist they talk about this.

She entered her office and dropped her camera bag on the floor near her desk. She walked to the lunchroom and filled her mug with black coffee. Instead of hanging around the pot to chat with Jenna and her other coworkers, who were already making plans for the upcoming weekend even though it was only Thursday, she slipped out and darted back down the hallway to her office.

She placed her coffee mug on the desk and plopped in the chair. At that very minute the phone rang and she snatched up the receiver, thinking that maybe Gerald was finally calling her. The minute she picked up, she flinched. What if it was a bill collector calling to pester her? She hadn't thought of that. She was tempted to hang up, but it was too late for second thoughts.

"Hello?" she asked cautiously.

"Hey, girl."

Lenora sighed with relief. It was her good friend Monica. Still no Gerald, but at least it was not the bill collector. "Hey, what's up?" Lenora asked. She and Monica talked to each other most days, but Monica wouldn't call at eight-forty in the morning unless she wanted something in particular. She was a surgical nurse at Columbia General Hospital and her workdays were pretty full.

"I wanted to catch you before you get going," Monica said. "Got a bit of a break since a surgery was canceled this morning. We still on for tomorrow tonight?"

"Tomorrow night?" Lenora asked, frowning.

"Friday night. Dinner at my place. Don't tell me you forgot."

Lenora grimaced as she remembered that they had tentative plans to meet for dinner after work, something they did about once a month. They had made the plans last weekend, before Gerald postponed their dinner date to this Friday night.

"I was going to invite Alise," Monica added. "We can ask her about any recent developments on our applications to The Girlfriends. I think they make the decision whether to accept or reject us pretty soon."

"You're right." Lenora was so occupied with work and thoughts about Gerald that the pending application had slipped right by her. The Girlfriends was one of the premier social groups for black women in the area. A lot of people thought all the members did was party, since the club sponsored huge dances and other social gatherings throughout the year. But fun wasn't all that the group was about. Most of the hundred and twenty women in the club were professionals, many of them doctors, lawyers, judges, and successful businesswomen. Each paid a thousand-dollar initiation fee and another five hundred dollars in dues annually, and much of it went to programs for needy women and children around the country.

Getting in was no easy feat, as the group was selective and applying was a six-month-long process. Applicants had to be sponsored by a current long-standing member and submit a seven-page application along with a résumé. They were also expected to attend at least two of the group's many functions throughout the year to give the members a chance to get to know the applicant. Finally the members voted. The club went through this process annually and admitted anywhere from three members to none at any one time.

The initiation fee and annual dues would be a stretch for both Lenora and Monica. But Alise was willing to sponsor them, and

Lenora figured that if the women of The Girlfriends would have her, she would find the money somehow.

"And I agree that it's a good idea to invite Alise," Lenora continued. "But I just can't tomorrow night. I'm having dinner with Gerald."

Monica sighed loudly. "You didn't tell me that. I thought you were seeing him some other night this week."

"I was supposed to see him on Monday, but he had to work late, so we postponed to Friday. Sorry, but I forgot to tell you."

"He's always postponing."

"No he's not. And he's got a business he's trying to keep afloat. That's not easy in this economy."

Stony silence.

"Look, Monica, what is your problem?" Lenora said with irritation. "We can always hook up with Alise over the weekend or next week."

"She's going out of town for a Realtor's conference next week," Monica said. "If we don't jump on it this weekend, it could be a while before we can catch her."

"So see if she can meet with us on Saturday. Can you do lunch or dinner on Saturday?"

"If you don't put it off again," Monica

said sharply. "You know I finally got invited out to a movie tomorrow night by this lab technician I've had my eye on here at work. I've been flirting shamelessly with him for weeks trying to get him to ask me out."

"So what else is new?" Lenora asked sarcastically. Her redheaded girlfriend had more men in her little black book than a rosebush had thorns. And if Monica saw a man who looked good, she wasn't shy about going after him. Once conquered, she moved on to the next one. She had been that way ever since her divorce ten years earlier.

"Very funny," Monica said. "I turned down a chance to get some good lovin' tomorrow night 'cause I thought we were going to hook up for dinner and maybe see Alise."

"I'm sorry about that," Lenora said.

"No, you're not," Monica countered.

Lenora chuckled. She had to admit to herself that she was only a little sorry. "Yes, I am. But I also know that you'll see to it that this brother asks you out again."

"You're right about that," Monica said, laughing. "Except he's not a brother. He's the cutest white dude I ever laid eyes on."

"Well, excuse me," Lenora said. "I forgot that I can't assume anything when it comes to you and your men."

"That's right. I'm an equal opportunity sister. Seriously, though, I think we have a better chance of getting into The Girlfriends this year than we did last, since we attended more of their social events. I'm excited."

"I hope you're right," Lenora said. "I was surprised when they rejected us last year with Alise sponsoring us."

"I know. That was frustrating, made me wonder if it's even worth all the trouble," Monica said. "You know how some people say they're a bunch of hard-partying snobs and not very organized."

"They're just jealous 'cause they can't get in," Lenora said. "The members know how to have a good time, but they do a lot of good deeds in the community. Like that charity event for sickle-cell anemia that we went to a few weeks ago. There's no harm in having fun while helping a good cause."

"Preach on, sister."

Lenora laughed. "You know I'm right."

"I have to run. Got a pre-op prep coming up," Monica said. "I'll call Alise during my lunch break and invite her to my place on Saturday for lunch. And you, no more canceling."

"Make that a late lunch," Lenora said. "It will probably be late afternoon, early evening before Gerald leaves my place."

"Whatever," Monica said. "Just please don't let him change your mind again. I'll get back to you tonight after I talk to Alise. Let's hope she can come. She might be doing something with her family."

"Will you stop being so negative? Jeez."

"Just keeping it real. I —"

"Hold on," Lenora said as Dawna walked into her office. Lenora covered the telephone's mouthpiece. "Yes?" she asked her boss.

"I need to see you now," Dawna said curtly.

"Be right there," Lenora said and Dawna walked off.

"I gotta go," Lenora said to Monica. "Go find that hot lab tech and get yourself some good vanilla lovin' tonight."

"I'll try my best," Monica said, laughing. "Talk to you later."

Lenora hung up and grabbed a notepad and pen. Whatever Dawna wanted, she didn't look too pleased. Then again, Dawna never looked pleased. The woman's smile, on the rare occasions it was displayed, looked more like a sneer.

Lenora entered Dawna's office and was about to sit in the chair across from the desk when Dawna held up her hand, palm out.

"Don't bother to sit," Dawna said. "You don't have time."

Lenora straightened her shoulders. "Okaaay."

"I got permission for you to shoot Ray Shearer and his crew at the Moss Building today."

"You mean the creepy place near Johns Hopkins that needs a ton of work done on it?" Lenora asked with disbelief.

"That's what I just said, isn't it?"

Lenora cleared her throat. "Yes, you certainly did." Although why the boss would want to feature such a hideous piece of property in the *Baltimore Scene* was beyond her.

"I went by there yesterday afternoon and finally was able to work something out with the manager this morning. Ray was also there when I went."

"So you met Raymond?" Lenora asked, noting that Dawna referred to him as Ray rather than Raymond.

"I hadn't realized how young he was." Dawna managed one of her infrequent smiles. "Or how charming. Both Ray and Steve were actually very nice."

So somehow Dawna had been able to get to these men and accomplish what she couldn't. Maybe the woman had a sweeter, gentler side to her that she revealed only for special people or occasions. Or maybe Dawna was able to get men to do what she wanted because of her stunning good looks. Lenora suspected the latter.

"Should I make it a before-and-after shoot?" Lenora asked.

"No, I couldn't get permission for all of that. You only have today."

Lenora almost choked. The grounds of the Moss Building were a photographer's nightmare. She stared at her boss in horror. "Are you serious? That place looks disgusting right now."

"I realize that, which is why I'm sending you to do the job. You'll think of a way to make us all look good. I'm depending on you."

"But it's impossible to make a place that shoddy look good."

"Use your imagination," Dawna said. "Focus on Ray. Fill the shots with his face. I don't know, but I'm sure you can think of ways to feature that hunk of chocolate goodness. And Linda will write the article. Talk to her to find out what angle she's using."

"Yeah, 'Nightmare at the Moss Building,' " Lenora said wryly.

Dawna smacked her lips and ignored the comment. Once Dawna had made up her mind about something, it was next to impossible to get her to change it.

"Here's the address," Dawna said, holding out a slip of paper. "Now go fix what you initially screwed up. I have every confidence that you can do this. You're my best photographer and I expect great things."

Lenora still had the address but decided not to mention that. Dawna was being nicer to her than usual, and Lenora didn't want to say or do anything to ruin that. Instead she accepted Dawna's offering and turned toward the doorway.

"And, Lenora," Dawna said.

Lenora turned and looked back at her boss.

"If you fuck this up again, your ass is mine."

Lenora shuddered as she shut the door to Dawna's office. She should have known that her boss could stay sweet only so long.

CHAPTER 7

Lenora pulled up to the Moss Building and gritted her teeth at the sight. She hadn't really grasped just how awful the place was when she was here before. Now that she knew she had to make this sorry site look good, at least in the background of her photographs, the ugliness of the place slammed her like a tidal wave hits the shore. She would give anything to be back at the luxury condo on the waterfront.

She got out of the car and stood there a moment before the tangled weeds, overgrown grass, and dead trees to think about how she might handle the assignment. Fortunately, the weather was cooperating somewhat. It was cloudy bright and a soft light illuminated the scene. This was her favorite kind of weather for outdoor portraits, and it would be easier to blur the background in her shots.

Linda, the author of the article, was also

aware of the problems with the locale, and together they decided to follow Dawna's suggestion and focus on Raymond and his crew members, with the angle being a new landscaper who would take on the toughest projects. If the weather held up, she might be able to pull this off. She exhaled and some of the stress drained from her body. She hadn't even realized how tense she was. After the unpleasant encounter with Dawna, she didn't even have the time to call Gerald.

She collected her photography gear from the passenger seat of the car, then crossed the parking lot toward two pickups. She scanned the grounds but didn't see Raymond or his crew and figured that they must be on the other side of the only building on the property. She walked in that direction, wading through the knee-high grass in her high-top sneakers; the place seemed more like a jungle with each step.

She stopped when she heard a noise behind her and turned to see Raymond pushing a wheelbarrow across the lawn toward her. "So you finally made it," he said.

She narrowed her eyes. There was something in his tone, as if he thought she made a habit of showing up late to her photo assignments. She was tempted to tell him that running behind was the exception for her, not the rule. But she needed to be on this guy's good side if she wanted to get quality photographs of him and his crew.

She managed a half smile. "Yes, I wanted to be sure . . ." She paused when she realized that he wasn't going to stop and chat. Instead, he strode past her toward a muddy, barren hillside in the distance. That was when Lenora noticed that Raymond was wearing heavy work boots, and the look of the rough hillside made her regret that she had worn her sneakers instead of her Timberlands, despite the warm spring weather. She slung her Nikon across her shoulder and hurried to catch up to him.

"Um, I know we got off to a shaky start, Raymond," she said, trudging awkwardly through the mud. "I hope we can put that past us."

He shrugged. "We're already past it as far as I'm concerned. And please, everybody calls me Ray."

At that moment she found herself imagining him saying the exact same thing to Dawna when he met her, and she felt a tinge of jealousy. It took only one visit for him to invite Dawna to call him Ray, yet two visits for her. "Ray it is then," she said. "I hope to get some good shots of you and your team, and it always helps if the mood and atmosphere are pleasant."

He let go of the wheelbarrow handles when they reached the hillside and turned to face her. "I hear you, and all the talk about moods and atmosphere and stuff is fine. But you should know that we're very short on time. The only reason Steve and I allowed you to come back here is because Dawna was pretty persuasive. She convinced us that you could maneuver around here without messing up our workflow. So I told her she could send you back today as long as you stay out of our way. I didn't promise that we would have a lot of time for posing and smiling or any crap like that."

Lenora nodded even though she was tempted to let him have it. The barbs about her comments on mood and atmosphere were not at all necessary. But this was work, and she would tolerate just about anything to get the shots for the magazine. "I get that. And I won't need a lot of posing and crap like that."

Ray chuckled good-naturedly at her obvious sarcasm and lifted the handles to the wheelbarrow.

"Maybe a few formal head shots later today, but for the most part I prefer candid shots," she said. "It's actually better if you all go ahead with your work and act like I'm not even here."

"Cool," he said, seeming genuinely relieved as he walked off.

She spent the next hour and a half photographing Ray and his crew as they worked. Her biggest regret was the sneakers she had worn. They were normally adequate in the spring but not on this assignment. The shoes were already damp and muddy, and she was doing a lot of slipping and sliding. God forbid she should fall and damage her equipment or hurt herself. But she had resolved to forget about all of that and focus on the job in front of her. She would pull out her foot massager tonight when she got back to the condo.

She took extra care to remain steady on her feet and not get in the way. At first the crew was uneasy about being photographed while they worked, but they were soon so wrapped up in their jobs that they seemed to forget she was there. That was exactly what Lenora wanted. She had worked hard over the years to perfect her ability to take photographs unobtrusively even under the most difficult circumstances. It started with the way she dressed for photo shoots — rubber-soled, ankle-high tennis shoes or boots and simple, baggy clothing in neutral colors. And she had learned early on that it helped to look as plain as possible when photographing men — little or no makeup, hair tied back in a ponytail. The less distracting she was, the easier it was to move around unnoticed.

As she looked through the lens throughout the day, she couldn't help but notice how photogenic Ray was, with his youthful good looks. The camera absolutely loved him. She had seen him only in his work jeans and T-shirts, but it was easy to imagine him wearing a suit or tuxedo. He was the complete opposite of Gerald in many ways. Gerald was far more cerebral and considerably older. Lenora didn't know Raymond's age, but she suspected he was just in his late twenties.

As good as Ray looked on camera, she needed to get a few close-ups. She had realized that it was a bad idea to interrupt him when he focused on a particular operation, such as uprooting a dead tree. She'd have a much better chance of catching him in an upbeat mood if she waited for the right moment, when he was between tasks. Waiting was a big part of photography. Waiting for the right light, the right mood, the right expression.

She finally saw Ray pause late that afternoon and quietly watch a couple of his workers. She thought it might be a good time to ask for those close-ups. As she approached him, he smiled. That was a good sign.

"Did you get what you needed?" he asked.

"I think so. I got some really nice, tight shots of you on the hillside with your crew."

"Sounds good."

"Now I'd just like to get a few of you alone, if that's okay with you?"

He glanced at his watch and that was when she noticed his hands — strong yet smooth, with scars that were likely characteristic of his chosen field of work. They were the hands of a man who used them often and well. He wore no rings whatsoever. No class ring, no wedding band. She wanted close-ups to capture the rugged beauty of those hands.

"You sure it'll be just a few?" he asked.

She nodded.

"So where do you need me?"

For a fleeting moment, Lenora had a vision of him posing naked. She shook her head for a second. Where the hell did that come from?

She cleared her throat and pointed toward a mound of dirt. The hands, she reminded herself, photograph the hands. "Can I have you pick up a shovel and pretend you're digging a hole?" While he went to retrieve a shovel, she changed to a macro lens. Then she got several close-ups of Ray's hands as he used the shovel in various poses. She looked around for another halfway decent background and found one near a huge weeping willow. The area was starting to look fairly nice, since some of the crew had worked there all morning.

"Next I want to get you standing near that tree where you all just put mulch at the base," she said.

He moved toward the tree and stood awkwardly, with his arms folded tightly across his chest. She smiled to herself as she changed to a telephoto lens. He might look good enough to be a model, but he obviously did not know how to pose like one. She took a couple of photos, hoping that would get him to relax. But he grew more tense with each shot, and she wasn't sure if he was always like that when his portrait was taken or if he was simply anxious to get back to work.

"Um, why don't you try to ease your shoulders back a bit?" she suggested.

"Didn't realize they were so tight."

"Try flexing your muscles like this," she said and rotated her own shoulders.

He laughed. "Am I that bad?"

"It happens," she said as he followed her instructions. "Your mind's in work gear and sometimes it's hard to shift." She looked around for something he could hold. That often helped put people at ease. "Let's get the wheelbarrow in the shot with you."

He brought the wheelbarrow back to the tree. She took his hands and showed him where to place them. Then she backed away and lifted the camera to her face. Through the lens, she could see that he had relaxed a lot. Now what she had to do was make sure she got all of that banging upper body in the frame.

"That wasn't so bad, was it?" she asked playfully when they were done. She had gathered all of her equipment, and he offered to walk her back toward her car.

He grunted. "Maybe not as painful as I thought it was gonna be."

"You loosened up a lot toward the end," she said. "That always helps."

He shrugged. "If you say so. Guess I just want to get my work done and get paid. Don't get me wrong, I love being a landscaper. I love taking something that's raw and rugged like this and making it look polished using nothing but my hands and a few tools. I'm just not all that comfortable doing it in front of a camera."

She glanced at his hands again, his ring-free hands. Did that mean he was single and unattached? she wondered. She shoved the thought from her head. What the hell difference did it make? None whatsoever, because *she* was attached. And even if she had been completely free, a good-looking twenty-something like Ray would never be interested in a chubby, plain thirty-seven-year-old like herself. She nodded. "I understand. I'm sometimes awkward or shy until you put a camera in my hands. Then my confidence surges."

He nodded. "I can tell. You're fearless with that thing."

She smiled.

"And I expect people to want to take pictures of my work," he added. "It's the nature of the business and I'm flattered that they like what I do. I just don't understand why they want to take pictures of *me*."

"You're getting popular in this area," she said. "That's what happens when you become as big a story as the work that you do. You need to start getting used to having your picture taken. There will be more attention in the future. Lots of people would kill to have that happen with their businesses." She thought of Gerald.

"You're right, and I hope you don't think I'm ungrateful or don't appreciate the recognition of my work. 'Cause I do."

They paused in front of her car, and she extended her hand. "It was nice to work with you." They shook and the touch was electrifying. Her breath quickened.

"Hope I wasn't too much of a pain earlier," he said.

"What?" She had barely heard him, she was so focused on wondering why his touch had affected her so. She had to work consciously to slow her breathing. "No problem," she said, laughing lightly at her momentary lapse. "Any issues we had earlier were my fault. I was really late to the first site."

"Still, I could have been a little nicer about it. I get that way sometimes when my work is interrupted."

"I understand."

He opened the car door and shut it for her after she was inside with all of her equipment. She rolled the window down, and he placed his hands on the edge of the door frame. In that moment of silence, as she looked up at him, she could hear her heart thumping. Was he going to lean in and kiss her? Or maybe ask her out?

"Would you like to get together for coffee or

lunch over the weekend?" he asked.

The fantasy lasted only a few seconds. Lenora realized that Ray had not actually said those words. He hadn't actually asked her out. Nor would he. Look at her. Thirty pounds overweight, a decade older, no makeup, baggy pants, sneakers, and burdened by a bunch of photography gear. Why would a man like Ray, who had everything going for him, want to go out with her? Dawna, she was not.

"Let me know when the piece comes out," he said and stepped back from the car.

She nodded. "The editor will be in touch with you. Thanks for agreeing to do this." She put the car into reverse and backed out. As she pulled out of the lot, she looked into her rearview mirror to get one last glimpse of Raymond Shearer as he walked back toward the site. In a way, she was glad that she would likely never see him again. The way her thoughts twisted into a knot when he got just a little bit close rattled her.

CHAPTER 8

Lenora hooked her Nikon up to the computer in her office and opened the photographs she had just taken at the Moss Building. She wouldn't actually do any editing or touching up herself. The magazine had a department for that. But she was always anxious to take a peek to see how the photographs turned out before e-mailing them to the editor. She also liked to organize them a bit and remove any really bad shots.

She frowned in study as the images appeared one by one in a slide show. Not bad, she thought, especially the close-ups of Ray's hands and the ones taken near the weeping willow. It helped that Ray was so photogenic. Hell, he probably couldn't take a bad photograph even if he tried.

She decided to make one print to take home with her. No harm in a digital image, right? She zoomed in on Ray's face in her favorite image and blew it up to 200 percent. Then she stuck a five-by-seven-inch sheet of premium glossy paper into her printer. When the photograph was printed, she stared at Ray's face.

He was *so* good-looking, she thought. A little hot-tempered, but even that was appealing to her. Although she sometimes came across really attractive men in her work, she had never met a man who held her spellbound after seeing him only once or twice. There wasn't anything wrong with finding other men attractive, as long as one didn't go overboard. But this was overboard. Ray was playing all sorts of tricks on her mind. Her head filled with thoughts of Ray and his beautiful, rugged hands. It seemed as if his fingers were in the room with her, and Lenora imagined them slipping under her T-shirt to fondle her bare breasts. Her tummy quivered with anticipation as she closed her eyes and let the silky fingers slip slowly down to her waist and around the curve of her hip. She held her breath as they unzipped her khakis and inched beneath her underwear to the crevice . . .

The sound of a door shutting down the hall broke the spell, and Lenora's eyes popped open. She blinked. What the hell was wrong with her? She needed to get ahold of herself. And quickly. She took a deep breath and tucked the photo of Ray into the bottom of a side desk drawer. Then she sent the remaining photos off by e-mail to Linda and deleted all copies from her own computer. That was risky in that there was a small chance the photos would get lost in transmission. But she had to get this man out of her computer and her mind. She had done more than enough drooling over a man who was not her boyfriend.

She picked up the wood-framed photograph of Gerald on her desk and thought back to when she took it. He had wanted a formal portrait for his business, so he was wearing a suit and tie in the photo. Gerald wasn't as sexy as Ray. He didn't have the chiseled abs or the fine facial features and smooth chocolate complexion that got her to swooning. But Gerald was steady, well educated, ambitious, and dependable when he wanted to be. He was the kind of man a woman took home to Mama.

They had been through many ups and downs together over the past three years, the worst time being when he cheated on her. And Gerald was now going through a fairly rough period with his public relations firm. It had survived the dot-com bubble burst as well as a former shady business partner who dipped into the till to the tune of nearly fifty thousand dollars. Now they were facing the weakest economy since the Great Depression. This was definitely taking a toll on the business and on Gerald, but Lenora was convinced that they would get through this just as they had everything else. She had to be patient and have faith in that.

She sighed and put Gerald's photo back down on her desk. That was more than enough daydreaming for one day. She needed to call Dawna to let her know that the photo shoot had gone well and that the images had been e-mailed to the editor. Even giving Dawna good news was something Lenora dreaded. Dawna would likely lecture her about not letting her work get behind again. After talking to Dawna, she would try to reach Gerald.

Lenora reached toward the receiver just as the phone rang. She picked it up to hear Gerald's voice.

"Hey, love," he said.

So he had finally decided to call her. "What happened?" she asked. "I thought you were going to call me last night."

"I got in real late, and I didn't want to disturb you."

"You could have called me this morning before you left for work."

"I was at my office before you even woke up," he said. "I honestly didn't want to disturb you. And at least I'm calling now."

"I don't mean to get testy," she said. "I was just expecting you to call last night. I waited and waited. You've been doing this a lot lately."

"I'll try to do better. Honestly."

She sighed. She was tired of this happening, but what could she do? Break up with him for not calling a few times a week? "How are things going with the client?"

"Well enough," he said. "I think things are looking up, but we're going to need to work on him more, a lot more."

"Uh-huh," she said, sensing what might be coming. "You better not be calling to cancel dinner tomorrow night, Gerald Thomas. We have reservations at the Iron Bridge."

"Umm." He paused and exhaled with regret.

"Dammit." She was so looking forward to a nice dinner together. She waited in aggravated silence for him to explain himself.

"I'm really, really sorry," he said. "But it honestly cannot be helped. We're renegotiating the terms of the deal because the client insists on it. He's losing money like everyone else in this economy."

She stifled a cry of frustration. "Is this the same client you've been meeting with all week?" She was trying hard not to get suspicious, but it was getting more and more difficult with him canceling their plans all the damn time. This was the second time in less than a week.

"Yes," he said. "We persuaded him not to walk away from the deal, but he still wants to scale the original plans back to save money. So we've got to meet with him again, and the best time for him is tomorrow evening. Sorry."

"I'm so sick of hearing you say sorry," she retorted. They'd had this discussion many times before. His work was always of the utmost urgency. Never mind their plans. *She* could always be put off. The client couldn't. "One of these days, you're going to put *me* first."

"Come on, Lenora. That's not fair. You always come first, you know that. But one of the things I love about our relationship is your flexibility. You understand what I'm trying to do, what I'm trying to build."

She said nothing. She was still trying to recover from this major disappointment.

"And you know that I'll make it up to you, right? In fact, I was going to suggest that we spend all day Saturday together. We can do lunch, dinner, a movie. Since it's the week-end, we'll have enough time to do whatever you want. Unless you have other plans."

She *did* have other plans. She was sup-posed to meet with Monica and Alise. And she had already moved the meeting with her girlfriends once to accommodate Ger-ald. But she didn't dare tell Gerald that. If she did, he would probably insist that she stick to her plans for a night out with the girls. And that wasn't what she had in mind to do. As much as she hated to cancel again on Monica and Alise, spending time with her man came first.

"Saturday will do," Lenora said reluc-tantly. "I'll call the Iron Bridge and try to reschedule." Monica was going to be livid, Lenora thought, but she would get over it eventually.

"Good," Gerald said.

"I guess this means you're too busy to come by tonight after work," she said.

"Afraid so. I'll be here late planning for tomorrow's big meeting with the client."

"I've hardly seen you all week."

"I know. I was thinking the same thing earlier today. I'll try to call tonight, but I don't want to promise and not do it again. If I get bogged down and it's really late when I get home, maybe not."

"I understand." Or she was trying to. She dropped the phone in the cradle. There was a time when that kind of news from Gerald would have led to an argument, especially in the period following the affair. She would have jumped up from her seat, closed her office door, and returned to the phone to have it out with him.

But she had learned that arguing with Gerald about anything that had to do with his business was a waste of time. If anything, it made him fight back harder. If they were going to be together, he expected her to be understanding about his work. It was his dream to run a successful business, and she had to come to grips with that and all it entailed.

She reached for the phone to call Dawna about the photos and then Monica to give her the news about the change in plans. That was going to be a tough call, but Monica would come around. They had been close friends since college. If Monica or Alise wanted to cancel because of something to do with their men, they knew that Lenora would understand.

It looked like tomorrow was going to be another lonely Friday night sitting up watching television, waiting for the lottery drawing, and hoping for a call from her boyfriend. At least she knew the lottery drawing would happen on schedule. The call from Gerald was a lot more doubtful.

CHAPTER 9

Lenora woke up on Saturday morning with a huge headache. As soon as she moved to sit up, her temples throbbed as if a gong were being struck repeatedly next to her bed. "Ugh!" She moaned and rubbed her forehead. That was when she realized that her mouth was as dry as sandpaper.

She opened her eyes to peek at the clock on her nightstand, but the view was obstructed by a half-empty bottle of Baileys Irish Cream. She grunted as she placed the bottle on the floor and noticed Paws standing at the foot of the bed, her head cocked to the side as she stared at Lenora. Paws was probably desperate for a walk.

She leaned up on her elbow and reached across the bed for the remote to shut the TV off. That was when she noticed the photo of Ray on the sheet next to her, and the long night of guilty pleasure with a man she barely knew flooded her memory.

She sat up, feeling guilty, and turned Ray's photo upside down. Then she wondered why she should feel bad. Gerald hadn't bothered to call for two days straight. Not Thursday night and not all day or night Friday. And when she dialed his number, she kept getting his answering machine. She suspected that she finally nodded off around midnight last night, since the last thing she remembered was the news going off and the late-night talk shows coming on.

"Damn that man to hell," she muttered. The last time she spoke to him was at work on Thursday. She was really getting fed up with his crap. Something wasn't right. Why would business meetings keep him out so late at night? Why did he get so occupied that he couldn't take a minute to call and check in on her? She had a bad feeling in her gut. She kept hoping that this would go away. Instead, it got worse with every postponement, every cancellation, every missed call.

She patted Paws on the head and gave her an "I'm sorry, you'll have to wait a bit longer" look. It was already 10:30 a.m., but she had to try to reach Gerald before she budged from this bed. She grabbed her cell phone off the nightstand and dialed his landline. If he answered that line, she would at least know he was at home, and it would be easier to believe that he simply got in late again last night and didn't call because he didn't want to disturb her. Whereas he could be anywhere if she called his cell phone and he answered that.

The landline rang and rang, and her anxiety grew. Sometimes she wondered why she even bothered with the man, but she couldn't imagine life without Gerald. She hung up and furiously dialed his cell phone. He answered on the third ring.

"Hey, baby. What's up?" he said.

Lenora's lips tightened. "Don't you dare act like everything is all right with us. Where the hell have you been for two days?"

"At the office mostly. I meant to —"

"You're lying, Gerald," she snapped. "Where are you now?"

"I'm not lying. And I'm at my apartment building now."

"Then why didn't you answer your landline just a minute ago?"

"Probably because I'm already outside my building, walking to my car, on my way to see you."

"Oh?" Lenora frowned, trying to figure out whether what he was saying made sense. He lived about thirty minutes away, in a high-rise apartment building in downtown

Silver Spring, and he parked on the street. If he had already left his apartment when she rang him, he would not have heard the phone. So he could be telling her the truth. Maybe.

"I still don't understand why you didn't call me last night," she said, still full of doubt. "Or the night before."

"I ended up sleeping at the office Thursday night. I was in meetings most of yesterday and didn't get home until two this morning. Then I crashed until about an hour ago. Frankly, I was exhausted and in no mood to talk about anything."

Lenora sighed deeply. Should she let it go? Again. What else could she do? She had a nagging feeling that something was off, but she couldn't find anything concrete. And if he was telling the truth, how could she fault a man for working hard to build his dream? "Okay," she said, her tone softer. "So we're still on for today, right?"

"Of course," he said. "I'm hopping in the car now. Should be there in around thirty."

"Cool." As soon as they hung up, Lenora glanced down and suddenly remembered that she didn't have much time to shower, dress, and walk Paws. It also dawned on her that she had yet to check the lottery numbers for Friday night's Mega Millions drawing. She had been so despondent about not hearing from Gerald that she forgot all about the ticket.

She picked the photo of Ray up off the bed, now feeling even more guilt about fantasizing half the night about another man. But she didn't have time to dwell on that. She quickly tucked the photo under the mattress, slipped into her flip-flops, and ran into the bathroom to get dressed.

CHAPTER 10

Gerald was a little late, but for once Lenora was thankful he didn't arrive on time. The extra minutes allowed her to get her head together, to banish all thoughts of Ray and come back to sanity. And that sanity was Gerald, her real-life, in-the-flesh boyfriend of three years.

She also spent several minutes searching for the lottery ticket, to no avail, despite practically turning the condo upside down. When the doorbell rang, she decided to postpone the search. She was excited to see Gerald and wanted to focus on him. Besides, he didn't really understand the whole lottery thing, since he believed that the chances of winning were close to nil. And he was right. In moments of clarity, she didn't really think she would win any money either. Gerald was her prize.

And he was looking good as he stepped over the threshold wearing navy slacks and a beige shirt that showed off his nice caramel-colored complexion. He was carrying a bottle of Baileys Irish Cream, which he knew was her favorite drink, and that explained why he was running a little behind. She accepted the bottle, wrapped her arms around his shoulders, and kissed him fondly. She missed her man more than usual, with him working late all the time. At least he was here with her now.

She placed the Baileys in the refrigerator, and he sat on the couch, picked up the remote, and flipped the television on. But Lenora had other ideas in mind. She was wearing cutoff blue jeans and she sat across his lap and straddled him. She removed his glasses and kissed him again, this time thrusting her tongue into his mouth. He seemed surprised to find her behaving this amorously so soon after his arrival, but he quickly got with the program. He shut the television off, and they slowly sank down on the couch with him on top.

The first thing Gerald always did when they began to make love was to nibble on her earlobe. In the beginning of their relationship, his thick mustache tickled her pleasurably no end. Then again, everything about him thrilled her in those early days. Not so much anymore, especially the ear nibbling. Probably because she always expected it, there was no surprise, no suspense. In fact, to her way of thinking, their lovemaking sessions had become too much like reading an instruction manual on how to assemble a piece of furniture. A, nibble on ear. B, undo clothing. C, enter. D, sit back and catch breath. Repeat.

Lenora wanted to toss the routine, try something different. She removed his head from her ears and guided it down toward her boobs. He resisted for a second and then his tongue slowly found its way down to her cleavage. He reached down, found the zipper to her cutoffs, and helped her slide them off her hips, along with her bikini undies. He knew that of late she preferred to keep her top on when they made love, because she was ashamed of her increasingly bulky tummy. So he lifted himself up above her on one arm and quickly shed his slacks. He moved to enter her, but she raised a hand to stop him. He looked at her, breathless but clearly puzzled. She smiled seductively and twisted their bodies around on the couch until she was on top of him. If he looked puzzled before, he was happy now.

She was just starting to really get her groove on when he flipped her around until he was back on top. What was wrong with him? Didn't he get it? They needed to try something to the side or do it on the floor. Anything but this again, she thought as he panted and pumped inside her. They used to enjoy trying new positions here and there, but lately Gerald always wanted the same old boring drill. When she asked why, he explained that he was simply too tired to be adventurous. He reasoned that the missionary position was familiar, relatively effortless, and always worked. She figured that it was better than no action at all, so she would spread her legs, close her eyes, and hope for the best.

Surprisingly, her desire mounted quickly that afternoon, likely still strong from the previous night of fantasizing. So she allowed herself to go there completely, to be consumed with thoughts of Ray. With his silky chocolate complexion, his beautiful strong hands. Warm sensations pulsed through her loins . . .

"You about to come?"

Lenora's eyes burst open at the sound of Gerald's voice. The question shouldn't have startled her. Gerald almost always asked it at some point in their lovemaking, usually prematurely. What he really meant was for her to have her orgasm now so he could have his turn. It wasn't a complete turnoff. At least it hadn't been in the past, since she was used to it. She either quickly did her thing or faked it.

But this time was different. This time he had interrupted an intense interlude with Ray, literally the man of her dreams. She didn't *want* to fake it. She shut her eyes tightly and tried to push Gerald's question out of her mind. She tried to bring Ray back.

"You feeling it yet, baby?" Gerald asked.

"Yeah," she lied with exasperation as thoughts of Ray vanished into the nether. She tightened her lips and waited as his pace quickened. Then he stiffened and finally climbed off her. She stared at the ceiling while he slipped back into his boxer shorts. Then she sat up, slid into her underwear, and glanced at her watch. Fortunately, that had wasted only nine minutes of her time.

It used to bother her immensely that their lovemaking had become so monotonous and often did absolutely nothing for her. At first she attempted to spice things up by introducing candles, music, sexy nighties. She shed a few pounds. She tried having long talks with Gerald. But her efforts had done little to improve the sex over the years.

If anything, it had become even blander as Gerald worked more and more hours.

He picked up the remote and leaned back against the couch. "That was nice, baby," he said. He wrapped his arm around her shoulders reflexively.

"Yeah," she mumbled. She grabbed the half-empty bag of potato chips she'd been snacking on before his arrival and watched the tube for a few minutes while he flipped channels. Why the heck did he do that all the time? It was so damn aggravating. You would think he had ADD or something. After several minutes of flipping, Gerald settled on something cheesy and violent, something she would never watch. Then Lenora heard it.

"Zzzzz."

She looked into his face. He had dozed off, mouth hanging open. How predictable, she thought. She sighed and nudged him with her elbow.

He awoke with a start. "Huh?"

"Are you really that tired?" she asked, not sweetly.

"Guess so. Tough times at work."

He closed his eyes again and she leaned up on one elbow and poked him in the ribs.

"Hey, c'mon," he said. He lightly slapped her hand away, but the more he brushed it away, the harder she poked until finally he was wide awake. "Okay, okay, I'm up. You happy?" He rubbed his face and sat up.

"If you're that sleepy," she said, "Why don't you go and get in the bed? I'm going to go get the food started."

"We're not going to Iron Bridge later?" he asked, yawning widely.

"No, I couldn't get reservations this late so I got the stuff to fix pasta here."

"That's just as well, 'cause I'm tired as hell." He reached for the remote control and flipped the television to a different channel.

She placed the chips on the coffee table, sighed deeply, and stood. He glanced up at her as she yanked her cutoffs over her hips and slipped into her sandals.

"What's wrong with you?" he asked.

"Nothing."

"You sure? You seem agitated."

She walked to his side of the couch, placed her hands firmly on her hips, and glared down at him. "Oh, so you noticed? Well, what do you expect? I haven't seen you for several days. You hardly ever even call me anymore. Then you waltz in, fuck me for all of five minutes, and doze off. You used to talk to me nonstop. You used to want to screw me nonstop. Now all you do is snore in my ear. Hell yeah, I'm agitated!"

"Damn! Where is this coming from?"

She realized her voice had climbed to a shriek during her outburst, but she needed to air this out. "Is that all you have to say?"

"It's been a rough couple of weeks," he added. "When I come here to be with you, I just want to chill. I thought that was what you wanted. But if you want to talk, let's talk." He switched the remote control off and patted the couch next to him. She ignored the hint.

"We used to get it on for an hour, sometimes even longer," she said. "Now I get ten minutes if I'm lucky."

He cocked his head and folded his arms tightly across his chest. She could see that his mood had shifted. She knew that it was dangerous to criticize a man's virility, but maybe she was finally reaching him.

"You're forty years old, Gerald," she added, her tone a bit softer. "Maybe you need some, you know, help."

His eyes narrowed. "Help?"

"Yeah. You ever think about getting a prescription for Viagra or something?"

"Viagra? Hell, no!"

"Why not?" she said. "It might be good for us."

"So I'm not twenty-five years old any-more," he said. "Or thirty-five, for that matter. But forty isn't exactly over the hill. I do fine for my age."

She knew better than to push a man too much about these things. "If you say so."

"Maybe it would help if you lost some of that weight you've been putting on lately," Gerald said. "Thought you were on a diet, but look at this." He pointed to the bag of chips on the coffee table.

Lenora gulped and sucked her gut inward. So he had noticed. She wasn't fooling anybody with the baggy clothes and keeping her top on during their lovemaking. "You saying you don't find me attractive anymore? Is that it?"

"I still find you attractive for now. But if you keep piling on the pounds, that might change."

Lenora wanted to melt into the floor. There was no worse feeling than having your man scold you about being too fat.

Gerald stood. "I'm going to go grab a beer," he said, as if he hadn't just hurled a whopping insult at her. "Can I get you a glass of Baileys?" he asked.

"You don't think it will make me too fat, do you?" Lenora said, her voice thick with sarcasm.

He ignored her comment and walked toward the kitchen. She waited for him to finish in the refrigerator. Then she walked in and removed peppers, onion, and garlic and placed them on the countertop. She reached for a knife and began to chop up the onion, her back toward him, her jaw set firmly in silence. She was determined not to speak to him. She was too embarrassed, too upset. He spoke the truth about her weight, but he picked a terrible way to tell her. All she did was suggest they do something to improve their love life. She didn't deserve this.

Gerald placed a glass of Baileys Irish Cream on the rocks on the countertop near her. She was tempted to say something nasty but held back. They had both said enough nasty things for one evening.

He sat at the small kitchen table and took a generous swig from his bottle while she chopped peppers. Neither said a word for several minutes. She remembered when she and Gerald couldn't get enough of each other, whether chatting or screwing. These days Gerald wanted less sex and talk and more tube. Yes, he was working hard. She got that. But a pair needed to spend quality time together to survive. She was beginning to wonder if they would make it as a pair. Or even if it was worth it to keep trying.

Gerald pierced the silence between them

with a loud burp.

"Oh, God," she said. She couldn't help but laugh. "That's disgusting. You've barely taken a sip and already you're burping."

He laughed too. "That's what beer does to an old man like me."

She stopped chopping and turned to look at him. "Is this what we've become, Gerald? A boring couple who insult each other?"

"Look, I'm sorry about the weight comments."

"Don't be. You were being honest. I know I've put on some extra pounds. I just wish you were nicer about telling me."

"So do I," he said, sounding genuinely regretful. "I'll do better in the future, as long as you watch the weight. And lay off the stuff about Viagra."

"I'm going on a diet this minute."

"Good. Now don't lose too much. I do like a woman with some meat on her bones."

"I hear you. And about our love life, we really have to do something to —"

He held up a hand. "I know. I have to do a better job and I will. Without Viagra. All I need to do is catch up on my rest and I will."

"When?"

"As soon as we get through the next couple of weeks at work."

Lenora nodded. She doubted that the

solution was that simple, but she wasn't going to push anymore today. She didn't see Gerald nearly enough, and when she did, the last thing she wanted was to spend the time arguing with him. "We act like two old married people," she said, smiling. "Only we aren't married."

Gerald glanced away. "Uh-oh," he muttered. "Not that word again." He took another swig of beer.

"Yes, I'm going there. We've been together for three years now, except for when we broke up for about two months." She had dumped him when she discovered a year into their relationship that he was having an affair with a woman in his office. Gerald insisted that the affair was purely about sex and that he still loved Lenora. It took him two months to convince Lenora of that, and she agreed to get back together with him only when the other woman quit her job and moved out of the state. "That's what most couples do when they've been together as long as we have, Gerald. They get married."

"I know and we will. Eventually."

"You always say that. When is eventually?"

"Soon."

"Your definition of soon and mine are like night and day."

"We're not that far apart. But I'm too focused on getting the firm back on solid footing to be a good husband to you now. And you deserve the best. Once we start paying ourselves decent salaries again, then I'll be able to think about marriage and starting a family and all that stuff."

"You don't have to be nasty about it."

"What do you mean, nasty?" he asked. "I'm just saying."

"You just called marriage 'that stuff.' Is that what you think of marriage? That it's a bunch of junk?"

"I did not say junk."

"It's all in the tone of voice, Gerald."

"Look, you need to cut a brother some slack. I'm out here trying to do something constructive to earn a decent living. You want to live a good life after we get married, right? I want us to be in a position to buy a nice house. And in this market that takes a lot of cash up front and flawless credit."

"I don't understand why we can't live here in the condo for a while and save together," she said. "A lot of couples do that, you know."

"Yeah, but that just makes everything harder, especially once the babies start coming."

"Not necessarily. We'd only have one house payment. And speaking of babies, I'm thirty-seven years old. I don't have a lot of time left. A couple of years at the most and my eggs go poof."

He drained his beer in silence and she knew she was losing him. He couldn't get her to see things his way so he just gave up trying.

"Don't I make you happy, Gerald?" Lord knows, she tried. She had forgiven him for the affair. She was patient and flexible about his work, for the most part.

"Of course," he said.

"Then what are you going to do about it?"

He sighed deeply and stood up. "Soon, baby, soon."

"I didn't ask you *when,* I said *what.*"

"Lighten up, will you?" He moved behind her and pinched her butt playfully.

She knocked his hand away. "Stop that."

He got another beer out of the refrigerator and went back to the couch, where he flopped down and put his feet up on the coffee table. "Before we know it, we'll be chasing babies around the house and reminiscing about the good old days when we were single and knocking back a few beers and some Baileys while walking around half naked."

She smiled halfheartedly. "You say that like it's something to dread. I look forward to it."

"That's not how I meant it," he said. "Jeez, can't you take a joke, woman?"

She shook her head even though he couldn't see her. Not when it came to marriage, she thought.

CHAPTER 11

Monica escorted Lenora to the dining room in her small townhouse, then moved into the kitchen. "Fix yourself a drink," Monica said, "while I pop the rolls into the oven."

"Can I help you with anything?" Lenora asked just as the doorbell rang.

"You can get that," Monica said. "It's probably Alise."

Lenora walked to the front door and let Alise in. The two of them exchanged air kisses and walked back into the kitchen, where Alise greeted Monica warmly. All three of them had gone to college at Hampton University in Hampton, Virginia, where they hung out together so much that other students used to tease them, calling them the Three Stooges, the Supremes, the three this or the three that. They had been more nerdy than trendy but were known for liking a good time as much as for hitting the books. Since their graduation, Lenora had stayed closer to Monica, but the three of them still got together several times a year.

Alise had always been the most glamorous of the three. She dressed fashionably and her short hair was always styled so perfectly that it looked like she had just walked out of the salon. She'd married a dentist, had children, and over time entered the "right" crowd — doctors, lawyers, accountants, and the like.

Today Alise wore an off-white designer pantsuit; Monica and Lenora wore simple cotton slacks. Monica, who was always on the prowl for eligible men and wasn't shy about admitting it, also had on a tight-fitting V-neck top that accentuated her perky boobs. Her long red hair fell seductively over her shoulders. Lenora had her hair pulled back in the usual ponytail, although she had taken the time to apply a little mascara and lipstick.

"Sorry to be late," Alise said as the three of them carried dishes full of lasagna, macaroni salad, bean salad, and even omelets from the kitchen into the dining room.

"Fix yourselves drinks," Monica said. "I made Bloody Marys and there's fruit juice and sodas in the fridge."

"I'll just take juice," Alise said. "Two o'clock on a Sunday afternoon, barely out of church, is early for a drink for me."

Lenora remembered her promise to Gerald to lose weight. "I'll just have water," she said as she opened the refrigerator door.

"Down on the bottom shelf," Monica said. "You must have had a late night, Lenora, if you're not drinking."

Lenora shook her head as she poured a glass of water for herself and juice for Alise. "I'm on a diet, actually. Gerald didn't leave my place until a couple of hours ago, but we weren't up all that late last night, maybe until midnight."

"Oh, so you two have become more of a first-thing-in-the-morning kind of couple," Monica said as she positioned a large tossed green salad and the rolls on the table. They all sat down.

Lenora scoffed. "I wish. All we did was watch the Sunday-morning talk shows."

"Sounds exciting," Monica said.

"At least he finally decided to show up," Alise said.

Lenora decided to choose her words carefully in response to that comment. She knew that neither of her friends really approved of Gerald and the way he had kept her dangling over the years by putting off marriage. Alise liked him even less than Monica did. After his affair, Alise felt strongly that

117

Lenora needed to dump him and move on. But Lenora had decided that people didn't understand her relationship with Gerald. She and Gerald had been through a lot together, and they understood each other in the way that long-term couples do. "What do you mean by that?" Lenora asked. "He always shows up."

"Didn't he cancel on you a few times last week?" Alise asked.

"That's different," Lenora responded with measured calmness. "He's busy at work. At least he called to let me know he couldn't make it."

"No good man would have you canceling repeatedly on your close friends," Alise said as she spread her napkin in her lap. "Sorry, that's how I feel."

Was that what this was about? Lenora wondered. She had moved their lunch meeting a couple of times due to Gerald's changing schedule, and Alise didn't like that. "He didn't know I was canceling meetings with you. I didn't tell him that. But I'm sorry about postponing twice. I really am." She was trying to keep this civil. She didn't want to turn this lunch into a fight with her friends about her man.

"You don't need to apologize," Alise said. "I still feel that if you want commitment, you need to find a man who wants the same thing. If this man won't marry you, move on."

"I've invested too much in Gerald to walk away at this point."

"What if he never marries you?" Alise asked.

"He will," Lenora said firmly. "He just needs a little more time."

Alise raised her brows doubtfully.

"Let it go, ladies," Monica said, interrupting before either could say more. "I invited you here to have some fun. This bitching back and forth about Gerald ain't fun. Now can we please say grace and move on?"

Alise nodded in agreement and rearranged her napkin. "I'm done. I've said what I needed to say. I'm only thinking of your welfare, Lenora. I don't mean any offense."

Lenora nodded. "None taken." She also wanted to move on. Although Alise could be exasperating at times with her rigid view of relationships, Lenora didn't want to fan the flames. Alise held the key to their entry into The Girlfriends, and that ultimately was what this meeting was all about.

They held hands and bowed their heads while Monica blessed the table. Then they all dug in.

"So did you go out with that lab tech guy

from work, Monica?" Lenora asked.

Monica nodded coyly. "Oh, yes. I managed to make the most of my evening after you canceled."

"And?" Lenora asked.

"All I have to say is that the dude is hung like a brother and can go all night. I plan to see him again real soon."

"Too much information," Alise said.

"Sounds like a typical evening for you," Lenora said.

Monica scoffed. "I wish it *was* typical. Sadly, nights like that don't happen often enough to suit me."

"That's because you're such a slut," Lenora said teasingly.

"I do try," Monica said, rocking seductively in her chair. "Bring it on!"

Lenora laughed. She was actually jealous of her friend. She felt lucky if she could get Gerald to go more than ten minutes once a week. But she didn't share that. The girls already had a low enough opinion of Gerald.

"In the interest of changing the subject, even at the risk of sounding boring, we just started house hunting," Alise said.

"House hunting?" Monica said with surprise. "But you all just moved into your current house, what, five or six years ago?"

"Seven. But we want to move up, and with the market being like it is now, we'd like to take advantage of the insanely low mortgage rates and prices."

"Lucky you," Lenora said. "You're in a position to take advantage of this crazy economy while others are barely holding on. Like me."

"I didn't mean it like that," Alise said.

"Oh, I don't fault you," Lenora said. "It is what it is."

"And since you're a Realtor you know exactly what's out there and where the bargains are," Monica said. "Take advantage of it."

"It's a great time to buy if you can," Alise said.

"Oh, sure," Lenora said. "All I have to do is find my winning Mega Millions lottery ticket, and I'll be ready to buy my McMansion."

"Winning lottery ticket?" Monica asked.

"I bought a ticket and lost it," Lenora said. "It would be just my luck that it's a big winner."

"You lost it on the street?" Monica asked.

"Hopefully not," Lenora said. "It's probably somewhere at the condo, provided Paws didn't get to it."

"Now that would be something, wouldn't

it?" Monica said, laughing. "If it was a multimillion-dollar ticket and Paws pawed it."

"Not funny," Lenora said. "Fortunately, I would never find that out since I let the machine pick. I have no idea what numbers I had."

"Are you really in trouble with your mortgage, Lenora?" Alise asked.

Lenora shrugged. "I'm all right for now. I can make the payments, but it's tight. I wish I had taken out more-traditional financing."

"Are you underwater?" Alise asked.

Lenora nodded. "I have one of those loans where I was making interest-only payments for a while."

"Ouch!" Alise said. "I wish you had consulted me before you did that."

"That makes two of us," Lenora said wryly.

"You live a charmed life, Alise," Monica said. "Here I am still living in a rented townhouse, and you're about to move from one mini-mansion to the other."

"She married a dentist," Lenora said. "Guess that helps."

Alise shrugged. "Nothing's stopping the two of you from marrying successful men."

"Yeah, like there are rich dentists popping out of the woodwork just waiting to be chosen by us," Monica said.

Lenora and Alise laughed.

"I'm just kidding," Monica said. "I'm proud that you did so well for yourself, Alise."

"So am I," Lenora said. "You'd never think we all hung out together in college."

"How soon do you think we'll hear from The Girlfriends?" Monica asked, looking at Alise.

"Any day now," Alise said. "The members just voted, but I don't know the results yet. A committee handles that. I imagine they'll let us know soon."

"You can't ask around and find out now?" Lenora asked.

Alise shook her head firmly. "The admissions committee is very guarded. The members won't even find out until just before they start sending the acceptance letters out."

"I heard that the women who are invited get letters first, then the rejects," Monica said. "Remember what happened last year, Lenora? Alise heard a week before we did."

"How could I forget?" Lenora responded. When Alise got her acceptance letter, Lenora and Monica were left wondering for several days what was going to happen to them. It was a tense time among the three friends, with Alise torn between joy and concern about the fate of her friends. Finally Lenora and Monica got their rejection letters in the mail. They were crushed.

"Hopefully things will turn out better for you two this year," Alise said.

"Maybe we need to do more than helping out at a few soup kitchens," Monica said forlornly.

"We have done more," Lenora said. "You volunteered to work with sick children. I've been active in journalism groups and conferences."

"But Alise is on the board for a local deaf school," Monica countered. "She's also won awards as a top local real estate agent."

"I do make a lot of connections in my work," Alise said. "I'm sure that helped me."

"Being married to a dentist probably didn't hurt either," Lenora said.

"I don't think it's about that," Alise said.

"I'm not so sure," Lenora said. "We all went to the same college together. We're all professionals and active in the community. Only real difference is that Monica and I didn't marry dentists. How many applicants were there this year?"

"Seventeen," Alise responded.

"What?" Monica exclaimed.

"That many?" Lenora added. "There were

only about a dozen applicants last year. Now I'm even more worried."

"Sounds like we probably shouldn't get our hopes up too high," Monica said to Lenora.

"Mine are already too high," Lenora said.

"Let's not jump to conclusions," Alise said. "Wait to see what happens."

"You're right, Alise," Monica said. "We have to have patience. And if we don't get in, you can keep inviting us to the affairs so we can get to know more of the members."

"We could always rob a bank and get rich," Lenora said, only half joking. "Or win the lottery."

CHAPTER 12

Lenora was a lot more upset about possibly not getting into The Girlfriends social club than she had let on at lunch with Monica and Alise. Getting into the club was almost all she and Monica talked about these days. Both of them had submitted a résumé and an application form along with three letters of recommendation and had agonized over making sure everything was perfect. They attended several events and parties throughout the year, trying to get to know the women. In short, they had spent months kissing butt for the second year in a row, perhaps only to be rejected because they weren't rich enough or connected enough. It would be monumentally disappointing if they didn't get in.

For now, she still needed to find the lost lottery ticket. So she searched while waiting for a phone call from Gerald. When he left her condo earlier that afternoon, he said that he and his partners were having drinks in Baltimore tonight with the client, the one they were working so hard to woo back, and that he would call when he was done. If it wasn't too late, he would swing by her place since it was sort of on the way back to his apartment in Silver Spring.

Waiting for Gerald had become such an aggravating pastime for her. She loved that he was a go-getter and wanted so much out of life. She just hated that his ambition meant so many lonely evenings for her.

She sat at her desk and decided to go through the clutter very carefully in hopes that the lottery ticket was buried somewhere in there. Each week the piles of envelopes grew taller as she tossed more bills on top. Major credit cards, department store cards, phone bills, utilities. The envelopes and the papers inside were nasty, evil, predatory things. She hated sifting through them but had no choice if she wanted to find that lottery ticket.

The only bills she made sure to pay on time every month were her mortgage and condo maintenance fees and her auto insurance. Those three bills alone devoured nearly all of her monthly income. For the other bills, she would pay a small amount most months, just enough to keep them out of collection. A couple of bills would sometimes slip by, like her Macy's credit card. She had gone insane charging furniture for the condo and making repairs to her aging Honda, and it finally caught up to her. The situation was a constant juggling act that kept her stomach in knots. She knew that if she kept it up much longer, one day it was all going to come tumbling down.

In all honesty, she shouldn't even be thinking about joining The Girlfriends. Where the heck was she going to get the thousand dollars for their initiation fee? She would have to borrow it, maybe from her parents. She had always figured that if she were ever lucky enough to get admitted, she would find the money somewhere.

If she and Gerald were married, none of this would be a problem. They would have two incomes, and she wouldn't have a stack of overdue bills sitting on the desk taunting her.

Lenora stopped looking for the ticket. She was only about halfway through the clutter, but her mind was on Gerald, not on some stupid piece of paper that was likely worthless. She couldn't take another minute of this wallowing in self-pity, waiting for her man to call and bring her to life. She was going to call him. It was already after nine o'clock. He couldn't possibly still be with the client, could he? Sometimes she wondered if Gerald was seeing another woman. She didn't want to believe that, but with the absences, the missed phone calls, and the lack of sex in their relationship, she couldn't help but be suspicious.

She reached for the phone on the table next to the bed but paused with her hand in midair. She should probably give him another few minutes to call her. She hated behaving like a jealous nuisance of a girlfriend. She didn't want to be that person, and Gerald didn't want to be with that person. If they were going to be husband and wife someday, she had to trust the man and give him the space to do his thing.

She walked to the bookshelf lining the wall next to her small desk and scanned the shelves. She noticed a couple of books about digital photography she had yet to read; now was as good a time as any to get into them, she figured. She picked one out, and as she passed back by the desk, an idea came to her.

She paused and stared at her laptop. Maybe if she looked at the winning numbers, she would get a feel for whether she might have won anything and decide if she should keep searching for the ticket. She did remember seeing the numbers 2 and 17 on her ticket. She sat in front of the laptop, turned it on, and googled the words "Maryland Lottery." She clicked the link to the lottery's web page. When the site came up, she looked down the side of the page to the winning numbers and saw both 2 and 17. The jackpot was at five million dollars, with a cash option of two million, two hundred and fifty thousand.

"Damn!" she said aloud. Getting two matching Mega Millions numbers was fairly unusual. Where was that stupid ticket? She reached for the shoulder bag dangling from the back of the chair. That was where she first put the ticket after buying it. She dug through the bag and all the compartments for the umpteenth time then dumped the contents on top of her desk. Still no ticket.

She glanced around the room and frowned. Where could that ticket be? The most likely place was in this very bag, where she always kept her lottery tickets until she tossed them. Had she lost it somewhere outside the condo? It would be her dumb luck that she had the winning numbers and had lost the damn ticket. Someone else would find it lying on the ground and become a millionaire. And she would be none the wiser but still poor as hell.

She eyed Paws, who was in her doggie bed nibbling on a chew toy. Nah, Lenora thought. She couldn't be that unlucky. That ticket had to be around here somewhere. She stood, walked to her dresser, and began opening drawers and digging through pajamas and undergarments. She even checked under the bed and beneath the pile of clean clothes in the armchair.

Still no lottery ticket. She was about to give up when she thought again about the numbers 2 and 17 and decided to go through the papers on her desk one more time. And presto! She found the ticket almost immediately, tucked between two files. She had taken the ticket out of her bag a couple of nights ago, gotten distracted when the telephone rang, and forgotten all about it.

Lenora sat back down and positioned the ticket up next to the computer screen. She realized at a glance that one of the two groups of numbers on the ticket was close to the six winning numbers. Her heart skipped a beat as she checked the numbers one by one. When she was done, she paused for a few seconds. Not only were 2 and 17 there, but all six numbers matched. What the hell? That had never happened to her before, not even close. She shook her head.

She had to have made a mistake. Better look again.

She started over, checking more slowly this time. When she finished, the numbers still matched. The pounding in her chest was deafening. She tried to calm herself so she could think straight. But that didn't do much good.

She jumped up. She had just won the jackpot!

A sharp pain started in the pit of her stomach and shot up to her chest. She clutched her waist and doubled over. She thought she was going to lose her last meal and was tempted to run toward the bathroom. But the pain soon dissipated.

She sank back down into the chair. She had just won the lottery big-time. She should be ecstatic, yet she felt queasy and ill. She would never have expected to feel this lousy right after winning so much money. This was good news, right?

Yes, it was fantastic. But it was also the end of life as she had known it for thirty-seven years. That was thrilling . . . and also frightening as hell.

CHAPTER 13

Lenora flew into the bathroom, where she wet a facecloth with cold water and placed it on the back of her neck. She had to get a grip or she would pass out. That was the worst thing that could happen when you lived alone.

She stared at her reflection in the bathroom mirror but hardly saw her face. All she saw was dollar signs. Big ones!

She had to tell someone. She ran back to her bed, grabbed the phone on the nightstand, and frantically dialed Gerald's number. Then she slammed the phone down. Did she really want Gerald to be the first to know? Or should she tell her parents first, even though they lived in another state? Or one of her girlfriends?

She flopped down on the bed, placed her fingers on both sides of her forehead, and rubbed in a circle. Paws had detected that something odd was happening. The pooch stood on the floor near the bed, staring up at Lenora and wagging her tail. Instead of picking Paws up and petting her, Lenora sat frozen, willing her breathing to slow down. Then she finally realized that, yes, she wanted Gerald to be the first to know. They were going to build a life together, right? Of course he should be first.

She picked up the phone again and dialed his cell number — or tried to. Her hands were shaking so badly she misdialed. She hung up and tried once more. Wrong again. She disconnected hastily and the third time dialed more slowly.

She couldn't wait to share this unbelievable news with him. But she was going to have to. He was either on the line or had his phone turned off. She hated it when she wanted to reach him urgently and couldn't. And it had never been more urgent than now, this very moment. She had mind-boggling, life-altering news to tell her man, and she couldn't even reach him. She grabbed her ponytail. She felt like yanking all her hair out. She felt like throwing something. Instead, she hit Redial and got Gerald's machine.

She left him a message to call her as soon as possible. She didn't want to get any more detailed than that in a phone message. Then she ran to her desk and sat down at the computer once more. She picked up the winning lottery ticket and triple-checked the numbers. When she realized that she was still a winner, she kissed the ticket ardently and held it close to her chest. "Thank you, sweet Jesus!" She was holding five million bucks in her hand.

She stood up. She had to squirrel the ticket away until she figured out what to do next. She knew that she probably had to take it to an office somewhere in Baltimore, but it was Sunday night. Nothing was open now. She had to tuck this precious baby somewhere safe until she could get to the lottery board.

But where? She glanced around the condo. She didn't have a safe or one of those fireproof boxes. That was when it hit her. What if there was a fire overnight and the place burned down? Very unlikely, she knew. But when you had this kind of money in your possession, you couldn't be too careful.

She figured she should tell someone and get some suggestions as to what to do with the ticket. For now, she tucked it into the bottom of a dresser drawer, right beneath her underwire bras, and decided to call her folks in Richmond. Lenora had left home shortly after college and never went back. Even though she loved her folks, Maryland was now home.

Her mom answered on the second ring. "What's the matter with you?" Mama asked. Lenora could tell by her mother's tone that she knew something big had happened. Lenora tried to steady her emotions by picturing her mother sitting at the wooden kitchen table in the house where Lenora had grown up. No doubt at this latish hour Ma's hair was up in rollers and she was wearing one of her many flowered housedresses. Daddy was likely nearby reading a book or magazine. Every night after dinner, her parents would sit around the kitchen table, sometimes with guests, and talk until bedtime.

"You're not going to believe it," Lenora said breathlessly. "I'm not sure I believe it, and I have the proof right here." Her efforts to calm herself down did not seem to be working. She hopped up to her feet and paced the floor. How the hell could she sit down now? This was too exciting.

"What is it?" Ma asked. "Don't tell me you're getting married."

Lenora laughed. "No, not that. Even better. Or maybe I should say almost as good."

"You won a million dollars," Ma said.

Lenora laughed again. "Nope. More."

"More what?"

"More money than that."

Silence.

"Ma, you still there?"

"What do you mean, more money than a million dollars?" Mama asked. "I was just joking."

Lenora heard her father's voice in the background. "What's this about a million dollars?"

Lenora couldn't hold it in any longer. "Ma, I won the Maryland Lottery. Five million dollars!"

"Lenora, you stop messing with me. That's not even funny. You trying to give me a heart attack?"

"I'm not kidding, Ma. I got the winning ticket right here."

"Oh, Lord!" Ma exclaimed.

Lenora could hear her father demanding to be caught up. She paused as her mother explained to him what was going on.

"Where is the ticket?" Mama asked.

"It's in a drawer. That's what I was going to ask you. What should I do with it? It would be just my dumb luck for a fire to break out in the building before I cash it. Or I'll get robbed on the way over to the lottery office tomorrow."

"Okay, Lenora, calm down," Ma said.

"The ticket is fine for tonight, as long as you don't tell every soul you know where it is. Have you told anybody else?"

"Only you."

"Good," Ma said. "Where do you have to take it?"

"I have to call tomorrow to make sure. Somewhere in Baltimore, I think."

"Your father said you should go to Kinko's or somewhere like that first thing in the morning and get a copy of the ticket made before you turn it in."

"Good idea."

"Where did you buy the ticket?" Ma asked.

"At a convenience store last week."

Ma smacked her lips. "Unbelievable."

"I know," Lenora said.

"Hold on," Mama said. "Your father wants to talk to you."

"Girl, you something else," Daddy said. "When did you find out?"

"Just now," Lenora said. "The drawing was on Friday, but I forgot all about the ticket until now. So I looked up the winning numbers online. Can you believe it?"

"No, indeed. What you going to do with all that money?"

"I haven't even had time to think about that yet, Daddy. I honestly don't know."

"Put it in the bank, but first find yourself a good accountant," he said. "The leeches will be knocking on your door as soon as they hear about it."

"Oh, God," she said.

"I'm not trying to scare you," Daddy said. "I just want to prepare you and make sure you do the right thing."

"I know."

"And anybody call that you don't know and say they related to me or your mama, you hang up the phone."

Lenora laughed.

"I'm dead serious," Daddy said. "When were you planning to take the ticket in?"

"Tomorrow, I guess." Lenora held her head in her hands. She could barely think much less plan this all out. "I guess I should take someone with me. Gerald or Monica. I don't want to go alone. In fact, I think I'll call Monica now and tell her."

"I wouldn't go blabbing to everybody you know," Daddy said. "They'll all be looking for a handout."

"You're right. But she's my best friend."

"I'm just saying you should be careful who you tell before you turn it in," he said. "And even after you turn it in. Monica is probably fine, but she's going to go and tell someone and then that person will blab, and before you know it, all of D.C. and Baltimore will know."

"I'll make Monica swear not to tell anyone."

She said good night to her parents and hung up, intending to call Monica. Instead she decided to try Gerald again. She really wanted him to hear the good news. Unfortunately he still wasn't answering. Well, she wasn't going to fret about it, not now, not when she had just become the Baltimore area's newest millionaire — at least before taxes and assuming she was the only winner. Even if there were other winners and after taxes, she had a big fat check coming to her. She would finally be able to pay off her bills and a whole lot more.

She picked up the stack of bills on her desk, held them high over her head, and let them tumble to the floor. She picked Paws up and held her as she danced on top of the bills and across the floor.

"Hot damn!" She placed Paws down and hastily dialed Monica's number.

"Let me call you back," Monica said. "I'm in the middle of watching *Obsession* on On Demand."

"This is way more important than a movie, girl," Lenora said. "You alone?"

"Yeah," Monica said. "Why?"

"Put your cell on speakerphone."

"What for?"

"Put it on speakerphone," Lenora repeated. "Hurry up."

"But what on earth for?"

"Just do it, Monica. You'll understand why in a sec."

"I'm telling you, Lenora, this better be good, making me miss my movie. Okay, it's on speakerphone. Go ahead."

Lenora screamed at the top of her lungs. "Ahh!"

"What the fuck is wrong with you, fool?" an exasperated Monica asked.

Lenora screamed again. She realized that she had been dying to do that. To let it all out was just what she needed. "Oh, girl, you're not going to believe this."

"Believe what?" Monica asked.

"I won the damn lottery!"

"Really?" Monica asked. "Seriously?"

"Yes, very seriously."

"How much you talking about?"

"Five million," Lenora said.

"Come again."

"You heard it right."

"Oh, my God! Are you sure?" Monica asked.

Lenora laughed. She understood why her friend was having trouble taking it all in.

She was having trouble herself and she had seen the ticket with her own eyes. She had held it and hidden it inside her drawer and still had trouble wrapping her mind around the enormity of it. She sat down on the bed. "Unbelievable, huh?"

"Did you just find out?" Monica asked. "The drawing was last week."

"I know," Lenora said. "I forgot all about the ticket and then I couldn't find it."

"Well, I'll be. What did Gerald say?"

"I can't reach him."

"Not even on his cell?"

"No," Lenora said.

"Any idea where he is that he can't answer his cell phone for you?" Monica asked, her voice thick with suspicion.

"Sometimes he turns it off when he's with a client or in a meeting and forgets to turn it back on."

"Lenora."

"Yes?"

"It's Sunday night."

"So?" Lenora asked. "He meets with clients on weekends all the time."

Monica smacked her lips loudly. "If you say so."

Lenora decided to ignore her friend's doubtful tone. She was too happy to even contemplate anything negative, especially when it came to Gerald. "I'm way too excited to be worrying about that or anything, for that matter."

"I hear you," Monica said. "I'm excited for you."

"I don't know how I'm going to sleep tonight."

"You won't. I'm not sure *I'll* be able to sleep. This is so unbelievable. I won't even be able to talk to you now."

"Don't be silly," Lenora said. "You going to be up awhile? 'Cause I'm too hyper to stay in this house."

"Come on over," Monica said. "I'll pop that bottle of bubbly I got last year for my birthday. I was saving it for when we get into The Girlfriends, but forget that, we can celebrate this tonight."

"I'll be right over."

"You know the press is going to come knocking at your door, right?" Monica said. "And everyone else. So be prepared."

"You don't have to remind me," Lenora said. "I work for a magazine, remember?"

"You planning to quit your job?" Monica asked.

"Please," Lenora said. "I haven't even thought that far ahead."

CHAPTER 14

Monica opened the front door of her townhouse holding the birthday bottle of Veuve Clicquot in one of her outstretched hands.

"Welcome to my humble abode, Ms. Millionaire," Monica said, smiling.

They hugged each other warmly.

"I'm so happy for you," Monica said.

"Want to see the ticket?" Lenora asked as she followed Monica into the kitchen and dropped her shoulder bag on the table.

"You brought it with you?" Monica asked, eyes wide with disbelief. "I would have thought you would hide that thing someplace safe in your house."

"Right here with me is the safest place I can think of now. What if my place burns down or gets robbed?"

"What if you're in a car accident?" Monica asked. "Or you get robbed in the streets?"

"That's not going to happen," Lenora

said. "You live only, like, ten minutes away from me."

Monica shrugged. "It's your ticket. Let me see, girl."

Lenora removed the ticket from her bag and cradled it in the palm of her hand as if it were a ten-carat diamond.

"Wow," Monica said. "Just wow. Why'd you pick those numbers?"

"I didn't pick them. I let the machine do it."

"You are one lucky sister," Monica said. "That's all I can say."

Lenora carefully placed the ticket back in her shoulder bag. She leaned back against the countertop and sighed deeply. "I'm still pinching myself mentally. How the hell did this happen?"

Monica retrieved two champagne flutes from the cupboard and placed them on the countertop near Lenora. "Don't drive yourself nuts trying to figure that out. You got lucky. Enjoy it."

"You're right."

"Did you ever reach Gerald?" Monica asked.

"I still haven't talked to him," Lenora said. "I was trying the whole time I drove over here. I'll try again in a bit."

"Mm-hmm."

"Don't you dare say a single word."

"I'm not," Monica said. "I'm thinking of saying a whole pile of words. I'm thinking I'd like to give you a good talking-to about that man and his disappearing acts. But you already know what I think."

"Just 'cause I can't reach the man doesn't mean he's up to no good."

Monica popped the champagne bottle and rolled her eyes skyward. "Whatevah!"

Lenora held up the flutes while Monica poured.

Monica took her glass and raised it toward Lenora. "To Columbia's newest, smartest millionairess."

"Maybe not after taxes," Lenora said. "And if anyone else won. But still, I'll drink to that."

They clinked their glasses and sipped.

Lenora placed her glass back on the countertop, then hugged her friend again. "Damn! Can you believe this?"

Monica laughed. "It's crazy, but believe it, girl. When are you going to cash the ticket? Tomorrow?"

"I don't even know," Lenora said, waving her hand. "My mind is all over the place. When should I claim my winnings? Do I quit my job? Where the hell is Gerald?"

"If it was me, I'd be at that lottery door

146

the minute it opens."

"That's what you would think. But honestly, sometimes I feel like I'm going to be sick just thinking about all this." Lenora frowned. "This changes so much. It changes everything."

Monica nodded with understanding. "I know. You seriously thinking about quitting your job?"

"I don't know," Lenora said. "I just don't know what I'm going to do. I mean, I hate my boss — no news there. But I love what I do."

"That boss of yours is a trip to hell, from what you tell me," Monica said. "Why stay if you don't have to? I mean, even after taxes you probably won more than ten years' worth of salary. Plenty of time for you to figure out what you want to do with your life."

"I love getting out and taking photos of people doing their thing. I love seeing my work in print. And I meet some very interesting people. Did I tell you about the landscaper I photographed last week?"

"No. What about him?"

Lenora touched her cheek with her hand. "Girl, talk about hot. He's a scorcher. He's tall, with a yummy chocolate complexion and the prettiest hands."

"Hands? You're gushing over a guy's hands?" Monica asked, blinking at her friend. "I haven't heard you talk about a man like this since you and Gerald became an item. How old is Mr. Chocolate Goodness?"

"I have no idea. In his mid- to late twenties."

"Whoa," Monica said. "This is getting weirder by the minute. You lusting after some guy in his twenties. That's my thing. That's the age where they can still go all night long. If you had any sense you would do him, but you don't so . . . Is it okay if I meet him?"

Lenora laughed. "You are too much."

"I'm serious," Monica said. "We can't let this hunk go to waste, can we? And if I know you, you're not going to want to cheat on Gerald."

"You're right about that," Lenora said. "But if I wasn't so into trying to make it work with Gerald, I'd be all over Ray. I won't lie."

"Fool."

Lenora shrugged. "Can't help it if I'm a one-man woman."

"Then introduce your best single girl-friend to Ray."

Lenora rolled her eyes skyward. "Not a

chance."

"Uh-huh. Is somebody thinking about cheating on their man?"

"Like you said, I'm not about to cheat on Gerald. Speaking of which, let me try him again." Lenora pulled her cell phone out of her shoulder bag. "I want to tell him the news so bad."

"I'll give you some privacy." Monica picked up the bottle of champagne and took it, along with her glass, to the dining room table while Lenora dialed Gerald's number. Lenora waited until his machine answered, then hung up, feeling frustrated that she couldn't reach him. But she had already left him several messages. There was no point in leaving another. Lenora followed Monica to the dining room table and sat across from her.

"Still can't reach him?" Monica asked.

"No. If I hadn't just won the lottery, I'd really be pissed. But I'm too happy to get mad about anything now."

Monica waved an arm. "Forget him for now. Want to go out for drinks or something to celebrate?"

Lenora held her glass up. "Girl, we already drinking and I have to drive back. Don't need any more booze than this."

"So how about we just get some dessert

somewhere. How about that place up the street that has those yummy Italian cakes?"

Lenora shook her head. "I have got to lose some weight. I promised Gerald. Besides, I really want to go home after I leave here and try to catch up with him. I just won big money in the lottery. I want to tell my man."

"I hear you," Monica said. "Well, unlike you, I do have to work tomorrow. So it's just as well. I couldn't have stayed out late anyway."

"We can do something special next weekend," Lenora said. "I'll treat you and Alise to dinner at a fancy restaurant."

Monica nodded. "That sounds like a plan I could get with. You know, you probably won't have any trouble getting into The Girlfriends now, with all your millions."

"I hadn't even thought about that."

"Well, think about it. And put in a good word for a sistah if I don't make it with you."

Lenora smiled. "That might not even be necessary. We might both already be in. Either way, you know I got your back. Will you promise me something?"

"You know I will," Monica said.

"Promise me that we won't let this money change things between us. I heard some weird stuff about how winning the lottery can change the winners and the people

150

around them. Don't get weird on me. And if I get weird or, you know, if I catch too much attitude, let me know I stepped out of line."

"Deal," Monica said. "But I've known you a long time. We've been close since forever. There's no way this will change you or me or our friendship."

Lenora reached across the table and squeezed her friend's hand. "Thanks."

CHAPTER 15

In the car, Lenora decided to try Gerald again. If he was at his place, she would drop by and give him the news. It was at least thirty minutes to Silver Spring, but she was too antsy to sleep and doubted she was going in to work tomorrow anyway.

This time Gerald finally answered. "What's going on with you?" she asked as soon as he said hello.

"What do you mean?" he asked.

"I've been calling and calling," she said. "Why didn't you answer your phone?"

"I was on a conference call with a client and one of my partners earlier. Then I turned it off while I worked on some papers. I just turned it back on."

"You sure have been spending a lot of time talking to clients lately."

"Yes, I have," he said. "But that's the nature of the business. I got your message when I turned it back on. I was about to call you."

"Are you home?" she asked.

"Yes. Sure am."

"Good. I'm going to stop by to tell you something."

"It's after eleven. You sure you want to drive all the way over here instead of telling me over the phone?"

"This is important," she said. "I want to see your face when I tell you. Unless you have a reason for not wanting me there."

"Actually, I'm getting excited to hear what this is all about. When will you get here?"

"Soon. I'm leaving Monica's now."

Twenty minutes later she parked in front of Gerald's high-rise apartment building on Georgia Avenue. She used her key to let herself in, then entered one of the elevators and rode up to the sixth floor. Gerald opened the door after the first knock and greeted her warmly with a hug and kiss. He was wearing a black bathrobe and had a white towel draped around his neck.

"Mmm, you smell nice," she said.

"Thanks," he said, toweling off his short wet hair. "Been working and didn't bathe all day, so I hopped in the shower after you called. Come on in."

She entered the living room area of the apartment, sparsely furnished with a few sleek contemporary pieces, dropped her shoulder bag onto a chair, and clasped her hands together. She wanted to share the news with Gerald before another minute went by.

"Have a seat," he said, leading her to his black leather couch. "I can see that you're about to burst. What did you want to tell me?"

She tried to contain herself as they sat next to each other. "Oh, God," she said, fanning herself with her hand.

"What's wrong?" Gerald asked. "You don't look good."

She took his hand in her spare one. "I'm fine. I'm just so excited I think I'm going to faint."

He knitted his brows. "Well, damn, go on, tell me what it is." He squeezed her hand. "I don't think I've ever seen you so worked up."

"That's because I've never been this excited, Gerald." She couldn't sit still for another minute. She jumped up from the couch and turned to face him. He was clearly baffled by her behavior and stared at her in silence. She reached out and pulled him up to stand in front of her. She needed to hold on to something to keep from passing out.

"Will you please tell me?" he pleaded. "Just say it."

"I won, Gerald!"

"You won? Won what?"

"The big one."

He frowned deeply. "I don't get it, Lenora. The big what?"

"The lottery, Gerald. I won five million dollars in the lottery!"

Gerald stared at her speechlessly. His mouth opened to say something and then closed. Lenora laughed at the expression on his face.

"Say that again?" he finally asked when he found his voice. "You won *what?*"

She nodded with excitement. "The lottery. Five million dollars."

"You aren't joking, are you?"

"No, I'm very serious."

Gerald let go of her hands and smacked a fist into his palm as he paced the living room carpet. "Damn!"

Lenora giggled. "I know."

She leaped into his arms and wrapped her legs around him. He fell back onto the couch with her on his lap, both laughing uncontrollably. When they calmed down, she pulled back to look into his face. He could not have looked more shocked if she had come in here and shot a pistol. "I hardly know what to say," he said. "Are you sure the numbers were right and you had *all* of them?"

She nodded. "Oh, yeah. I checked them, like, fifteen times."

"Damn!" he repeated. He hugged her and she slid off him and onto the couch next to him. They looked at each other and burst out laughing again. "You know that this is going to change your life, right?" he said.

"No kidding!" she said. "It's going to change *our* lives, Gerald. We're a couple."

He took her hands and squeezed them tightly.

"I can tell you're stunned," she said.

"No doubt about that," he said. "Aren't you?"

She nodded.

"So, tell me . . ." He paused and exhaled deeply to gain control of his emotions. "When did you buy the ticket?"

"On Thursday after you called and postponed our date. Guess I have to thank you for doing that, or I might never have stopped to buy a ticket. I would have been rushing home to start dinner for you."

He nodded, an ironic smile creasing his face. "Glad I could be of help."

She laughed. "I just realized that I won a few hours ago. I completely forgot to check the ticket and then I lost it until tonight."

"When do you plan to go to wherever it is you have to go to claim your winnings?"

"I'll call tomorrow."

"Just call? Don't you have to go there?"

"I will," she said. "Eventually."

"Eventually?"

"What's the rush? I have plenty of time. It's weird, but a part of me is real nervous about winning all this money. I have butterflies in my stomach. I don't know why."

"It's a pretty damn big deal, but you'll be fine," he said. "And I'm here to help out if you need anything."

They were still holding hands, and she lifted his and kissed it. "Isn't this exciting? You always talk about how you want to be more established before we take our relationship to the next level. And then this happens. Now we have all this money."

"Whoa," he said. "I'm happy for you, I really am. But it's your money. You won it."

"Don't be silly," she said. "We're a couple. We've been together for three years now. What's mine is yours."

He smiled and kissed her lightly on the lips. "It makes me feel real good to hear you say that. Right now I want you to focus on yourself. Don't even think about me. People are going to start coming out of nowhere asking for a handout. So prepare yourself for that. You're going to need to develop a thick skin and be willing to tell people to back off and get lost."

"I know. Long-lost cousins and all that."

He let go of her hands and leaned back against the couch. He laughed. "This is unbelievable. Have you called your folks?"

"They were the first people I told when I couldn't reach you. Then I went over to Monica's."

"Sorry it was so hard to catch me for a while there, baby."

She clutched her stomach again. "Oh, God. I get these waves of pain shooting through my stomach." She held one hand out and watched as it trembled. "I'm shaking like a leaf."

"I see. You have to try to calm down." He put an arm around her shoulders and kissed her — a long, slow tender kiss. She felt her nerves steadying and her body began to relax. She didn't know why she had felt so anxious in the first place. Her finances had just gotten a huge much-needed boost. Good-bye, bill collectors. Hello, new house, new car, new everything.

But first it was time to ramp up her sex life. She yanked Gerald's bathrobe open and ran her hands across his broad chest as she leaned in and kissed his neck. "Whoa, baby," he said, sliding down on the couch. "You need to win the lottery more often."

She smiled. "I won't argue with that."

CHAPTER 16

After a night of some of the best lovemaking that she and Gerald had enjoyed in a long while, Lenora headed for home. Their night of passion wasn't as wild as those they had experienced after they first met, but it was way better than anything that had happened over recent months. If it had been up to her, they would still be going at it, but Gerald left for work at six-thirty that morning despite her pleas that he stick around in bed longer. He insisted that he absolutely could not afford to go in late. So she got up reluctantly and had a quick cup of coffee with him as they planned the day out. She would drive back to her place, walk Paws, shower, and dress. She would call the lottery board as soon as it opened at 8:30 a.m. and then drive out there. He would call her around noon to see how it went.

That was the plan. And it worked fine up to the part where she took Paws for a brisk stroll around her building. But as soon as she came back up to the condo, her stomach started acting up again, twisting and turning to the point where she could hardly catch her breath. She stripped down to her underwear, climbed into bed, and pulled the sheet up over her shoulders. As if she sensed her pain, Paws hopped up beside her and rested her head in her lap.

What was the matter with her? On the one hand, she was ecstatic about the money and couldn't wait to get out and start living her new life. No more worries about not being able to make mortgage payments or bill collectors pestering her. She could easily buy just about anything she wanted. Car, house, new cameras and equipment. Then there was the total freedom that came with that kind of money. No longer would she have to go to work and face her evil boss if she chose not to. *Oh, how sweet the thought.*

But there was a flip side to all this, stuff no one else had to think about. Yes, she could quit her job, but what would she do with her time? She couldn't lounge around the house all day long. She had long dreamed of having her own photography studio, but that involved huge risks. That had become all too clear as she had watched Gerald and his partners struggle to keep

161

their business afloat. What if she started a studio and failed to land clients? What if she wasn't so good at managing the finances? All sorts of things could go wrong if she went down that path.

The truth was, she had no idea how to handle the money. She had heard so many horror stories of people coming into large fortunes and mismanaging them badly or hiring people to help who swindled them out of every dime. Given her dismal financial track record, she couldn't assume that she would do any better. Chances were that she would make a complete mess of it.

She stared at the ceiling. Maybe she could ignore the money or give it all back. She closed her eyes for a second and opened them again. How silly, she thought. She couldn't possibly do that. Nor did she really care to. What she wanted was a magic way to become a master at handling the money. But this wasn't going to happen. She had to figure this all out on her own.

She would have to work hard to avoid the pitfalls. And that meant taking her time and moving cautiously, thinking through every angle before she made a move. She probably shouldn't quit her job right away, even though others would expect her to and she was certainly tempted. In fact, it was a wonder she hadn't already picked up the phone and quit.

But as much as she despised Dawna, now more than ever she needed to know what her days would be like. That sense of security would vanish the minute she quit her job. She would also miss not seeing her photos in print on the pages of a major local magazine.

She sat up and patted Paws on the head. Now that she had made what seemed like a sound decision about her job, she felt a little better. She was going to fire up her laptop and gather as much information from the lottery board's website as she could. Given her mental and physical state, the fewer surprises when she went there, the better.

She swung her feet around to the floor, and a sharp pain shot across her belly. She clutched her waist and grimaced as she ran to the bathroom. She threw the toilet seat up and leaned over, but nothing came out. She sat on the floor next to the toilet and waited until the crummy feeling passed. Then she stood and let out a deep gust of air.

Damn these nerves. That's all this was, she was sure. She just wished they would go away, she thought as she reached for her toothbrush. Maybe getting into the routine of her day would help. She bathed and slipped into a pair of running pants. Eating anything now was out of the question. Perhaps a quiet walk would soothe her. She put the leash on Paws, who was thrilled to get two walks in one morning,

In front of her building, gardeners were edging the lawn along the walkway and placing mulch at the bases of flower beds. The grounds of the building were well maintained — this was one of the reasons she bought her condo here — and she had seen the workers out there many times before. But now they reminded her of Ray. She found herself wondering where he was working that morning, what he was up to. She also wondered what he would say if he knew that she'd won millions in the lottery.

As soon as she got back upstairs, she removed the photo of Ray tucked under her mattress. In all the excitement, she had forgotten about it. She had also forgotten how young and photogenic he was, she thought as she stared at the photo for a minute. Then she smacked her lips in annoyance. Why was she doing this? Why was she even thinking about Ray? She had just spent a passionate night with her boyfriend, the best in a long while. And more than likely she would never see Ray again.

She shoved the photo back under the mattress and went to get a glass of juice. Before she could decide what to do next, she noticed that the message light on the wall phone in the kitchen was blinking. She was surprised to discover that it was Gerald. She wasn't expecting a call from him until later that afternoon.

"Hey, baby," Gerald said in the message. "Sitting here at my desk thinking about you. I just wanted to say hi to Maryland's sexiest millionaire and wish you luck at the lottery board this morning, but it looks like you may have already left. I'll catch you later tonight to see how it went."

She smiled as she hung up the phone. It was sweet of him to take the time out from his busy workday to call, she thought as she put on a pot of coffee. She wished he would do that kind of thing more often, but better occasionally than never.

Back at her desk, she turned the laptop on and sat down to learn as much as she could about what to do when you win the lottery. By the time she looked back up, she realized that it was nearly nine and she had yet to call the office. She picked up her cell phone and dialed. Dawna wasn't in yet, so she left a message with Jenna to tell the boss that she had some urgent personal business to take care of and wouldn't be in today.

She gleaned a lot of information from the website and decided to drive straight to the lottery board. She turned the computer off, and the minute she stood, her stomach heaved. She covered her mouth and made a dash for the bathroom. Nothing came up, and the squeamish feeling soon subsided. Damn, how was she going to get through the day if this kept happening? One step at a time, she told herself. She had to manage somehow.

She walked to the closet and rummaged through her clothing, trying to pick out something nice to wear. She was a millionaire now. Her usual jeans or shorts with sneakers no longer seemed appropriate. She wished she didn't feel so queasy and could fully enjoy all the good stuff that was happening to her. It had been ages since Gerald did something frivolous like calling in the morning from his office to offer words of encouragement. He used to leave messages like that on her phone almost daily when they first met. The renewed attention from him had to do with the money she had won, but that was fine. She knew that Gerald really loved her. If he had just won the lottery, no doubt she'd be paying a little extra attention to him as well. It was exciting, and he wanted to be a part of it. That was understandable.

She pulled a skirt off the hanger and another pain shot through her stomach. She dropped the skirt onto the floor and clutched her stomach as she made her way to the bed. She buried her head into the pillow and tried to will the pain away. She didn't understand this. She should be on her way to get her check, not in bed writhing in agony. This was crazy.

The phone rang. She reached across the nightstand to pick it up and immediately recognized Alise's voice.

"Congratulations!" Alise said. "Monica just told me."

Lenora was startled. This was the last thing she expected. She was going to have to call Monica and insist that Monica keep quiet about the money from here on out. Not that she minded Alise knowing, she simply would have preferred to tell Alise herself in her own time. "Thanks," Lenora said.

"That's it?" Alise asked with a chuckle. "I expected you to sound a lot more excited than this. Aren't you happy?"

"Of course. I hoped Monica would wait until I was ready to start telling people, that's all."

"Sorry," Alise said. "You didn't want me to know?"

"It's not that. I just . . . oh, never mind."

"You don't sound good," Alise said. "You definitely don't sound like someone who just won several million dollars."

"Is that what Monica told you? It was only five million, and much less after taxes."

"Oh," Alise said. "*Only* five million dollars. Poor you."

"You know what I mean. And to tell you the truth, I feel like I'm coming apart. I can barely think straight."

"I can imagine," Alise said. "Or maybe I can't. Not too many people could imagine what it's like to win that much money. But I'm sure it will all work out for you."

"Thanks," Lenora said.

"Have you gone down to claim your winnings?" Alise asked.

"No, not yet."

"Really?"

"I checked on the website," Lenora said in response to Alise's obvious surprise. "I have a hundred and eighty-two days to claim my winnings. That's, like, six months. So, there's really no rush. It's fine."

"Right," Alise said after a brief pause.

"I know it seems strange that I'm not running down there the minute it opens, but the money isn't going anywhere. Really, what's the rush?"

"None, I guess," Alise said.

"It's odd how this has affected me physically and emotionally. I mean, I'm thrilled that I won, but I'm getting these weird thoughts and feelings that I never expected to have."

"Like what?"

"Mainly fear. It's a huge amount of money, and I worry that I'll screw it all up. Or how other people will act around me once they know."

"I hear you. I've heard stories about that kind of money changing people's lives. And not always for the best."

"I always assumed that was because the people's lives were screwed up to begin with," Lenora said. "Now I'm not so sure. It's like someone put my life and all my history in a blender and shook violently. Nothing makes sense. I literally get sick to my stomach when I stand up."

"That doesn't sound good."

"I know," Lenora said. "I'm hoping it's nerves and I'll get over it soon."

"That's what I was thinking. Eat lightly for a day or two. Are you taking anything for your stomach?"

"I'll have Gerald bring me something later

today. He's being a real sweetheart about it."

"Well, you just be careful with him," Alise said.

Lenora frowned. "Meaning?"

"This kind of money will change some of the people around you."

"Not Gerald," Lenora said firmly.

"Mmm."

"I can't believe you're saying this, Alise. You don't even know Gerald that well. Trust me, he isn't like that."

"Maybe not," Alise said. "You're right, I don't know him that well. I just know how people are."

"Thanks a lot for the vote of confidence in the man I'm going to marry," Lenora said sarcastically.

"Just looking out for you," Alise said. "Don't get so defensive."

Lenora rolled her eyes to the ceiling as they mumbled good-byes and hung up. Lenora felt worse than she had before the phone call. She groaned, turned over on her side, and decided that she would wait a day or so to go in and claim her winnings. She was going through too many changes now. She needed to rest and give her mind and body some time to adjust. The money would still be there when she felt better and was

ready to deal with all the changes that lay
ahead.

CHAPTER 17

Lenora woke up when she heard Gerald opening the door to her condo that evening. She lifted her head and peered at the clock as Paws jumped from the bed and ran to greet Gerald. It was 5:30 p.m., and Lenora realized that she had been drifting in and out of sleep all day long.

She sat up and tried to straighten her hair as Gerald approached the bed. He sat beside her with a concerned expression on his face and gently touched her forehead. When he had called to check on her at lunchtime, she had asked him to stop and get her something for her stomach.

"You feeling any better?" he asked as he placed a bag from Walgreens on the table next to her bed.

"Maybe a little," she said.

"How long you been sleeping?"

"Off and on all day pretty much."

His eyes grew big. "You've been sleeping

all day?"

Lenora nodded. "Just about."

He touched her forehead again. "You don't feel hot or anything."

"It's mainly my stomach. But I also feel woozy when I stand up."

"I brought you some Pepto-Bismol. Let me go get you a spoon."

When he returned, he had removed his suit jacket and loosened his necktie. He opened the bottle and poured a couple of spoonfuls for her.

"That should help," he said as he replaced the cap on the bottle.

"Hopefully," she said.

"You don't sound optimistic." He rubbed her legs gently beneath the covers.

"That's 'cause I'm so upset with myself," she said. "Why do I feel so lousy?"

"It is what it is," he said. "You didn't even get down to the lottery board, did you?"

She shook her head. "I told you, I've been in bed all day. But I'm definitely going in tomorrow."

"Do you think you should see a doctor?"

"No. I'll be fine by tomorrow."

"You want me to go in late and take you to the lottery board in the morning before I go in?"

"That's not necessary. I know how hectic

things are at your office."

"I can manage a couple of hours before I go in," he said. "This is a pretty big deal for you."

"I know," she said. "And thanks. But I can take care of it."

"That's all well and good if you do, but in case you don't get down there tomorrow, you should let me put the ticket in a safe-deposit box at the bank. The longer you wait and keep it in that drawer, the more likely stuff could happen."

"Nothing's going to happen." She didn't want anyone else messing with her lottery ticket, not even Gerald. It wasn't that she didn't trust him. It was just another of the strange feelings she was getting since winning the money.

"You don't know that," he said.

She waved him off. "I'm going down there tomorrow."

"What? You don't trust me with it?"

"Of course I trust you. But the ticket is fine, Gerald."

"Suit yourself," he said, exhaling loudly. "At least see a doctor if you don't feel better by tomorrow."

"I'll be better by then. I'm sure of it."

"I've never seen you act this way," he said. "Usually when you're sick for more than a day, you run straight to the doctor."

"Why are you making a big deal out of this?" Lenora asked. Everyone was acting so odd, and it was starting to freak her out. "I need you to hold me and comfort me," she added. "Not to interrogate me."

"Sorry." He removed his shoes and slipped into bed beside her. He put his arm around her and she rested her head on his shoulder and closed her eyes. This was more like it, she thought.

"Is the medicine helping any?" he asked after a few minutes.

"I just took it."

"Probably just nerves," he suggested.

"Why on earth would I be nervous?" she asked sarcastically.

"About the money," he said. "That's a lot of dough you won."

Lenora realized that her sarcasm had gone completely over Gerald's head. They weren't connecting. She removed her head from his shoulder and sat up straight. "I was kidding."

"About what?"

Lenora sighed. "Nothing. I'll be fine. The ticket is fine until I get down there to the lottery board."

"If you say so. I'm done talking about it," he said and stood up. Lenora watched with more than a bit of surprise as he walked to the kitchen, opened the refrigerator door, and removed a beer. He popped the cap and sat in front of the television.

She had never expected him to be so short on sympathy for what she might be going through emotionally after this major up-heaval. It felt like a bomb had exploded in her life. And Gerald had walked off to drink a beer and watch the tube.

Was Alise right? Was the money going to come between them?

CHAPTER 18

She tossed and turned all night in agitation. By late Tuesday morning, it felt like she hadn't had a minute of sleep. Still, she dragged herself out of bed to walk and feed Paws. She circled the building on that clear spring day and took lots of deep breaths, hoping that the fresh air would revive her.

Early that morning, Gerald stood over her for several seconds before leaving for work. She suspected that he wanted to say something to her, but she pretended to be asleep. She was as baffled by her sudden illness as anyone. Yet she was sure it was nothing but nerves and that it would pass. She didn't need Gerald bugging her about it, and she didn't need any doctors. What she needed was patience. She wished Gerald could recognize that.

The telephone rang as soon as she and Paws entered the condo. She walked into the kitchen and looked at the caller ID, hoping for the first time since they met all those years ago that it was *not* Gerald calling. She was in luck, but not by much. It was the office. She had completely forgotten to call in and let them know that she was taking another day off. She picked up, expecting to hear Jenna's voice.

"Lenora?"

Uh-oh, Lenora thought. It wasn't the receptionist. It was the boss.

"Hi, Dawna," she said. "I was about to call Jenna."

"To tell her that you're on your way to work, I hope," Dawna said. "You're already late. It's almost ten o'clock."

"Actually, no. I'm not feeling that well."

"Yesterday, Jenna said you were going to be out all day taking care of personal business. Now you're saying you're sick. Which is it, Lenora?"

Boy, what a bitch, Lenora thought, rolling her eyes to the ceiling. "Both, actually," she responded. "Some personal stuff came up that made me ill."

"What the hell does that mean?" Dawna asked.

Lenora grimaced. Talking to Dawna was always such a chore, and wanting to hold back information didn't help the situation. But she was determined to keep her secret

178

a secret, at least for now. "I can't explain today, but I will soon and you will definitely understand."

Dawna smacked her lips loudly. "The only thing I will understand is you getting your ass back into this office today," Dawna said. "There's work to be done. The photos of Ray and his crew are back from the editing department, and I want to go over them with you. I have questions about some of the selections, and I need a second opinion."

"I'm afraid I'm not up to it today, Dawna. Can Patrick do it?"

"No, he can't. He doesn't have your eye for this kind of detail. You know, I'm really getting annoyed with you, Lenora. Are you sure you want to keep your job? Because I'm beginning to wonder."

Look, lady, I'm sick! That was what Lenora wanted to shout. But she didn't. "Of course I do."

"Then I suggest you get in here within the hour unless you're so sick you need to be in a hospital bed." With that, Dawna slammed the receiver down.

Lenora jerked the receiver away from her ear. How did someone become so evil, so vile? she wondered. It was as if the woman had been placed on the planet to make Lenora's life miserable.

She walked to the bed and picked up the bottle of medicine on the nightstand. After struggling frantically to twist the safety cap off, she put the bottle to her lips and chugged several tablespoons' worth. Then she took a shower.

What she ought to do was go down to the lottery office, get her money, and quit once and for all. The hell with that woman. She didn't need this aggravation. And she didn't have to put up with it anymore.

But she wasn't ready to do that yet. She was determined not to act in haste and make a bunch of changes in her life that she might regret later. She had to take this slow and steady to preserve her sanity. She just wished everyone else would go along with her program.

After a brief but tense meeting with Dawna, Lenora sat at her desk and gulped more medicine while she played her office phone messages. She was surprised to discover that one of them was from Ray. He called the day before to ask how the photographs turned out. She listened to his voice and found herself smiling for the first time in days. He sounded so young and upbeat.

Fortunately Dawna had just sent the photographs of Ray to her by e-mail so that

Lenora could review them prior to a second meeting later that afternoon. She flipped through the images on her computer and especially liked the ones in which he stood near the weeping willow. He took such joy in his work and it showed.

She didn't know what had come over her when she foolishly deleted all of his images from her computer last week. Or with that silliness at home in bed with the one print photo she kept. Call it temporary lust-insanity. Whatever it was, she was embarrassed now just thinking about it. Ray was charming and cute beyond words, but he was just another man, a very young one at that. There was no reason to act like a fool about him.

She decided to call him back before reviewing the photographs for her meeting with Dawna. Talking to Ray would be a welcome relief from all the crazy things going on in her life now. She searched through the business cards on her computer until she found his number and put in a call to him. The phone rang and rang, and she was about to hang up when she heard his voice.

"Hi, Ray. It's Lenora."

"Who?"

"Lenora Stone from the *Baltimore Scene*

magazine. Remember? I'm returning your call."

"Oh, hey," he said. "I'm onsite and the phone almost slipped out of my hand. I didn't hear you at first. I assume you got my message. How are you?"

What a question. Her whole world had been flipped inside out. But she didn't need to tell him about that. "Oh, I'm hanging in there. How about you? How have you been?"

"Still working at the Moss Building, but it's coming along nicely now. You wouldn't recognize it."

"Good to hear that. Although I'm not surprised it turned out well. You're good at what you do."

"Thanks," he said. "So how did the photos turn out?"

"I just saw them. They look fantastic."

"Really? Do you think you could send me a few if I give you my e-mail address? Having a feature with photos in the *Baltimore Scene* is kind of a big deal for me."

Lenora smiled. She loved the sound of his voice. It was so pleasant. And so far removed from all the chaos in her life. Still, the smart thing to do would be to chat a bit, send him a couple of watermarked images that he couldn't copy or use, and move on. She was oddly fascinated by Ray, so it was probably wise not to cultivate a relationship with him. After all, she had a long-term boyfriend. She and Gerald were going through a rough spot, but Lenora was confident that they would get through it just as they had all the others.

"I can e-mail them to you, but they're going to have a watermark on them. Or I can print a few out and bring them to you if you'd like." What was she thinking? She knew that she should *not* do this. Besides, she was a somewhat geeky, overweight photographer, and he likely had beautiful women falling at his feet. He didn't have time to see her.

"That sounds good," he said, and she smiled in giddy surprise. "How about Friday around noon?" he asked. "We'll be wrapping up here, and my workload should be lighter by then. I can meet you at my office."

"Sounds perfect," she said. They hung up and Lenora stared into space. She could hardly believe what just happened. She walked into her office not thirty minutes ago and now she had a date to see Ray on Friday. Well, not a date in the usual sense. More like a meeting.

She would have loved to spend more time

daydreaming about what had just transpired and what it all meant. But with the upcoming meeting with Dawna and other staff members, she didn't have time. So she turned back to her computer and began reorganizing the photos of Ray for the magazine feature. She selected a few that she thought would be good for the cover and sent them to the shared photo printer down the hall. When she stood to retrieve the photos, she realized that her stomach was completely free of pain.

Chapter 19

Gerald called before she left her office for the meeting. He was happy to hear that she was feeling well enough to go into the office and asked when she planned to visit the lottery board. She assured him that she would go after her meeting. She halfway believed that when she said it, but as soon as they hung up she knew it wasn't true. She would go when the time was right, not a minute sooner, and it didn't feel right just yet.

When she reached her condo that evening, the spicy aroma of Gerald's pasta sauce greeted her the moment she walked in the door. She was startled to find that he had already let himself in and started dinner. He used to cook for her often but hadn't in many months.

"This is a nice surprise," she said as she dropped her camera bag on the couch along with a bag of medicine from the drugstore.

"I already walked Paws," he said. "So

relax, unwind."

"Really? And you're cooking, too? Next you'll tell me you scrubbed the bathroom down," she teased as she bent over and petted Paws. She entered the kitchen, peeked over Gerald's shoulder, and took a good whiff. "Smells yummy. But I'm afraid I can only have a taste. I'm on a low-fat diet starting today. No more excuses. I really have to lose some weight."

"You might want to hold off and start that diet tomorrow," he said. He scooped a bit of the sauce into a small spoon, blew on it to cool it, and fed it to her.

"Mmm. Delicious," she said.

"It needs to simmer for another thirty minutes to bring out all the flavors. I figured you were up for a nice meal since you sounded pretty good when we talked earlier. How's the stomach?"

"Much better," she said. "I stopped and picked up some more medicine as a precaution. I think I'll take some now. Be right back."

She entered the bathroom with her stash of medicine and opened the bag. What she removed was a package of weight-loss pills, though, not medicine for her stomach. She didn't want Gerald to know that she was using diet pills. He would probably feel they

186

were unsafe and lecture her about losing the weight the old-fashioned way, with less food intake and lots of exercise. She didn't want to hear that. She needed to drop the weight fast — preferably by her meeting with Ray on Friday. Unfortunately, it would be impossible to shed more than a few pounds by then, but she had to at least start. Every ounce would help.

She scanned the directions on the bottle, took her first pill, then hid the package at the top of the medicine cabinet. When she walked back into the kitchen, Gerald was placing a single red rose in a glass bud vase on the kitchen table. She jerked back in amazement.

"Wow, that's nice," she said. "Who are you and what did you do with my boyfriend? Kidnap him?"

Gerald laughed. "I know this has been a tough time for you and I want you to take it easy. Hope this little bit helps."

"It helps a lot." She bent over to smell the rose then kissed him. "Thanks."

"How'd it go today?" he asked, walking back to the stove to stir the sauce as she sat at the table.

"Good." She knew what Gerald really wanted to know. "I didn't go down there," she said before he could ask. "Not yet."

He turned and stared at her. "All right." He was clearly surprised but trying to pretend otherwise. "What happened?" he asked.

"Nothing happened. I'm just not ready."

"Well, when will you be, Lenora? I don't mean to push. I really don't. But I'm beginning to wonder if you'll ever get down there to claim your winnings."

"Don't be silly," she countered. "How could I let that much money go?"

"Do you even know how much you'll actually collect?"

"Depends on how many winners there were. I'll call tomorrow to find out."

"I already did that today. It's public information. There was only one winner. You."

Lenora blinked with astonishment. It somehow made winning feel even more real to hear him say that she had won the entire prize. But she also found it disturbing that he took it upon himself to check on *her* winnings. "I can't believe you called before I could get around to it."

He chuckled with sarcasm. "I just told you that you were the only winner, and you're complaining about me calling down there? You're unbelievable."

"I could say the same thing about you. I

can't believe you did that." She had a mind to tell him to back the hell off and let her handle this at her own pace. But she didn't want to turn him off completely. "Never mind," she said, flicking her wrist. "It's done now."

He sat down across from her. "Look, I'm trying my best to understand what's going on with you. But I honestly don't get it. You won the lottery, but you act like something bad happened to you."

"I admit that I'm not myself. I'm not. But have you thought about what I might be going through emotionally? This is a *lot* of money. What if I slip up and do something stupid? I used to wonder why people sometimes took weeks and even months to claim their winnings. Now I understand it in a way that only someone who has actually won this kind of money can probably understand. They were waiting to get their heads together."

"Maybe you're right, and I'm just on the outside looking in at this point. Someone who can't possibly understand what you're dealing with." He raised both hands, palms out. "If you want me to back off entirely, that's what I'll do."

This was exactly what Lenora was afraid of. That he would get defensive and turn a cold shoulder. Why did this have to be so difficult with him? "That's not what I want, Gerald. I want you to support me without pushing. I want you to be there for me."

He nodded slowly.

"I'm not asking you to back off altogether," she continued. "At times I probably need some prodding, but you don't have to be so relentless. Sometimes I feel like I'm going nuts and I don't need you to pile it on. Try to have faith that I'll see this thing through eventually."

He reached across the table, gently took her hands, and looked into her eyes. "Okay, I'm not sure I understand your thinking, but I'll try my damnedest to be better about this with you."

"Thanks. I appreciate that." This was one of those times when she and Gerald were so far apart they could be night and day. But at least he was trying. He was here fixing dinner for her and attempting in his own way to work with her. How many women could say that about their men?

It was enough to make her feel guilty about meeting Ray on Friday. But not so guilty that she was going to cancel. Besides, she and Ray were meeting just to look at photographs. No harm in that.

CHAPTER 20

As Lenora pulled into the lot in front of Ray's office building near Little Patuxent Parkway in Columbia, Maryland, on Friday afternoon, she reached a decision that she had fretted over for days. She would not tell Ray about the money. Yes, it was now a huge part of her life, but it also complicated things. The few people who knew about her lottery winnings — Gerald, Alise, and Monica — all acted different around her now.

Monica was calling way more than usual, sometimes several times a day, to the point of really getting on Lenora's nerves. Especially since all she talked about was how the money would help them get into The Girlfriends.

"Girl, we are so in as soon as you let them know about all the money you won," Monica had said when she called early that morning as Lenora was about to walk out the door for work. This was after they had talked until midnight the day before during a break in Monica's night shift at the hospital.

"When do you plan to start telling more people?" Monica asked that morning. " 'Cause whenever I talk to people we both know, I have to watch what I say about you."

"When I'm good and ready," Lenora said firmly. She was standing at the phone on the kitchen wall, camera bag dangling from one shoulder, car keys in hand, ready to leave.

"Well, how soon do you think that'll be?" Monica asked. "I'm not trying to push you or anything, you know. Just asking."

"It sure feels like you're pushing," Lenora said. "When I am ready, you'll be one of the first to know."

"That's what you said the other day."

"And I'm going to say the same damn thing tomorrow and the next day when you ask me again."

"Whoa," Monica said. "You don't have to get an attitude about it."

"If I have an attitude it's 'cause I'm tired of you asking me the same thing over and over. 'When are you going to start telling people? When are you going down to the lottery office?' Not to mention that it's eight-thirty in the damn morning and I have to get to work. Don't you have surgical patients waiting for you to start an IV or plump their pillows up or something?"

"Good-bye," Monica said and hung up on her.

Alise was behaving in exactly the opposite way. She had stopped calling altogether after they had gotten into a tiff about Gerald when Alise insinuated that the money would change him.

So she wasn't even going to mention the money to Ray. She didn't want Ray and the easygoing relationship they were developing to change. She wanted to keep things nice and simple. She might not even see him again after today anyway.

Ray worked in one of the office parks scattered around Columbia, and Lenora found a parking space in front of the address to Ray's unit, checked her lipstick in the rearview mirror, and hopped out. She wasn't sure whether to knock or just enter but decided to try the knob. The door opened and she stepped into a large, neat one-room office with three desks lined up against one wall. On the opposite side were file cabinets, a long narrow table, and a few odd hard chairs. Yard tools hung from hooks along both walls.

A woman who appeared to be in her fifties sat at the desk nearest the door. She smiled and beckoned for Lenora to enter. At the far end, Lenora saw Ray seated with his work boots propped up on his desk and the phone to his ear. The middle desk was unoccupied at the moment, although someone obviously worked there, given all the papers, folders, and pencils on top of it.

"Hi," Lenora said to the woman. "I'm here to see Ray."

The woman glanced back at Ray, and he smiled and gestured for Lenora to come and sit in a chair in front of his desk. He covered the mouthpiece as Lenora approached. "I'll just be a minute."

The other woman gathered her shoulder bag and left, probably for lunch, Lenora thought as she sat and placed the folder holding the photographs on the edge of Ray's desk. She leaned back and looked around. It seemed like a busy office, she thought as a telephone rang. Ray quickly said good-bye to the person he was talking to, pressed a button on his phone, and picked up on the line that was ringing. Lenora hoped he wouldn't feel that she was intruding and regret agreeing to meet with her.

"Yes, yes," he said softly. "I got it. Look, can you call back around one? My secretary just left for lunch. She keeps the schedule and she should be back by then. Right, right. She'll set you up." He nodded and listened for another minute. "Sure thing. We'll talk soon." He hung up, swung his feet to the ground, and smiled at her.

"Sorry about that," he said.

"No problem. I hope it isn't a bad time for us to meet. You seem to be really busy."

"It's fine," he said. "Things are a little crazy, but I'd rather be too busy than not enough. So how are you?"

"I'm doing good," she said, reaching up to smooth her hair. She wished she were skinnier, prettier, and more charming, she thought. Otherwise she was fine. "A lot has happened since we last met."

"Oh. At work?"

"No, personal. But I don't want to get into that now," she said. "Maybe another time. How have you been?"

"Busy, as you can see," he said. "But it's all good."

Lenora wondered if that was a hint that he wanted her to move quickly with this so he could get back to work. Shame on her for bringing up personal stuff. "Um, I brought the photos for you."

He scooted closer to the desk as she opened the folder. "I'm looking forward to seeing them," he said.

She turned the folder to face him. "This shot of you standing by the tree with your workers in the background is one of my favorites. We'll probably use that as the lead photo, maybe even on the cover."

"The cover? Really?"

She nodded. "The managing editor loved the photos and the article."

He nodded as he sifted through the photographs, one by one. "These are damn good," he said. "I don't know how you managed it, but it doesn't even look like we're at the Moss location."

"Thanks," she said. She could feel her cheeks getting warm at the compliments coming from Ray. "I love what I do, for the most part."

"For the most part?" he repeated, glancing up at her. "What don't you like about it?"

"Some of the people I work with," she said. "Like my boss, the managing editor."

He nodded. "Met her a couple of weeks ago when she came to the Moss Building. Is she difficult?"

"You could say that."

Ray smiled. "So no female bonding going on there, I take it?"

Lenora smiled. "You would be right about

that. But I didn't come here to burden you with my work troubles. I really do enjoy my job, especially getting out with my camera and looking over a scene to figure out how to make it all look good. It's like a blank canvas."

He looked at her with understanding. "Our work is similar in that way. I love being in the field, seeing things take shape as I mold the land with my hands and a few tools."

"So how did you get into landscaping?"

"By accident, really. My grandma passed away, and my mother inherited the house. It had several acres and the grounds were in terrible shape. I was working for the Interior Department then, in a boring desk job, but I dabbled in yard work. When Ma got a bid to clean the place up and it was in the thousands, I told her I would do it myself on weekends and evenings for half that amount. She agreed. A couple of the neighbors liked what I did and asked me to fix up their properties. Eventually I had so much work that I quit my regular job and did landscaping full-time."

"That's very interesting how you fell into it," she said. "Sounds like you were meant to do this."

He nodded. "I think so. There have been

some real rough times, no doubt about it. At one point I thought I was going to have to go back to the nine-to-five. I wasn't getting enough residential work to stay afloat. Then I caught a break, landed a contract to do the landscaping for a new luxury apartment building. Haven't looked back since."

"I hope you talked about all of this when you spoke to Linda for the article that she's writing about you and your work," she said. "It's a wonderful story."

"And these are wonderful photos," he said. He went back to the first photo and flipped through each of them again, one by one.

Lenora watched in silence and slowly found herself transfixed on his hands. She loved the size, the shape, the color. They were rugged yet gentle, soft yet strong, and his movements were so precise. She shifted her eyes to his face as he studied the photos. Not only was he extremely attractive, he was also intelligent and very interesting to talk to. He was the complete package, the kind of man most women fantasized about.

And the kind of man who would never give a woman like her a second thought romantically or even as a close friend. At least not before she came into money. That single fact could change the landscape for her entirely, she thought. She might not have much in the looks department, but she had lots of money. Actually, she was loaded.

She cleared her throat. She couldn't believe she was planning to go through with this wild idea in her head. But if she was going to do it, she didn't have a lot of time to think it over and that was probably just as well. No doubt she would chicken out if she thought it through. It could backfire big-time, it could . . . No, no. She wasn't going to go there.

"Remember when I mentioned that a lot was going on in my personal life?"

Ray looked up at her. He nodded. "Yes. Is everything okay?"

"Other than getting the surprise of a lifetime, everything is fine. I won the lottery."

He lifted his brows. "Really? Judging from your face, it was a lot."

She smiled. "Five million."

He whistled and his eyes popped wide open.

She laughed at the reaction. She was loving this sudden enthusiastic attention from him.

"When did this happen?" he asked.

"I found out on Sunday."

"You weren't kidding when you said a lot

had happened since I last saw you. Congratulations!"

"Thanks."

"So what's in store for you now? That must change everything."

She sighed at the thought. "It will be a lot less after taxes, but I'm still in shock, trying to wrap my head around it. I haven't even gone to claim my winnings yet."

"My understanding is that you have months to claim it."

"A hundred and eighty-two days."

He waved a hand nonchalantly. "Then it's not going anywhere. Give yourself time to adjust."

"That's what I'm trying to do, but everyone seems to think I'm moving too slowly. They think I should have been down at the lottery office the first weekday after I won."

"You have to do what's right for you," he said. "Don't make any rash decisions. Take all the time you need."

"That's exactly what I intend to do." Finally, someone who understood, Lenora thought. Even if he barely knew her, at least he saw her point of view. That was refreshing. She wasn't expecting Ray to suddenly drop down on one knee and propose due to her revelation about the lottery or even to want to get involved with her. But she liked him. Perhaps the money would pique his curiosity about her enough that he would want to be friends. Having a friend who won the lottery could be pretty cool. "Not to change the subject too suddenly, but do you mind if I take a few shots of you now?" she asked. "Your expression since I told you is priceless. My camera is right in the car."

He laughed. "You really know how to lay on the surprises. I don't have to pose or anything, do I?"

"No. I prefer candid shots."

He nodded in agreement, and she ran outside and grabbed her camera bag from the trunk of the Honda. She returned and asked him to act natural, to do what he normally did at his desk. He leaned back and put his feet up while she circled his desk and fired away.

"By any chance, do you work on the side?" he asked. "Wait a minute. You don't need freelance money." He laughed.

"I never did it only for the money," she said quickly as she lowered her camera. "It's something I love to do and don't plan to stop. At least not yet. What do you have in mind?"

"I need some photos for a brochure I'm putting together for my landscaping busi-ness." He chuckled. "Or at least I've been trying to. I could use some help with the layout. Actually, I need someone who can put the entire thing together. All I've got so far is a few paragraphs that I wrote about my background."

"I'm your girl," Lenora said, trying to keep her cool. "I've worked on more brochures than I can count."

Ray got up, walked to a cabinet across the room, and returned with a file full of sample brochures. He said he had saved them as examples of what he liked. They stood side by side at his desk, their arms brushing now and then, and Lenora felt a little woozy with excitement. It was the first time she had been so close to him. But as they pored over the brochures and he shared his thoughts and ideas, she quickly shifted into work mode. They were in her realm now, discussing what she loved best. She talked about some of the brochures and other freelance work she had done over the years, and he seemed impressed.

"Can you work up an estimate for the brochure and fax or e-mail it to me? Or call me when it's ready." He reached across his desk, picked up a business card and handed it to her.

She took it and gathered her things. She had what she wanted, an excuse to see him again. "I should be able to get back to you by Monday."

She was all smiles as she left his office and walked to her car. She couldn't believe she actually pulled that off, she thought as she climbed into the driver's seat. She was going to see Ray again. They were going to work together. It had been a long time since she'd felt so excited about spending time with someone.

For a few brief moments, as she waited at a traffic light, she allowed her mind to wander to thoughts of driving back to Ray's office, strolling in, and seducing him right on his desk. Her thoughts traveled back to the tingling sensation that flooded through her body as they stood next to each other, arms touching. She fantasized about what it would feel like to have him on top of her, deep inside her, making mad love to her.

The light turned green and she snapped back to reality. She realized, of course, that if she was going to work with Ray she had to get past this insane crush on him. She already had a man, someone she had been with for years. She had no reason to moon about someone she barely knew.

No doubt Gerald was going to think she was nuts for considering freelance work when she had just won five million dollars.

So would Monica and Alise. Now that she thought about it, maybe it *was* nuts. She had just won a boatload of money and had yet to go claim it. Instead, she was accepting freelance work that would pay her a couple of thousand dollars at most. Did it even make sense? Not really. Was she going to do it? Probably.

Nuts or not, she wasn't feeling sick anymore. In fact, she was happy for the first time in days. On Monday morning, she would go down to the lottery board with the golden ticket and claim her winnings. She was beginning to realize that all that money could bring a lot of good things into her life. She wasn't even sure why she had freaked out about it. The money wouldn't change her life in a bad way if she didn't allow it to. She would be sensible about how she spent it and get good advice. Hell, she could afford to get the best damn advice in the world.

She smacked the steering wheel and laughed out loud. She was a millionaire! It was about time she started acting like one.

CHAPTER 21

She walked out of the Maryland Lottery headquarters in Baltimore at ten on Monday morning and decided to celebrate by buying a new car. Her dream car, a BMW. She knew exactly where the dealership was near Baltimore. It was as if she had been planning this day all her life.

"BMW 750Li, here I come!" she announced as she exited the building and headed for her beat-up Honda. Thing was so old she was almost embarrassed to drive it onto the BMW lot, but she quickly got past her shame when she saw all the shiny new luxury automobiles. They seemed to be waiting for her, and she spent more than two hours roaming around the showroom on Baltimore National Pike, looking at color combinations, features, and options. By the time she settled into her new cashmere silver BMW, it was past noon.

Lunchtime traffic would be a bear, but

she decided to drive to Gerald's office forty minutes away in Silver Spring anyway and offer to buy him lunch. Lately he had been much more flexible about leaving work to have lunch or dinner with her. It was amazing how much more available people had been since she won the lottery. She dialed Gerald's cell number while sitting in the lot.

"Hello?" came a woman's voice.

Lenora frowned into her phone. Had she dialed wrong? "Hi, who am I talking to?"

"Robin. Gerald stepped out of his office. Oh, wait. Here's Gerald now."

Lenora heard a light rustle and Gerald came on the line. "Hello?" he said.

"Hi, it's me," Lenora said.

"Hey, baby," he said warmly.

"Who was that?"

"Oh, that's Robin."

"I know her name is Robin. She just told me. What's she doing answering your cell phone?"

"She's a coworker. We were going over some papers and I stepped out. My cell was on my desk. She was nice enough to pick it up."

"Seems rather presumptuous of her. Cell phones are pretty personal. She knows you that well?"

"She was only trying to be helpful."

"Mm-hmm."

"Come on, Lenora," he said. "Don't be that way. She's just a coworker."

Lenora wasn't sure what to think. People didn't normally go around answering other people's cell phones unless they were close. The whole thing seemed weird, but it could be entirely innocent, nothing more than a coworker helping out as Gerald said. Gerald had never given her any real reason not to trust him since the affair. And yet he *did* have an affair, which was what made incidents like this, when they popped up once in a while, so nerve-racking.

But Lenora decided to give him the benefit of the doubt. Besides, she wanted to give him the good news. "Guess where I am," she said.

"I have no idea. I hear traffic. In your car?"

"Right. But not that raggedy old Honda. That thing is ancient history. I'm about to leave the car dealership and drive down Baltimore National Pike in my brand-new BMW."

"What?"

She giggled like a schoolgirl. "Yes. You heard right."

"So does this mean you finally went to the lottery board?"

"Yep."

"Damn," he said. "You mentioned that you were going this morning, but I thought you would probably change your mind again."

"Nope, not this time. I finally did it."

"Oh, man. How was it?"

"Scary but exciting," she said. "They want me to go back and pose for a photo holding one of those giant-size checks, but I told them I'd think about it. I'm not sure I want to do that."

"Don't do it," he said. "They put that in the newspaper. When people see it, everyone and their mama will start calling on you with their hands out wanting some."

"I know," she said. "I'm going to have enough trouble with that without any publicity once the word gets out."

"So which model did you get?" he asked.

"750Li."

He chuckled softly. "Of course. When do I get to see it?"

"How about now? I was going to swing by your office and buy you lunch to celebrate if that works for you."

"That works just fine for me. Can't wait to see it."

"Let's meet at the restaurant next door to your building in about forty minutes," Lenora said. "You going to stay at my place tonight?"

"If you'll have me."

"What do you mean? Of course I will."

"I'm kidding," he said. "You have all that money now. For all I know, you might have other ideas about what to do with me."

"Don't be silly," she said. "We're still a hot couple."

"Does that mean you still want to take things to the next level?"

She blinked. "If you're saying what I think you are, I'm shocked."

"Is that a yes or a no?"

"A yes, of course," she said without thinking further.

"Glad to hear that," he said. "I'll have to see what I can do about it."

That was odd, she thought after they said good-bye and she pulled off. Gerald might finally be about to propose to her, and she would have expected to be much more excited. Instead, she felt like she needed to think about it. So much had changed.

Lenora smacked her cheek. What the hell was she thinking? Of course she wanted to marry Gerald. She had wanted this for years. Now was not the time to get stupid just because she had the hots for some young thing. She had a silly crush on Ray, nothing more. She would get over it soon enough. She was probably already past it.

So why haven't you contacted him to give him an estimate for the freelance brochure job, as you promised him you would? a tiny voice in her head asked. *If you're in control of your emotions when it comes to Ray, what are you scared of?*

The truth was, her attraction to Ray was as strong as ever. As much as she tried to avoid it, she fantasized about him several times a day and drooled over his photograph at night. Ray was all kinds of trouble, and Lenora wasn't sure she could trust herself alone with him. So last night she made up her mind not to contact him. She had a good thing going with Gerald and she didn't want to mess with that. Everything was finally falling into place, and if she didn't do anything foolish, she had a feeling that this could be the beginning of a long, happy life for her with Gerald.

She decided to try to reach Alise at her office next. They hadn't talked for several days, since the last time they spoke the conversation ended badly. But Lenora decided that morning on her way to get the BMW that she wasn't going to hold grudges. She had known Alise longer than she'd known Gerald. They'd had a lot of fun times together. And Alise had been driving BMWs for years. She'd love to exchange notes about the car. It was the perfect excuse to call her old friend and make amends.

Alise picked up on the third ring.

"Hello, Alise," Lenora said. "Got some time to talk?"

"A little," Alise said. "I'm meeting a client to show a house and I have to leave in a few minutes. What's up?"

"I'm sorry if I was short the last time we spoke," Lenora said. "I was going through a rough spot."

"Don't worry about it."

"Good. Glad we got that out of the way. Guess what?"

"What?" Alise asked.

"I bought a BMW."

"Really?"

Lenora nodded into the phone. "I'm about to pull off the lot."

"How exciting for you. Which model did you get?"

"The 750Li," Lenora said. "Same one you have."

"Ah, no," Alise said. "I've always had the 500 series."

"Really? For some reason I thought you drove a 750."

"Nope, not me."

"Well, the 750 drives like a dream, girl," Lenora said.

"No doubt."

"Now I know why you like them so much, Alise. I think it's spoiling me for anything else ever."

"Lucky you."

Lenora thought there was something odd in Alise's tone. Normally Alise had so much to say — often too much. Today she hardly uttered more than a sentence at a time. "Where do you take it for service?" Lenora asked.

"Always to the dealer."

"Even for small jobs like oil changes?"

"Yes."

There it was again. The ultra-short comment. So unlike Alise. "Thanks for the advice."

"Of course. I'm so sorry to have to cut this short, Lenora, but I really have to go meet this client."

"No problem," Lenora said. "We'll talk another time."

Alise didn't even bother to say good-bye. She just hung up. Lenora stared at the phone for a second. What was that all about? Could Alise still be upset about their last telephone call, when they had the spat about

Gerald? Or maybe Alise really was in a rush or had some personal things going on. Lenora shrugged. She wasn't going to let this drag her down. Not now. She had already spent too much time since winning feeling depressed.

Forty minutes later Lenora pulled into a parking lot in Silver Spring near Gerald's office building. She drove around the lot until she found a spot near the wall situated so that only one car would be next to hers and the chances of someone nicking this beauty would be lowered.

When she walked into the restaurant, Gerald was already in a booth waiting for her. He stood and waved, then gave her a warm hug and kiss before she sat across from him. He motioned for her to move closer and she slid across the leather seat. Lenora liked the new positive energy she felt coming from Gerald.

"You look gorgeous," he said as he placed his hand over hers on the table. "You look happy."

"I am. I feel relieved, refreshed. It's thrilling to realize that you don't have to worry about money. I feel fifty pounds lighter, even though I've only lost about five."

"That much? Five pounds in a week is

nothing to sneeze at."

She didn't tell him that she had some extra help with the diet pills. "I don't know why I waited so long to go to the lottery office. It was so silly of me."

"Don't beat yourself up about it. Better late than never. You needed some time, that's all."

She nodded as the waiter approached the table with a bottle of champagne. "I already ordered this," Gerald said as the waiter popped the cork and filled their flutes. "I hope you don't mind."

"I would have preferred wine," she said. "Or a glass of Baileys."

"Come on," he said. "This occasion begs for champagne. Don't you think?"

"You're right," she said. Even though she wasn't crazy about it, if ever there was a moment for champagne, this was it.

He raised his glass and she followed suit. "To Maryland's cutest, smartest, sweetest millionaire." He said it with lots of enthusiasm but not so loudly that others in the lounge would hear above the faint music in the background.

She laughed. "I'll drink to all of that."

"So tell me more about what happened when you went down there," he said.

"Well, I decided to take the single cash

payment instead of getting annuity payments over the next twenty-five years. It's a lot less money, but you get it all now."

"How much less?" he asked.

She leaned close to him and whispered in his ear.

"I don't know," he said. "I might have taken the annuity payments. I'd have to do the math."

"The idea is to invest it so it can earn interest," she said. "I've been reading up on this."

"Hey, it's your money. You wanted to handle it on your own, and I'll support your decisions whatever they are. What color is the car?"

"Cashmere silver," she said with an uppity air.

"How much?"

She leaned close again and filled him in with a whisper.

He nodded knowingly. "That's about what I thought."

"I could have ordered something more customized, but I was too excited to drive one off the lot today. And I can always afford to order another one later if I want."

"Baby, you can order up a Bentley or Rolls if that's what you want."

Her eyes grew big. "Ooh," she said. "Don't

put ideas into my head."

Gerald laughed.

After lunch, they decided that he would walk her to the BMW and they would ride around downtown Columbia a bit before he went back to the office. They approached the BMW 750Li and Gerald circled around it, nodding admiringly; then he sat in the passenger seat and looked it over inside.

"You like it?" she asked from the driver's seat.

"What's not to like?" he asked. "Although I might have gotten a different interior color, this is a beauty in any color."

She dangled the keys in his face. "Want to take it for a spin?"

He took them from her. "I was wondering when you were going to ask me that."

They switched sides and Lenora could see how pleased he was as he sat in the driver's seat. He removed his cell phone, placed it in a small compartment on the dashboard, and started the ignition. He smiled and nodded with approval as the engine purred.

"Nice," he said. He leaned over and gave her a kiss on the lips before he carefully put the gear into reverse.

"What I wouldn't give to drive something like this every day," he said as they exited the lot and headed down Colesville Road.

216

She smiled. "Let's go pick something out for you next weekend."

"Whoa," he said, clearly surprised. "I'm not expecting anything. No, you wait until you get your finances in order. You got a few bills to catch up on, don't you? We have plenty of time."

His cell phone rang as he was attempting to make a left turn into traffic. So she picked it up. The moment she saw the caller's first name, she stiffened.

"It's Robin Lewis," she said as he completed his turn. He took the phone from her, pressed a button, and put the phone back in the compartment. Rarely did Gerald let his phone go unanswered. He would sometimes tell the person on the line that he would have to call them back later, but he almost always picked up.

"I'm shocked you didn't pick up," she said. "You never do that."

"It can wait until I get back to the office."

"That the Robin who answered your phone when I called earlier?"

He nodded reluctantly.

"Is that why you didn't want me to hear the conversation?"

"Not at all," he said. "I just want to be careful. I'm driving a brand-new, very expensive car that I'm not used to handling.

I don't want to mess it up."

Something about this was really starting to bother Lenora. Who was this Robin? And why was she popping up all over the place? "Is she going to be there when you go back?"

Gerald took her hand as he pulled up in front of his office building. "Yes, she's going to be there. We work together. Look, Lenora, it's been two years since that happened. When are you going to learn to trust me again?"

She smiled thinly. She really wanted to do that. He had done nothing to cause serious suspicion. But she was having a hard time putting his cheating to rest. Obviously it didn't take much to dredge the memories back up to the surface. A simple phone call from a female coworker and it was as if it had all happened just yesterday. "You're right."

"I'll come by your place after work for dinner," he said. "That is if you still want me to."

She nodded. "Of course."

He exited the car and she came around and climbed into the driver's seat. It was a high traffic area lined with No Parking signs, and they kissed quickly on the lips. Then she drove off.

CHAPTER 22

When Lenora heard Gerald enter the condo that evening, she was in the kitchen mixing apple martinis. The drinks were to lighten the mood after the tense lunchtime drive in her new BMW. She wanted them to relax and enjoy the meal she had prepared of blackened salmon, grilled corn and peppers, and frozen yogurt topped with fresh strawberries for a lightweight dessert.

She peeked around the corner from the kitchen and saw that he was changing into shorts and a T-shirt. He winked at her and sat down on the love seat in the front room to change his shoes. She went back to her cocktail shaker and filled it with ice, followed with vodka. She added apple juice and Sour Apple Pucker and shook. Then she filled two plastic martini glasses. This would be the last time she used these cheap martini glasses. Later this week she was going to shop for some kick-ass crystal.

Gerald came and stood behind her at the sink. "Mm, that looks delicious," he said.

She picked up one of the flutes, turned, and lifted it to his mouth. "What does it need?" she asked.

"Tastes fine to me," he said, smacking his lips generously.

She nodded in agreement and they took their glasses and sat on the couch in front of the television. They were about halfway through their drinks when Gerald turned the volume down on the TV, then took her flute and placed it on the coffee table next to his. He removed his eyeglasses and she knew exactly what was coming. Their once-weekly alphabet-soup lovemaking. A, nibble on ear. B, get naked. C, enter, missionary style. D, catch breath.

This time there actually was a little more variety to the routine. As she lay face up, one leg thrown over the back of the couch, a little black beetle of some kind slowly crossed the ceiling above them. Lenora stared as it stopped and started repeatedly in its trip to the other side of the room. She made a bet to herself that Gerald would wrap up his business before the beetle finished its journey.

She won the bet. The beetle was a little more than halfway across when Gerald lifted himself up off her and pulled his boxer shorts back on. She sat up and giggled uncontrollably as she slipped her clothes back on.

"What's wrong with you?" Gerald asked, staring at her in puzzlement.

She shook her head. "Nothing."

"No one laughs at nothing," he said.

"You are so right," she said. "Must be the martini."

"Half a martini and you're drunk?"

"Empty stomach." She couldn't bear to tell him the truth — that watching the bug cross the ceiling was more suspenseful than sex with him. She exhaled deeply.

"So tell me," he said. "What's it feel like to be rich?"

She leaned back on the couch. At least talking about the money should be interesting. "It freaked me out at first."

"So you admit that now."

She nodded. "I was scared to death."

"I know."

"Everyone else was thinking and talking about all the good things the money would bring me, but I was thinking about what I could lose."

"You mean like that beat-up old Honda?" he teased.

She laughed. "Or a job with a boss I

always complain about anyway."

He lifted his brow. "You're thinking of quitting?"

"I've thought about it. But thinking is the operative word. At least now."

"Not before you find something else, I hope," he said. "You won a lot of money, but it won't be enough after taxes to live on forever unless you're real careful about how you spend it. A BMW doesn't fall under 'real careful.' "

"Oh, I'd start something of my own. Like a business selling my photos to greeting card companies or a photography studio. What do you think?"

"I like the idea, but that kind of thing takes a lot of time and work to set up," he said. "You can't rush it. You need to plan carefully before you quit your job. And it wouldn't hurt to wait a year or two for the economy to come back."

"But with the money I won, I could afford to set up a photography studio, even to buy a small building somewhere in Baltimore and support myself while I build the business slowly. That's something I've dreamed about. And now I can do it."

"No doubt that's exciting. All I'm saying is to take some time to think it through. Look at the numbers. I can help you there.

Talk to other photographers who have done this and ask the hard questions. Be realistic about what they tell you, because once you take the plunge, it's difficult to undo. You see what our firm is going through. We're even starting to talk about shutting down."

Lenora's eyes widened. "What? You never told me things were that bad. When did this come up?"

"We've discussed it, but not seriously until we lost the client last week. That was a huge blow after all the effort we put into trying to hold on. With the way things are going recently, we have to put that on the table as a real possibility."

"I'm so sorry to hear this. Why didn't you tell me before?"

"You were going through your own stuff when all this was going down. You weren't feeling well, and I didn't want to burden you further."

Lenora shook her head with disbelief. "I'm shocked that it's come this far, Gerald. Now I understand why you've been putting so many hours in. I'm sorry I was such a nag about it."

He nodded with appreciation.

"What about taking out another business loan?"

"Normally that's what we would do. But

that's not going to happen in this financial climate. Banks aren't exactly scrambling over each other to make loans to struggling PR firms."

"Maybe I can help. How much do you think you all would need to keep going until the economy turns around?"

He put his hands up, palms out, in protest. "Absolutely not. I'm not expecting you to do anything like that. That's your money, not mine."

"We're a couple, Gerald, and we have been for years. I'm happy to help if I can."

He shook his head firmly. "This is my problem. I'll work it out with my partners."

"Don't be so stubborn," she said. "If I can help, you should let me."

"Let me talk it over with my partners," he said. "They may not even want to go forward. And the only way I would accept such an offer is if we considered it a loan. We would pay you back every cent. That's the *only* way."

"Fine," she said. "Just let me know. I would do this for you even if we weren't a couple. We've known each other for so long, and I know I could depend on you to pay me back."

That was Gerald, she thought as he picked up the remote and turned the volume back up. Reliable, dependable. *Boring.* Let's face it. They got along, and she enjoyed his company well enough. He would make a good business partner, a great friend. But did she really want this man as her lawful wedded husband for the rest of her life? It was something to think about.

CHAPTER 23

Monica called on Friday night to tell her that she was meeting Alise for lunch on Saturday afternoon and suggested that Lenora join them. Lenora wasn't sure that was a good idea, given the way Alise had acted so cool when they last talked. But she agreed to meet them and even offered to treat her friends to dinner.

"Did you tell Alise that I was going to be here?" Lenora asked Monica from across the table at P.F. Chang's China Bistro.

"I tried to reach her this morning but couldn't," Monica said. "I left her a message."

"So she might not know I'm here, depending on whether she checked her messages."

"Is that a problem?" Monica asked.

"Last time I spoke to her she was real chilly. It was like she didn't want to be bothered with me."

Monica frowned. "Why would she act

like that?"

"Beats me," Lenora said. "I have no idea."

"There she is," Monica said, waving toward the entrance. "I think you're probably imagining things, Lenora."

"Maybe," Lenora said as Alise walked up to the table.

"How's it going?" Alise asked as she slid into the booth next to Monica.

"Fine," Monica said. "It's good to see you."

"Sorry to be late. I had to take Junior to the ballpark this morning. Hello, Lenora."

Lenora smiled. "Hi, Alise."

After the three of them ordered, Alise shook her cloth napkin out and placed it in her lap. Lenora buttered a roll. Neither spoke and they avoided each other's eyes. That was when Lenora knew for certain that something was going on with Alise, although exactly what she wasn't sure.

"So tell us what you've been up to since you won the lottery, Lenora," Monica said.

Lenora swallowed her bread and cleared her throat. "It took me more than a week to claim my winnings. I was freaking out."

"I know," Monica said. "What was that about?"

Lenora shrugged. "Nerves, I guess. For some reason, I obsessed about all the negative things the money might mean rather than focus on the positive. Anyway, I'm completely over it now."

"Good." Monica nodded absentmindedly and looked at Alise. It was obvious to Lenora that Monica had caught on that Alise was not her normal, chatty, and opinionated self. "I saw the new BMW outside," Monica said. "Very nice."

"Thanks," Lenora said.

"Did she tell you she got a new BMW?" Monica asked Alise.

Alise blinked. "Yes."

"Did you see it outside?" Monica asked.

"How could I miss it?" Alise replied.

Lenora and Monica exchanged glances. What kind of response was that? Lenora wondered. Was Alise jealous about the new car? And that Lenora now had an even bigger and better model BMW? If so, Lenora couldn't believe that Alise could be so shallow.

"I love the color," Monica said. "What color is that?"

"Cashmere silver," Lenora said. She could take it no longer. Alise had always been a little on the uppity side, but this was different. She was standoffish and distant. "What's going on with you, Alise?" Lenora blurted out.

Alise lifted a brow. "Excuse me?"

"Why the attitude?" Lenora asked. "And it seems to be directed only at me. Did I do something? 'Cause I don't get it."

"I'm noticing it too," Monica said. "Is everything okay with you, Alise?"

"Everything is fine with me," Alise responded.

"The last time we talked, you hung up on me," Lenora said.

"I did not hang up on you."

"You didn't even bother to say good-bye," Lenora said. "That's hanging up, last I heard."

Alise patted her short hair in place, as if it needed straightening, and frowned with irritation. "I don't remember that. But I *do* remember that when I called you to congratulate you on winning the lottery, you acted like you didn't want me to know anything about it."

Lenora was stunned. Alise was still griping about *that?* "Of course I wanted you to know, Alise. Don't be silly. I just would have preferred to tell you myself rather than have someone else blab about it before I had a chance." Lenora stared pointedly at Monica.

"Uh-oh," Monica said with a little embarrassment. "I didn't mean any harm. I didn't think it would be a problem telling Alise."

"Exactly," Alise said. "What was the big deal about her telling me?"

"I just . . . my mental state wasn't the best at the time," Lenora said. "I wanted to tell people myself in my own time."

"We've known each other for years," Alise said. "I was trying to be nice, and I was taken aback by your reaction. I thought you would be pleased to hear from me. And then when I mentioned Gerald, you nearly chewed my head off."

"What do you expect?" Lenora said, her voice rising. "You never liked Gerald, but insinuating that he would try to take advantage of me because of my money was plain wrong. It was insulting."

"I never said he definitely would," Alise snapped back. "I suggested that you be careful. You have to be realistic about these things."

"Ladies, can you tone it down?" Monica held her arms out, trying to keep the peace. "People are starting to stare."

"Gerald is not like that," Lenora said, ignoring Monica and the other people. "And you don't know him well enough to assume that he would take advantage of me. And if you don't know what you're talking about, you should keep your opinion to

230

yourself."

"Believe me, that's exactly what I plan to do from now on," Alise retorted, folding her arms defiantly.

"C'mon, you two," Monica said. "People are really staring now. It's embarrassing."

Lenora rolled her eyes skyward and glanced away from the table. People *were* staring, but she was too agitated to care. "You need to talk some sense into your friend," Lenora said.

"I'm sorry if I caused this by running my big mouth," Monica said.

"You didn't make her a snob," Lenora snapped as the waiter came to the table with their appetizers. "No need for you to apologize."

Alise stood abruptly and the waiter backed a hasty retreat. "I don't have to take this. I'm going to the ladies' room." She glanced at Monica. "You need to talk some sense into *her.*" With that, Alise walked off in a huff.

"Damn," Monica said. "I've never seen you two argue like this. You all would get to bickering once in a while, but nothing this heated."

"I'm not sure what the hell is going on with her. But whatever it is, it started after I won the lottery."

Monica sighed loudly. "You don't really think she's jealous about the money, do you?"

"What else would it be? When I called to tell her about the BMW, she barely said a word, especially after she found out I have a bigger model than she does. And the crap about Gerald was totally unnecessary. I don't comment on her husband and his motives. She should shut the hell up about my man. Alise has always been kind of materialistic, but she was basically fine as long as she was the one with most of the material. Now that I have more . . ." Lenora paused and shrugged.

"I agree that she can be a little materialistic at times, but she's fun to be around and she's got so many connections. Not to mention that we've known her for so long."

"She *used to be* fun. Not anymore. I'm tempted to get up and leave and call you some other time. I can only take so much of her."

"Please stay, at least until she catches us up on what's happening with our applications to The Girlfriends?"

Lenora rolled her eyes.

"Please?"

"Only for you," Lenora said.

"I wonder what's taking her so long?"

Monica looked toward the ladies' room.

"With any luck she slipped out on us," Lenora said, only half joking.

"Don't say that," Monica said. "You two need to kiss and make up."

"Yeah, right," Lenora said as Alise came out of the restroom and sat back at the table. Several moments of tension-filled silence passed between them as they each fiddled with their food. Finally Monica spoke up.

"So can you two quit acting like bitches?" Monica asked.

Lenora and Alise both smiled stiffly but remained silent.

"At least long enough to talk about The Girlfriends," Monica continued.

"I do have news about that," Alise said quietly as she dipped her calamari into the sauce. "I only came back to fill you in on that. The president called me last night and told me the formal letters will go out next week. Lenora has been accepted."

"Really?" Monica said. "Congratulations, Lenora!"

Lenora started to clasp her hands together with joy but then paused and looked at Alise. "What about Monica?"

"I suspect that Alise didn't mention me for a reason," Monica said.

"I'm so sorry," Alise said, shaking her head. "You didn't make it."

Monica's face fell.

"Oh, I'm sorry, too," Lenora said, rubbing Monica's back. She glanced at Alise for an explanation.

"Don't look at me," Alise said. "I just found out last night, and I was as surprised as you two are now."

Lenora frowned as the waiter approached the table with their main courses. Why would one of them be accepted by the club and not the other? If anything, Lenora would have thought that Monica was the most qualified. As a surgical nurse, she had a higher-paying job.

"Carla did mention you winning the lottery when she called last night, Lenora," Alise said. "Said to tell you congratulations. Maybe that had something to do with it."

Lenora stared at Alise. "How did she even find out I won?"

"I assumed you told someone in the club," Alise said.

"No, I didn't," Lenora said.

Alise's face was filled with doubt. "You sure?"

"Of course I'm sure," Lenora said. "How could I possibly be mistaken about something like that? I've told hardly anyone."

Alise was really bugging the hell out of her, Lenora thought.

"All I know is that a couple of weeks ago, just before you won the lottery, I heard that both of you were going to be rejected again," Alise said. "Now suddenly, you're in and Monica's not. How do you explain that?"

"You're assuming that I was accepted only because of the money, and I resent that," Lenora said.

"What else am I supposed to assume?" Alise asked, raising her voice as if she thought Lenora had suddenly gone deaf. "Two weeks ago they were going to turn you both down. What has changed since then besides the money you won?"

"This is crazy," Lenora responded, her voice rising to match Alise's.

"You have to admit it looks like more than a coincidence," Monica said.

"So you agree with her?" Lenora asked. "You think the money was the only reason I was accepted?"

"Well, look at the timing," Monica said. "I'm just trying to keep it real."

"Fine," Lenora said, folding her arms defiantly across her chest. Both of her friends had turned against her. She couldn't believe this was happening.

"What else do you think it could be, Lenora?" Monica said. " 'Cause I'm all ears."

"I attended a couple of functions that you missed because you had to work those nights," Lenora said. "Maybe that helped me."

"They said I wouldn't be penalized for that since I was working," Monica said.

"Right," Alise said. "I doubt seriously it had anything to do with that, especially since it appears that the decision to reject you was changed suddenly. I've never heard of that happening before."

"It's the money, honey," Monica said. "Don't worry about it, Lenora. It is what it is."

"Is that just another reason why you've been acting so nasty toward me lately?" Lenora asked Alise. "Not only are you jealous about my new car, you think I was admitted to your precious club for the wrong reasons."

Alise stood up, reached into her purse, and tossed a couple of bills on the table. "That's it. I said what I came to say. I'm leaving."

Monica stared at Alise, obviously dumbfounded. Lenora looked down and lightly tapped her fingers on the table.

"Are you serious?" Monica asked Alise.

Alise leaned over to kiss Monica on the cheek. "I'll call you over the weekend." She left the table without so much as a nod in Lenora's direction.

"Wow," Monica said. "What just happened?"

Lenora shrugged. "Alise and I haven't been all that close since college. Not like you two are. We come together mainly because of you."

"But you've never argued like this."

"You're right." Lenora didn't want to keep saying that she thought Alise was jealous about the money. But this was by far the most explosive disagreement they'd ever had. She didn't know what else to think.

"I'm really sorry that you didn't get in," Lenora said.

"No worries. I admit I'm jealous that you got in and I didn't, but I'm also happy for you."

"Thanks," Lenora said. "And now that both Alise and I are members, it should make things easier for you next year."

Monica shook her head sadly. "*If* I decide to reapply. I'm beginning to think I'm wasting my time. Maybe it's not in the cards for me."

Lenora nodded with understanding.

"Think I'll order something decadent for

dessert," Monica said. "I could use some soothing about now. How about you?"

Lenora patted her waistline. "I'll pass on that, but you go ahead. Maybe I'll nibble on yours."

"You are looking slimmer these days," Monica said after asking a waiter for the dessert menu. "How much have you lost?"

"Ten pounds and counting."

"You look amazing," Monica said. "How did you do it?"

Normally Lenora told Monica just about everything, but she decided against telling Monica about the diet pills. With everyone reacting so unpredictably around her these days, Lenora felt guarded. And as a nurse, Monica might very well have a negative view of diet pills. "Oh, just watching what I eat and taking longer walks with Paws."

After the way this crazy meal had gone, Lenora didn't want any further discord.

CHAPTER 24

It was getting harder to drag herself out of bed and into the office, Lenora thought as she tossed the covers back. And Monday mornings were the hardest. She sat up and slipped her feet into her flip-flops. Just when she was starting to feel good about the money, something happened to rattle her nerves. She couldn't get the bitter meal she had shared with Monica and Alise on Saturday afternoon out of her mind.

Lenora had heard that a change in fame or fortune could strain old friendships. A relationship could be one way for years, with both parties pretty much on equal ground. Then unexpectedly one of them became famous or rich and the dynamics changed forever. People who had been kind and tolerant of each other for years suddenly became petty, jealous, intolerant.

The spat with Alise was exactly the kind of life-altering event she had dreaded when she won the money; in fact it was why she got so sick. She didn't want the people around her to change suddenly. But she was done with worrying about how her winnings might hurt her, her relationships, or anything else. From now on, she was going to enjoy her newfound wealth no matter what. If Alise or anyone else wanted to fall in place, fine. If not, she was moving on.

She turned on the shower, stripped down, and stepped in. She and Gerald had talked about house hunting over the weekend. She had the money to buy her dream house now, and he was excited for her. Now *that* was the kind of change she looked forward to and how she wanted to spend her time.

Gerald had expressed some strong opinions about where they should look. She would listen to him since they had been close for so many years and she valued his judgment. But she didn't have a ring on her finger yet. In the end, it was her money and her decision.

"Northern Virginia is too far from both our jobs and there's too much traffic," he had said last night at dinner. "We really should stick to the area north of D.C. and south of Baltimore."

"*We?*" she said, holding her left hand out in front of him prominently. "As long as I don't see a diamond ring on this finger, there is no we, at least not when it comes to buying a house."

"Oops," he had muttered as he smiled knowingly. "Fair enough."

The telephone rang as she stepped from the shower. She hastily draped a towel around her body and ran to the phone on the wall in the kitchen, noting that the clock said 9:05 a.m. She didn't have time to look at caller ID as she grabbed the phone on the fourth and final ring. She at least knew that it was not a bill collector. She had paid all her bills off and was finally completely caught up on her mortgage payments.

"Lenora?"

She recognized the voice of the receptionist at her office. "Morning, Jenna."

"Good morning," Jenna said. "You know why I'm calling."

"Dawna?" Lenora asked.

"Yep. She said she wants to see you in the office within thirty minutes unless you're laid up in a hospital somewhere."

"I hear ya. Did she say why? Any particular project?"

"No, but I think it's got to do with the job in West Baltimore for the September issue," Jenna said. "Peterson called in sick again and the feature is backed up."

"Crap," Lenora muttered. As the setting for the critically acclaimed television production *The Wire,* that area of Baltimore was known nationally for rampant drugs and crime. And West Baltimore could be such a depressing area visually, with rundown buildings, dirty streets, and people who looked like they had lost all hope.

But it was none of those things that most bothered Lenora about this assignment. It was Peterson. He had a way of squirming out of his assignments when they became difficult. He invariably became sick or busy with a funeral clear across the country. "She knows I don't want to take that on. Nobody does."

"What do you want me to tell her?" Jenna asked.

Lenora thought to say that she was sick herself. But she was already on shaky ground with the boss, and that could lead to dismissal before she was ready. She wanted to leave on her terms, not Dawna's. "Does she sound mad that I'm not in yet?"

"Put it this way," Jenna said. "She ain't happy, I can promise you that."

Lenora sighed deeply. "Tell her I'll be there as soon as I can."

Lenora dropped the receiver in the cradle. She couldn't believe that Dawna was letting

Peterson get away with this crap again. She stomped back into the bathroom. She would go into the office as planned, but she was going to take her sweet time and was absolutely not going to accept Peterson's crummy assignment. It was his idea to feature West Baltimore, let him see it through. No way, no how was she going to do it. The days of Dawna tossing her around like a rag doll were over.

CHAPTER 25

An hour later, Lenora pulled into the lot in front of her building and carefully parked the new BMW at the far edge, which was almost deserted. She wasn't prepared to tell them yet that she had won the lottery, and she didn't want anyone asking questions or wondering how she could afford such a car. She would tell them when she was ready and not a day sooner.

She smiled at Jenna as she stood at the front desk and retrieved her phone messages. "Is Dawna available now?" Lenora asked.

Jenna nodded. "She's in her office waiting for you."

Lenora debated whether to go straight in to see Dawna or to try to slip by Dawna's cracked office door and duck into her own office first to check her inbox. She decided to head for her own office. The confrontation with the wicked witch of the *Baltimore*

Scene could wait.

She had barely gotten past Dawna's door when it flew open. Lenora stopped cold and turned to see Dawna in her doorway wearing a tailored black pantsuit, a fresh white linen blouse, and a scowl.

"Morning, Dawna," Lenora said with studied cheerfulness. "Lovely day, isn't it?"

Dawna didn't say a word. She stepped back stiffly and motioned for Lenora to enter her office. Lenora strolled in and Dawna shut the door behind her. Dawna walked behind her desk, sat back in her executive chair, and tapped her fingers together.

"Before you even say anything about the West Baltimore assignment, that's not for me," Lenora said, sitting in the chair across from Dawna. There, she'd gotten in the first word, Lenora thought. Gone were the days when the boss could walk all over her.

"You've been missing work a lot recently," Dawna said. "Or you're late. What the hell's going on?"

Lenora frowned. " 'Scuse me? I thought you wanted to talk about Peterson's feature."

Dawna straightened up and folded her arms across her waist. "Forget that. What I want to know is why you're taking off work so much. You were out or late four days last week and again today."

"I always call and talk to Jenna whenever I'm not coming in."

"That's not what I asked you, dammit," Dawna said.

As they glared at each other across Dawna's desk, Lenora knew that she had to choose her words carefully. Something was up, because this wasn't what she had been led to expect. She didn't want to lie out-right, but she wasn't ready to reveal much of what was going on in her personal life yet either. Dawna might use the knowledge of her lottery winnings against her. "Something came up, something personal, and it made me sick for a while."

Dawna frowned doubtfully. "For more than a week?"

"It comes and goes."

"What on earth is it that made you so sick?"

"I'd rather not go into it," Lenora said firmly.

"Oh, really?" Dawna scoffed. "Well, you'd better come up with something better than that, Ms. Stone. You do know that when you're out sick for more than three days in one week, a note from a doctor is required. I assume you have one."

Lenora was well aware of the rule. She had never been out sick for more than a day or two prior to this, but others on the staff had been and the rule was never enforced for them. She shook her head. "No, I don't have one. I haven't been to the doctor's office."

"Then I'd suggest you go and get one."

"But I'm not sick anymore," Lenora protested.

"That's your problem."

"How am I going to get a note from a doctor? *I'm not sick anymore.* And the rule has never been enforced before."

"That was before I got here," Dawna said sternly.

Now that Lenora thought about it, Dawna was probably right. Still, she didn't have a doctor's note and there wasn't much she could do about that. "You ever heard of anyone going to a doctor for an illness that's passed?" Lenora retorted with scorn.

Dawna stared at her. "I need a doctor's note before you resume work. That's the rule."

"Well, it's a dumb rule."

"When you return with the note, we'll talk about your next assignment. And I need you back in here by tomorrow morning with the note. It can't wait longer than that. Otherwise, I'll have to let you go."

Lenora couldn't believe what she was hearing. She stared at Dawna, speechless. This was incredible, even for Dawna.

"And another thing," Dawna said. "Are you doing freelance photography?"

Lenora blinked rapidly. "Why do you ask?"

"Because that's what I heard."

"Exactly what have you heard?" Lenora asked.

"That you're working with Ray Shearer outside the office."

Now where did she hear that? Lenora wondered. Especially since she hadn't talked to Ray for days. "So what if I am? It's on my free time. I can do what I want on my time."

"That depends. You found Ray through the magazine, and if there is a conflict, you could have a real problem on your hands."

"There's no conflict."

"Tell me exactly what you're doing for him so I can determine that," Dawna asked.

"It's none of your business." Lenora hadn't even started the assignment with Ray and wasn't sure she would at this point, but she wasn't going to tell this bitch a thing.

"Fine, Lenora," Dawna said. "I'm going to have to let you go."

"You're not serious. You always say I'm

your best photographer."

"That doesn't mean you're irreplaceable."

Lenora sat in silence for a moment. But she quickly recovered, squaring her shoulders. "You intended to do this all along, didn't you?" she asked. "The stuff about the assignment in West Baltimore was just a ruse to get me in here, wasn't it?"

Dawna didn't say a word. She just shifted her arms from around her waist and placed her hands firmly on her desk.

Lenora stood and backed away. "Fine. You can take this job and shove it. I don't need it. I won money in the lottery — a lot. I never have to work again if I don't want to."

"Yeah, right, you won the lottery. And I'm dating the fucking King of Jordan."

"If you don't believe me, check the web. But I really don't even care whether you believe me or not. I'm so tired of your pompous attitude. I'll just get my things and go."

For once, Dawna seemed to be speechless as Lenora turned and left. She passed by Jenna's desk on the way to her office and noticed the receptionist staring at her wide-eyed.

"For real?" Jenna asked. "You won the lottery?"

Lenora stopped. "Yes. Crazy, isn't it?"

"Damn, girl!" Jenna exclaimed. "Why are you even here?"

Lenora smiled. This was supposed to be a happy time, and it was amazing how spending a few minutes around her boss could quickly make her forget that. The new young editor in the office next to Lenora's heard the commotion and came out. "Did I just hear that you won the lottery?" Julie asked.

Lenora nodded. Now that the news was out around the office, she actually felt relieved.

"How much?" Jenna asked. "If you don't mind me asking."

"Like I said, a lot. Let's leave it at that."

"Really?" Julie said. "Well, congratulations."

"Thanks."

"So you're leaving, from what I overheard," Jenna said, nodding toward Dawna's office.

"Looks that way," Lenora said.

"Good luck wherever . . ." Jenna paused as Dawna came out of her office and looked at Lenora.

"I'd like to talk to you in my office again, if you don't mind," Dawna said.

Lenora reluctantly followed Dawna back toward her office. She promised herself that if Dawna dished out any more abuse, she was not going to hang around. But Dawna seemed to have calmed down. Lenora hung in the doorway to be on the safe side.

Dawna sat and beckoned toward the chair in front of her desk. "Sit down," she said.

Lenora hesitated.

"Please," Dawna added.

It wasn't often — indeed, maybe never — that Lenora had heard that word from her boss's mouth. She warily moved to the chair and sat stiffly on the edge. She did not trust this woman, no matter how nice she pretended to be.

"I heard you speaking with Jenna and Julie. Congratulations on your winnings. Now I understand why you've been out so much."

"Thanks," Lenora said. "Is that all?"

"Well, no," Dawna said. "Why didn't you tell me you won the lottery? A lot of this could have been avoided."

"I had my reasons."

"I understand," Dawna said. "It's a personal choice. But if you had explained to me what was going on, I might have understood why you were taking so much time off. As it was, I had nothing to go on except that you were calling in sick almost daily yet you had no doctor's notice."

Lenora nodded. "I hear you."

Dawna smiled as much as she was capable of doing. "I realize that I can be difficult, but this is an extremely tough business to run, particularly since I'm new at the *Scene*."

Lenora wanted to roll her eyes skyward. To her way of thinking, there was no excuse for acting like a bitch all the time. Dawna was the meanest woman alive — or at least certainly the meanest she had ever met. But Lenora decided to keep her thoughts to herself. She really didn't care why Dawna was so nasty all the time because she no longer had to put up with it. "Fine, no arguments here."

"I have a question," Dawna asked. "After you won the lottery, you didn't quit your job right away."

Lenora nodded in agreement.

"How long did you plan to keep working?"

"I honestly don't know. I was still trying to decide what to do. I really do enjoy the creative side of my work as well as meeting new people and getting out in the field."

"In that case, it's fine if you want to stay. We will have to work something out about the freelance assignments, but I'm sure we can come to an agreement."

Lenora tightened her lips. She shook her head. "Thanks, but no thanks. I really think it best that I end things here."

"Why not take some time to think about it? I'll be honest, Lenora. You really are the best photographer we have by a mile. I would hate to lose you. I would even offer you more money to stay, but you obviously don't need it. What I do promise is to lighten up on you, if that will help."

Lighten up? Lenora wondered if it was even possible for this woman to lighten up. Still, maybe she shouldn't make a snap decision. Dawna was offering her time to mull things over. It couldn't hurt to accept that. Lenora nodded. "All right. I'll think about it."

"Good," Dawna said. "How much time will you need?"

"A few days?"

"Sounds fine," Dawna said. "Why don't you call me early next week and we'll go from there."

Lenora agreed and quickly made her exit from Dawna's office. Because the option to return was still available, she didn't need to clear out her office yet, so she decided to leave. As she walked back to her car, she dialed Gerald's number on her cell phone. She couldn't wait to tell him what had just happened with her boss.

Unfortunately, Gerald wasn't answering his cell phone or his office line. That probably meant he was in a meeting. Gerald and his partners had let their receptionist go to save money and now relied on answering machines. She left a message on his office line but was disappointed not to be able to reach him. It wasn't every day that she had the upper hand on Dawna. She dialed Monica's number, hoping to give her the blow-by-blow account. Same thing — no answer.

She was about to call her mom when her phone rang. She checked the caller ID and was surprised to see that it was not Gerald calling her back. It was Ray. Lenora couldn't believe she was seeing his name on her caller ID. She was late getting back to him with an estimate for his brochure, but she never expected him to follow up with her about it. She figured he would have forgotten all about her by now.

"Hi, Ray," she said.

"Hey there. I've been waiting anxiously to hear back from you."

"Yes. I'm sorry. I've been meaning to contact you. I got hung up with other things." And scared, she thought. Scared of what this man did to her mind and body when she was around him. It was baffling and embarrassing.

"I figured you were busy, given all that's happening in your life," he said. "And although I wondered about the brochure, I really called to see how you're doing."

She sighed deeply. "Things have been pretty crazy at work and with a couple of my girlfriends, but I'm managing."

"Anything I can do to help?" he asked.

She laughed. "If you have a minute, I could definitely use a sounding board."

"I'm all ears."

"You'll never believe what happened at work today. I . . . oh, never mind. I don't really want to burden you with my problems." She didn't know this man well enough to unload on him.

"It's not a burden at all."

"Okay, here it goes." She reached her car and opened the door. "It's about my boss, Dawna. It's kind of a long story." He couldn't cause harm over the phone could he? she thought as she climbed into the car. And if he was willing to listen, why not tell him?

She sat in the car in the lot and proceeded to tell him in detail what happened with Dawna. She started with a little background about the rocky relationship she'd always had with her boss. Then she told him about

255

the strange firing and rehiring episode that had just taken place, all because she didn't go into work for a few days and returned without a doctor's note.

"Do you think you'll stay there?" he asked when she was done.

"I'm really leaning toward not going back."

"Have you given much thought as to what you'll do with your time if you don't stay? You're too young to retire."

"That's why I stayed as long as I did after winning," she said. "What would I do? But lately I've been thinking about branching out on my own, starting a photography studio or something."

"That sounds perfect for you. It's not as easy as a lot of people assume to start a business, even a small one, but you have a lot of talent. If you work hard, you should do well."

Ray had actually done something similar, and he obviously knew his stuff. His business appeared to be thriving, unlike Gerald's. "Do you ever regret starting your own business and wish you were back at a nine-to-five?" she asked.

"Never. Absolutely not."

"Really?"

"Okay, maybe I shouldn't be so hasty to

say never," he said. "The first year or two, there were some hairy moments, I won't lie. I seriously underestimated the time and money I would need to reach the break-even point. But I persevered and now I definitely feel that striking out on my own was the best thing I've ever done. Sure, I made a lot of mistakes in the beginning, and I'd do many things differently if I was starting out now. For instance, however much you think you need to make it through your first year, double it."

Lenora listened to Ray and realized that he was a gold mine of knowledge and information. "I'd love a chance to pick your brain."

"And I'd love to share what I know. How about you bring that proposal to me and we talk?"

"I'll do that. Do you have time this week?"

"Hold a sec," he said. "Let me check my schedule."

She had jumped on the meeting with Ray without giving much thought to it. He was so pleasant and easy to talk to, a welcome change from her conversations of late with those normally around her. But could she handle a face-to-face meeting alone with him? Suddenly she realized that she didn't feel nearly as infatuated with him as she had before. He had barely crossed her mind over the past few days. "I'm in the field all week on a job," he said. "And since it's a rush job, I'll be working late, probably until dark. Can you meet over the weekend? Say Saturday afternoon? If not, it will have to wait until next week."

"Saturday works for me," she said. Normally she liked to leave her Saturdays open in case Gerald wanted to get together. He often didn't know whether he would be free until after work on Friday. But Lenora looked forward to meeting with Ray and exploring the possibility of launching her own photography studio.

They decided to meet for lunch, location to be decided later, and he gave her more information about what he wanted included in the proposal for the brochure. When they were done, Lenora noticed that Gerald had tried to call her while she was talking to Ray. She debated whether to try to reach Gerald while she was still parked but chose to drive home and call him later. She was eager to get behind her desk and work on the proposal for Ray.

CHAPTER 26

Gerald worked late most evenings the rest of that week, and for once Lenora did not mind. It gave her more time and space to work on the bid for Ray's landscaping business. She and Ray spoke on the phone several times during the week to flesh out the details of exactly what he did and did not want included in the brochure. Lenora decided to prepare a mockup, so it was taking up a lot more of her time. But that was fine with her. She welcomed the opportunity to do something new.

Monica called on Friday evening just as she was about to wrap up her work on the mockup and walk Paws. They decided to meet for coffee.

"Treat's on me," Lenora said as she flipped off her computer. She stood and stretched. It had been a rewarding and productive week. Some nights she worked on the proposal until two in the morning. A break with her girlfriend sounded perfect, especially since Gerald was working late.

"No arguments from me, Miss Millionaire," Monica joked. "I wouldn't have it any other way."

Lenora was placing the leash on Paws to walk her before she met Monica when the phone rang again. "Is this Lenora Stone?" asked a strange voice on the other end.

Lenora rolled her eyes skyward. Undoubtedly one of those annoying telemarketing calls. They always came at the worst possible moment. Then again, no moment was good for one of these meddlesome calls. "Who wants to know?" Lenora asked.

"My name is Peter Jackson. I'm calling from the *Northeast Dispatch* newspaper."

Lenora's stomach dropped. Was this what she thought it was? A reporter calling about the lottery win. God, she hoped not. So far she had done such a good job of avoiding publicity. She wanted it to stay that way.

"Are you Lenora?"

"Yes," she said reluctantly.

"Hi, Lenora. Congratulations on winning the lottery. I wanted to ask a few questions."

Dammit! How did they find out about her? "This will have to wait until another day," she said curtly. "I was about to go out."

"I only need a few minutes of your time. We plan to run a story in tomorrow morning's edition, so we really should talk now."

"What if I don't want to talk?"

"Then we'll print the piece without your input based on our research and talking to some of your coworkers. But I'd hate for you not to share your thoughts, since the story is about you."

"You talked to my coworkers?"

"I didn't, but another reporter did, I think."

Oh, hell. Lenora flopped down on the edge of her bed. "Go ahead, but I don't have long."

"So how did you feel when you realized you'd won the money?" Peter asked.

"Great at first. Shocked but excited. I'm still shocked, to tell you the truth."

She could hear computer keys clacking in the background. "You said you felt great at first. What does that mean? Did something happen to change that?"

"Mm, not really. It dawned on me eventually that this kind of money was going to change my life, and I wasn't feeling so hot for a while."

"Really? Was it nerves?" Peter asked.

"Probably."

"How long were you sick?"

"A day or two."

"What were the symptoms?"

Lenora hesitated, wondering why he needed so much detail. "Do you really need to know all that? I'm fine now."

"Glad to hear that," he said. "So, what are you planning to do with the money?"

"I just bought a new BMW. I plan to start looking at houses soon. That's it so far."

"That's a nice car," he said. "What model?"

"750Li. I always dreamed of owning one and now I do. I couldn't be happier with it."

"Sounds great. Did you quit your job as a photographer?"

"That's still up in the air. I love my work, but my boss is another story."

He laughed lightly. "That's the story of bosses everywhere probably. What's going on with yours?"

"She's too controlling, too demanding. A real pain at times. And now I don't have to put up with her if I don't want to."

"I understand," he said, keyboard clacking away.

"I'd like to start my own business eventually," she continued. "Something to do with photography."

She had expected Peter to ask her more

questions about her plans to start a business. Instead, he quickly moved on to other subjects, firing off one question after another.

"What did your boss say when you told her you won the lottery?"

"At first she didn't believe me. Then she acted like she was my new best friend."

"What does your boyfriend think of all this?"

"He's fine," she said. "Very supportive."

"How did your family react?"

"Do you have a financial adviser?" And so on and so on.

Lenora looked at her watch impatiently and began to cut her responses short. This was taking way too long. But she didn't want to be rude and find out later that he had written something negative about her.

"Did you take all the money now or installments?"

"I took all of it."

"Why the cash payment instead of an annuity?"

"That seemed to be best for me."

As if he sensed her attention waning, he quickly thanked her and said good-bye. Lenora rushed out to walk Paws. As they circled the building, Lenora thought back over some of her responses to the reporter's questions. She thought about the people who might read the article. Gerald, Monica, Dawna. She was beginning to suspect that she had blabbed too much. If he printed what she had said about Dawna, she might have blown her chances for reemployment at the *Baltimore Scene.*

She tried to cast her worries aside as she ran back up to the condo and dressed to meet Monica. But thoughts about the interview kept intruding even when she met Monica an hour later.

"That was really dumb," she said to Monica after they both ordered flavored coffee. "If Dawna sees the article, I'm done at the magazine."

Monica shrugged. "I think the *Dispatch* is basically a giveaway. There's a good chance she won't even see it."

"Someone could see it and tell her about it."

"Stop thinking the worst. And even if she sees it, so what? You don't need that job anyway. I doubt you were ever going back now that you're developing freelance opportunities."

Monica had a point. "You're probably right. But it was nice thinking I had the option."

"So are you still meeting the landscaper

tomorrow?"

"Yes, I'm really looking forward to that."

"You over your crush on him?"

Lenora waved a hand nonchalantly. "I'm so past that. This is all business. Besides, I'm spoken for."

"Sounds like what's best for you," Monica said. "Now if it was me, I'd probably be all over Ray. But you need someone more stable, more predictable. Someone like Gerald."

"You make Gerald sound so boring."

"Not at all. He's perfect for you."

"And you obviously don't think I could handle a man like Ray," Lenora said.

"No way. You would do something stupid like fall in love with him and get burned."

"Don't be so sure. A part of me has always wondered what it would be like to be like you."

Monica frowned. "And what am I like? I'm dying to hear what you think."

"Very available when you're attracted to someone. You go after what you want and you have few hang-ups."

Monica nodded. "No arguments there, but that's not you. So don't even try it."

Lenora laughed.

"Have you talked to Alise since we were at P.F. Chang's?" Monica asked.

Lenora stiffened. "Nope."

"That's too bad," Monica said.

Lenora shrugged. "She changed after I won the money. And she's too uppity."

"That's Alise. She's always been that way."

"True. Maybe I'm just less willing to tolerate it now."

"You mean since you won the money?" Alise asked.

Lenora nodded. "I don't know. For some reason it makes me less tolerant of crap like hers."

"I think you two need to sit and talk," Monica said. "If I arrange something, will you come?"

"Like what?" Lenora asked cautiously.

"I don't know. A meeting at my place. I'll slip out, let you two talk."

"Hmm."

"C'mon," Monica pleaded. "It can't hurt to try. You were friends for so long."

Lenora nodded. "All right. But she may not even want to come."

Monica nodded as Lenora's cell rang. Lenora dug the phone out of her bag and noticed that she didn't recognize the number.

"Should I even answer this?" she wondered aloud, then decided to pick up before she got a response. "Hello?"

"Lenora Stone?"

Something in the woman's voice made Lenora regret picking up. Was this another nosy reporter? "Who's calling?"

"My name is Lindsey. I'm with the *Columbia Post*."

Lenora covered the mouthpiece. "Damn," she whispered to Monica, "I knew I shouldn't have answered. It's a reporter."

"You're kidding," Monica said.

"I wish. How on earth did they get this number?"

Monica shrugged. "The word is out, girl."

Lenora went back to the phone. "I'm very busy now."

"This will only take a minute," the reporter insisted.

"I don't have a minute. I'm with friends."

"Just a couple of quick questions. What do you plan to do with the money?"

Lenora held the phone in front of her face and stared at it with disbelief. She had told this woman she was busy. "Sorry, but you asked for this." She pressed the button to hang up and shook her head as she dumped her phone back into her bag. "I can't believe how pushy these reporters are. It's like they're from another planet."

"You're a hot item now," Monica said. "A celeb."

"This is the last thing I wanted, you know that. All this attention. I wonder if Dawna called them."

"Why would she do that?"

"Who knows," Lenora said. "The woman is insane. But these reporters started calling right after I told her I won."

"However they found out, you'd better get used to them calling," Monica said. "Things are probably going to get worse before they get better."

"I sure hope you're wrong about that."

CHAPTER 27

The ringing telephone jolted Lenora awake. She forced her eyes open and checked the clock. It was placed at an angle and was hard to see, so she struggled up to reach it, cursing under her breath the entire time. Whatever the hour, it was Saturday and too darn early for anyone to be calling.

She got doubly upset when she noticed that it was only 7:15 a.m. If this was another one of those crazy reporters, she was going to yell at the top of her lungs until his ears fell off. She was really getting disgusted with this.

"Yeah," she snapped as she grabbed the phone on the third ring.

"Hey, Lenora."

It was another unfamiliar voice. "Who is this?" Lenora said curtly.

"It's Melanie Franklin. Your cousin."

Lenora frowned into the phone. She had no cousin named Melanie. And she didn't know any Franklins. "Sorry, you must have the wrong number."

"I don't think so. My mother is Stephanie Johnson. She and your mama are cousins."

Lenora still didn't know who this woman was. Had never heard of her. But Lenora's mother's maiden name was Johnson. And this caller had a slight southern accent, just like her mother. So maybe the caller really was a distant relative — a very distant one.

"We met at the family reunion down in Virginia a few years ago," Melanie continued.

"Oh, right," Lenora said, pretending to remember as she struggled to sit all the way up. The reunion was actually more like ten years ago, but it seemed as if Melanie really was a relative. As distant as the relationship was and as annoyed as she felt about being disturbed at seven on a Saturday morning, this was family. She had to try to be civil. "How are you?"

"I'm doing all right. I heard you won the lottery. Congratulations!"

"Oh, thanks," Lenora said, rubbing her eyes to fully wake herself. "You're definitely an early riser."

"I am these days anyway. Got a lot on my mind."

"Oh?"

"Lost my job a few months ago because of the economy."

"That's rough," Lenora said, starting to feel anxious about what she suspected was coming.

"Ain't it the truth," Melanie said. "I'd probably be all right with my savings, but I bought a house a few years back. I spent all my savings trying to keep up with the mortgage, and now I'm having a real hard time trying to make the payments. And I can't sell 'cause I owe more than it's worth."

"Uh-huh." Been there, done that, Lenora thought. Please don't remind me.

"Yeah, I'm probably going to lose this house," Melanie said.

"I really am sorry to hear that. Don't you have family who can help out?" Lenora regretted the words the moment they slipped out.

"That's exactly why I'm calling," Melanie said. "I was wondering if *you* might be able to help me."

Lenora pinched her lips tight. "Actually, what I meant was your parents or siblings or someone closer like that."

"My dad died a few years ago and my mom lives with me. That's one of the reasons I bought the house, to have room for her since she has diabetes. And she really

271

doesn't have much except a small social security payment."

"I see."

"And my brother . . . you know about him?"

"Can't say that I do."

"Girl, he's wasted," Melanie said. "He hasn't worked in years. He never could keep a job, and what money he gets he spends on booze. I'm not even sure where he's at right now. He's worse off than me."

Lenora sighed deeply. She knew this was coming. She had been expecting it ever since she won. But she also thought she would easily be able to say "No, get lost." The reality was different. This was her mom's family. And that meant it was hers, too. "How much money are you talking about?"

"My mortgage is about twenty-five hundred a month," Melanie said.

"How much are you behind?"

Lenora could hear Melanie shuffling through papers on the other end of the line. "A few months now. If I could get caught up on those payments, that would be a big help. Girl, you don't even know."

"Uh-huh."

"And I got some medical bills I still owe on 'cause I don't have health insurance anymore. I had surgery on my knee and I got arthritis in my hands real bad. I take pressure medicine, but I haven't been able to buy that for months now, trying to keep the lights on. I could go on, but I don't want to burden you too bad."

"How much are the medical bills?" Lenora asked.

"About five thousand. Yeah, that's about right."

"So you need about twelve or thirteen thousand altogether?" Lenora asked.

"Fifteen should do it," Melanie said. "There's a few other bills I owe on. I'm hoping that by next month I can find a job since the economy is getting a little better and I'm out here looking every day. Then I'll be able to handle the bills myself again. I mean, I hate to even ask you for this kind of money, but I'm pretty desperate." Melanie laughed nervously.

"It's fine. I'll send you a check this week."

"Really?" Melanie said, her voice clearly excited. "Oh, Lord. I don't even know how to thank you."

"Don't worry about it." The truth was, while it was a lot of money to Melanie, it wasn't much to her anymore. She wouldn't even miss it.

"I'm going to include you in my prayers,"

Melanie said. "You had some real good luck lately so you're obviously blessed, but we can all use more praying, right? Oh, yeah. How have you been feeling lately?"

"Excuse me?" Lenora asked.

"The article in the *Dispatch* said you haven't been feeling good since you won. Everything all right?"

Lenora explained that she was fine now and then took Melanie's address. All the while she could feel her body temperature rising. She wasn't upset with Melanie. No, she was mad at the *Northeast Dispatch* for intruding into her private life and publishing her business all over the place.

As soon as they hung up, Lenora got out of bed and switched on her computer. She no longer got newspapers delivered to her door. Instead, she read her news online or watched CNN.

She checked the home page of the *Northeast Dispatch* and was horrified to realize that this online site was a sort of regional version of the *National Enquirer.* Across the page were titles with phrases like "sex psycho" and "love-murder triangle" — one sensationalistic story after another. She found Peter Jackson's article about her lottery winnings and read it. She couldn't believe how titillating he had made the story. It was one of the tamer pieces in the trashy rag, but it was still garbage.

She realized that she had said too much as soon as she and the reporter had hung up. But she prayed that Peter would show a little mercy. Instead, he zeroed in on and exaggerated every single vulnerability. He talked about how the winnings freaked her out and how she was "violently ill" and "bedridden" for a week. How the first thing she did when she recovered was to run out and buy a luxury car. Worst of all, he said that she loathed her "bitchy" boss at the *Baltimore Scene*. Lenora couldn't believe how this reporter had maliciously twisted her words to create a more sensationalistic story.

By the time she finished reading the article, she was close to tears. She sat back and stared at the computer with disbelief. But as angry as she was with this Peter person, she was also extremely upset with herself. Why hadn't she kept her mouth shut? Why didn't she check the publication out before agreeing to talk? Well, there wasn't anything she could do now except pray that no one would read this junk besides Melanie.

She picked a tissue up from her desk and dabbed the corners of her eyes. She needed to clear her head. She did not want this clouding her mind when she met Ray for lunch. She blew her nose and focused on getting up and ready for her meeting.

A few hours later, just as she started to apply a little blush to her cheeks, the phone rang. She thought to ignore it, believing it could be another nuisance reporter or a needy relative, but then decided to answer. It could be Ray calling to cancel or something. She really hoped not. She was so looking forward to their meeting.

She walked to the kitchen and picked up the wall phone when she saw that it was Gerald.

"Hey, what's up?" came Gerald's voice on the line.

She was surprised to hear from him. He had said he was going into the office that Saturday morning and would call her later tonight. She leaned against the countertop, relieved that it was not a reporter. "Hi, I thought you were working all day today."

"Changed my mind. I made more progress than I expected to, so a few hours is enough. Thought I would give my woman a call and maybe drive out your way when I leave here in a few. What you got planned for this afternoon? Shopping?"

"Actually, I'm about to go meet a client."

"On a Saturday?"

"It's a freelance job," she said. "I'm designing a brochure."

"Still, on the weekend? Seems odd."

"This was the best time for him."

"You said him? Who is this?" Gerald asked. "You never mentioned this before and you usually tell me everything. Or you used to."

"He's that landscaper we did the feature on for the *Baltimore Scene*. He liked my work a lot and asked if I'd help him with the photographs and the layout for a brochure for his business."

"Cool," Gerald said. "Just surprised you never told me before now. So how long do you expect to be out?"

"It's hard to say."

"It can't take that much time to talk about a little brochure."

Lenora hated it when Gerald belittled her work. "*A little brochure,* as you put it, can take a lot of planning to do right. And it may not be just a brochure. He needs materials to promote himself. Business cards, flyers, e-mail blasts, things like that."

"And you're going to do all of that?" he asked.

"We're going to talk about me doing it. Yes."

"Sounds like this could get involved," Gerald said.

"If I'm lucky. It's not like I have a regular job anymore."

"You would if you took up Dawna's offer to go back to the magazine. But you aren't, are you?"

"I've decided not to. I'll let her know on Monday."

"A mistake, in my opinion."

"I've always wanted to branch out on my own, but I was reluctant to take the plunge. Now that I have the money, it's time."

"I'm not against it," he said. "I like the idea. I just think you should hold on to your job at the magazine until you know the freelance work is going to be a success. The money won't last forever if you're not careful."

"I promise to be careful. Have some faith in me."

"I do have faith in you. What I'm saying . . ."

"Look, I don't mean to interrupt, but we'll have to talk later." She stood up straight. "I need to run now or I'll be late for my meeting."

"We definitely need to discuss this more," he said. "I've already done what you're planning in a way. I know the risks."

Yes, but not how to avoid them, Lenora thought. Ray knew how to start a business successfully and keep it thriving even in bad times.

"I hear you," she said.

"I also worry about the effect that both of us running businesses will have on our relationship. It's so demanding. It will be hard to find time for each other."

Lenora paced the kitchen floor with a raised eyebrow. He never worried about how much they were apart when he was the one running a business and working all the time. Now that she was thinking about doing it, suddenly he was concerned about their time together. "We'll have to work all that out. I really need to go now."

"See?" he said. "That's exactly what I'm talking about. Already you don't have time to talk to me."

"You know what? You're starting to bug me," she said. "You're the one who was always tied up before. You never had a problem with us being apart when it was about *your* business. Now that it's about *me,* you want us to be together all the time."

"Well, damn," he said. "I guess I'll let you run off to your precious client."

"Gerald, that's not fair. They're all precious, especially when you're starting out."

"You're right," he said. "Sorry. So how long will you be out? An hour or two?"

"Um, probably more like a few."

"Mm-hmm. I'll come by there around three then."

"Why don't I call you when I'm done?" she asked. "In case it takes more time."

"Fine," he said. "You do that."

Lenora could tell by Gerald's tone that he was not pleased when they hung up. There was a time when Gerald's mood really mattered to her. She would have made sure all was well with him before hanging up. But she had already lost enough valuable time. She had only a few minutes left to throw on some lipstick, slip into her sandals, and gather her files for the meeting with Ray. By the time she walked out the front door a little later, Gerald was already long gone from her thoughts.

CHAPTER 28

Thirty minutes later, Ray was pulling a chair out for Lenora as she approached him in a small café in Columbia. She liked that he was the one who had arrived first. With Gerald, she was almost always the first to arrive, sometimes by thirty minutes or more. This used to aggravate her no end, and she and Gerald had argued about it many times over the years. Still, no matter how much she complained, Gerald would not change. She had pretty much given up and learned to bring her book reader along or to spend the time checking e-mail messages on her BlackBerry.

There was no need for that today. She and Ray hugged, and he smiled warmly as he helped her into the seat. A waiter approached as she placed her bag and briefcase into a spare chair and took their drink orders. The waiter left, and Lenora immediately reached for her briefcase. She removed the proposal and mockup and slid them across the table toward Ray.

"Everything's there: goals, tasks, timeline, fees. And it's all negotiable." She desperately wanted this job for the creative possibilities. The money was unimportant. She smiled and waited for his response.

"You look very nice today," he said.

She laughed awkwardly. "Oh. Thanks."

"You're welcome."

"I was pretty abrupt, I guess," she said. "Sorry. I've been working on all of that and I'm in a business frame of mind."

"That's fine," he said. "I get like that myself at times. Although the scent you're wearing would throw any man off his game, business or otherwise. It's very nice."

Lenora was silent for a moment. Was Ray flirting with her? She found him so attractive, and she wasn't confident that she could keep a level head if this man came on to her.

"Thanks. So, um, about the proposal," she said, pointing to it awkwardly. "Feel free to ask questions if you have any." Get the conversation back to strictly business, she told herself. She had thought she was over her odd obsession with this man. But he had her on edge immediately, so she was beginning to wonder about that.

"Looks like you've been real busy," Ray said, flipping through the pages of the proposal and looking over the mockup.

She waited silently for him to finish and made sure to keep her eyes off his hands. They tended to drive her a little crazy. Instead, she focused her gaze on the others in the restaurant.

"I do have a question," he said. "How many revisions of the brochure and flyers do I get?"

"As many as it takes to satisfy you. I want you to be happy." The minute Lenora said it, she regretted the way the words came out.

He obviously had no regrets. He looked into her eyes and smiled charmingly. "I like the sound of that."

She gulped and reached for her glass of water. Clients didn't often flirt with her, especially good-looking ones. Her tongue was tied in a knot. She took a big sip of water, cleared her throat, and tried to find her voice.

"Sorry," he said. "I'm embarrassing you."

"Maybe a little," she admitted with a nervous laugh.

"Didn't mean to do that. But there's something different about you."

Yes, like the money, she thought. It was

amazing how people changed right before your eyes when they learned about it. "It's nothing bad, I hope," she said.

"It's definitely all good."

She clutched her hands together tightly in her lap. She could feel the heat rising in her neck. The effect this man had on her couldn't have been any greater if he had reached under the table and laid his hand on her leg.

"Thanks," she said. "Should we get back to the brochure?" She craved his attention, but it made her nervous as hell.

He nodded. "Of course. That's why we're here."

"One thing I thought about as I wrapped it up last night was whether you would prefer one brochure that does it all or smaller separate brochures."

"Tell me what you're thinking with the smaller brochures," he said. He picked one up and held it as she talked. He sounded a lot more serious, and for that Lenora was grateful. This felt much safer.

"You said you want to include general information, like how many years you've been in business, your areas of expertise, and some of your bigger clients. You also want to include information about your fees and lots of photographs to illustrate some of your completed jobs. I could see dividing all that up into two or three small brochures instead of one big one."

"I see what you're saying," he said. "You've done this before for other clients. What do you suggest?"

"It really depends on your preference. Both approaches have advantages." She spent the next several minutes elaborating on her thoughts and ideas until finally he decided that he wanted to see more mock-ups.

"You saw my office," he said. "Things are hectic at times. When a client comes in or calls, whether it's a business client or a home owner, I don't want to have to search for the right brochure or wonder whether my receptionist gave a client the right one."

She nodded as she took notes over her shrimp salad sandwich. "That bodes well for one brochure that includes everything."

"On the other hand, I could see having different brochures for different clients. That's why I'd like to see more mockups before I decide."

"Fine," she said. "Makes sense."

"When can I see the revised mockups?" he asked, placing his hamburger down on the plate.

"I should have something for you in a

couple of days."

"Good. Now that we've gotten that out of the way, can I see you again?"

She sucked in her lips and glanced away. "You mean about the brochure?"

"Actually, I had something personal in mind. Like a movie and dinner."

She put her pen down on the table. Did Ray just ask her out on a date? Yes, he did. She was blown away. This wasn't the kind of man who asked women like her out. In fact, no man had asked her out since she started dating Gerald. She had thought the money would change her world. But thinking and seeing it unfold were two different things.

A lot of women — Monica, for sure — would be all over a man like Ray if he seemed even vaguely interested, no matter the reason. But now that the opportunity to go out with a man with movie-star appeal was banging at her door, Lenora was scared to open it. This was where she should tell Ray that she was almost engaged and be done with it. Go back to her simple, predictable life.

Then again, almost engaged was not engaged. She didn't really have to bring that up, did she? She could do what Gerald had done two years ago — lie about being attached and go have fun. But she had never cheated on a man before and she wasn't going to start now. She and Gerald had built up a good thing after much hard work. She didn't want to ruin that.

"I'm flattered you even asked," she said to Ray.

"Hmm. Sounds like a 'but' is approaching," he said with a regretful smile on his face.

She nodded. "I'm sorry, but I'm in a relationship."

"I didn't realize. I should have asked."

"I'm surprised *you* aren't involved with anyone," she said.

"I never said I wasn't."

"I see," she said, nodding. Of course he was.

"I hope my invitation doesn't make things awkward between us and that we can still work together," he said.

"It's not a problem," she said. She really wanted the work now that she had decided not to return to the magazine. So he was going to have to be on his best behavior. They both were.

"Good," he said. "I'm very much looking forward to what you come up with."

They arranged to meet again at Ray's office on Monday afternoon and then went their separate ways. As Lenora drove home, her mind kept drifting back to the moment when he invited her to dinner and a movie. The fat, geeky girl who men never noticed had just been asked out by a hunk. Not only that, she had turned him down. It was either the smartest or the dumbest thing she had ever done, and she hadn't made up her mind which yet.

That night in bed with Gerald, Lenora found herself thinking of Ray. At first she fought it. She closed her eyes tightly and tried to focus on the man on top of her — the man she was in love with, the one she wanted to marry. It didn't work.

When Gerald planted warm kisses on her tummy, she envisioned Ray's soft lips. When Gerald slid his fingers up her thigh, she thought of Ray's rugged hands. She couldn't shake the thought of Ray no matter how hard she tried.

Gerald must have noticed something, too. "You all right?" he asked after he rolled off her and lay on his back, his caramel-complexioned body glistening with perspiration as he tried to catch his breath.

"I'm fine. Why do you ask?" As if she needed to wonder. She knew exactly why he was asking. She had lain there like a log in the dirt the entire time they made love.

"You've been distant all evening," Gerald said. "The only time I got any kind of a reaction out of you was when I touched your thighs."

Lenora swallowed with guilt. She didn't have a response, at least not one she could share with Gerald. How did you tell your man you were thinking about someone else while making love?

"So I was out of it a bit," she said.

"A bit? You had about as much life as a mummy in a tomb. I thought we were trying to ramp up our romantic life. Whatever happened to that idea?"

A man called Ray, that's what happened, she thought. "I'm sorry. I'm tired, I guess."

"Tired? Why are you so damn tired? You haven't even been going to work."

"All the excitement of the past couple of weeks."

"You need to transfer some of that excitement to our lovemaking."

"Right," she said. Time to change the subject. "I'm going to start looking at houses this weekend."

"What? When were you going to tell me about this?"

"I'm telling you now," she said. "I contacted an agent earlier this week. A member of The Girlfriends. She's going to take me around to different neighborhoods in my price range."

"And your price range is?"

"I told Deanna around one to one and a half million."

Gerald whistled. "That sounds like a lot, maybe close to half your winnings after taxes."

"I've looked on the Internet, and to get what I want, that's what I have to spend."

Gerald looked doubtful. "Maybe you need to revise what you want then. Why don't you consult a financial planner before you start spending big like that?"

Lenora frowned. "Why would I need a financial planner to buy a house? That's silly."

"No, it's not," he said firmly. "You need to put a big chunk of the money away before you spend it all. A financial planner can help you set up the investments first."

"I'm not going to pay for the entire house. I'm going to make a down payment and take out a loan. Then I'll invest some later."

Gerald shook his head with disapproval. "Will you please listen to me? You're going about it all wrong. It's a mistake to buy the house first and spend anywhere near a million on it, loan or not. You don't need that much house."

Lenora set her jaw firmly. "I'm not going to argue with you, Gerald. I know what I want. And it's my money."

He sighed. "You're exactly right. I still hate to see you squander it. Will you at least promise me that you'll save or invest half of your winnings?"

"Okay, promise." Anything to get him to calm down. She didn't want to argue. She didn't *need* to argue. It was *her* money. In the end, she could do whatever she wanted.

"And do you mind if I tag along for this little adventure in big estate land?"

Lenora was surprised that he had offered to join her on a house hunt. "Really? I didn't ask you to come because I didn't think this would be your kind of thing, especially at this early stage. You never want to go shopping with me."

"For clothes, no," he said, turning up his nose. "That's not my thing. But a house is different."

"Of course you can come," she said. "I'd love to have you join us."

He put an arm around her and she snuggled against him. "About tomorrow night," he said. "Let's go out for dinner, someplace nice where we have to get all dressed up. It's been a while since we did that. That all right with you?"

"That's more than all right with me," she said. "I look forward to it."

She closed her eyes while Gerald picked up the remote control to the TV. Ray was messing with her head again for a while there, but she was past that now. Gerald was being extra sweet and attentive, saying and doing things he hadn't since the early days of their relationship. So what if she occasionally fantasized about another man. All women did that.

No doubt Gerald's improved behavior and all the attention from him had to do with the money she won. She was no fool. Still, if it had taken a lottery win to reignite a flame in him, so be it. She knew that Gerald honestly loved her. She couldn't say that about any other man, including Ray.

CHAPTER 29

The house-hunting trip started out badly. Deanna was young, in her early thirties, and Lenora could sense that Gerald was suspicious of her ability to deal with properties of the size and price range for which she was searching. He started pumping her with questions almost immediately after all three of them climbed into Deanna's Lexus, with Lenora in the passenger seat and Gerald sitting behind her.

"How long have you been selling real estate?" Gerald asked.

"About six years now," Deanna responded as she pulled out of the parking lot in front of Lenora's condominium.

"She's been very successful at it," Lenora said.

"That may be true, but how many houses have you sold in the million-dollar price range?" Gerald asked.

"Actually, I've only sold two properties in

that range," Deanna said. "My next highest sale was for about three-quarters of a million, and that was in Ellicott City last —"

"So how many have you sold at three-quarters of a million plus then?" Gerald asked before Deanna could finish.

Deanna paused and narrowed her eyes. She seemed to sense that she was being grilled. "A few," she said briefly. "I admit that my primary market is generally the four-to-six-hundred-thousand-dollar range, but I know the areas that you're interested in very well. I've lived out here all my life."

"So you have very little experience in our price range."

"C'mon, Gerald," Lenora said with exasperation. "Is this necessary?"

"Is what necessary?" Gerald responded. "A few questions?"

"You're interrogating her," Lenora said.

"That's fine," Deanna said, waving her arm with studied nonchalance. "He's looking out for you."

"Thank you," Gerald said to Deanna. "I'm glad you understand that. Any agent with any amount of confidence should expect a few questions."

Lenora rolled her eyes skyward and looked out the passenger window. Asking a few questions was one thing, she thought.

Gerald's line of questioning, not to mention his tone, was something else entirely. Deanna was a fellow member of her new club, and Lenora didn't like the way this meeting was going. But it wasn't her job to defend Deanna in a business arrangement. Deanna had been doing this for a while now, and she had likely worked with clients who were more difficult than Gerald. Lenora told herself to relax.

"Where are you taking us first?" Gerald asked.

"To a wooded area nearby with older homes."

"Older homes don't generally have the modern features that you find in newer homes," Gerald said.

"Such as?" Deanna asked.

"Large gourmet kitchens with new appliances, a real priority for Lenora. Big master bathrooms with soaking tubs, and plenty of storage and closet space."

"That's true," Deanna said, and Gerald nodded with confidence.

"Unless they've been updated," Deanna added. "And at the price range we're looking in, the houses are often very tastefully updated, especially kitchens and baths since the home owners can afford it. You also generally get more bang for the buck with older homes. Some people think they feel more solidly built."

Lenora smiled. Score for Deanna. If Gerald didn't settle down, she was going to pull him aside and remind him that this was *her* house they were shopping for and that she could handle the deal, questions and all, by herself.

"That's a good point," Gerald said. "But with a new house, you're the first to own it."

"I asked her to show me older houses first," Lenora said. This was a total lie, but she wanted Gerald to shut his trap. This was supposed to be a pleasant trip to look at houses for *her*. Instead, Gerald had taken over as if he thought he was buying a house for himself.

Lenora turned back to face Gerald and gave him a "Please stop this now" look.

"If that's the case, fine," Gerald said. "This is Lenora's show."

Lenora turned back around in her seat. Hopefully she had put an end to the nonsense.

They pulled up in front of the first house, a large French country manor style with stone and stucco siding.

"How much is this going for?" Lenora asked.

"This one is $1,150,000," Deanna said as she double-checked the listing.

Gerald whistled. "Really? For this?" He shook his head with disbelief.

"It's about five thousand square feet and it's on two acres," Deanna said. "Plus it's a wooded area with mature trees."

"So you essentially pay for all the trees," Gerald said sarcastically.

Deanna shrugged. "A lot of people like having mature trees."

"Me included," Lenora said.

"I never knew that," Gerald said.

"Well, you do now," Lenora said curtly.

"Um, let's look inside," Deanna said. "It's got a lot of quality craftsmanship."

"Which I also like," Lenora said pointedly.

Gerald was noticeably quiet as they walked through the house, which had stunning wooded views from all of the rooms.

"It may look a little small for a million-dollar house from the outside," Lenora said as they left and Deanna placed the keys back into the silver-toned Realtor lockbox. "But the details are outstanding. I really liked the updated kitchen and the landscaping."

"I have to admit the landscaping is nice," Gerald said. "I just think you could get

more for your money in other neighborhoods."

"Such as?" Lenora asked.

"Prince George's County has some nice
upscale areas where you can get a mansion
for a million bucks," he said.

"I know, but I prefer Howard County,"
Lenora said as she and Gerald followed
Deanna down a flower-lined pathway back
to the car.

Gerald lifted his arms. "Prices are too high
to buy out here, if you ask me. But it's your
call. I'm just offering advice."

"Then can you please stick to doing that
and only that?" Lenora said.

"That's what I have been doing," Gerald
said. "Or so I thought."

"No, you've been criticizing everything."

"If you don't want to hear what I have to
say, let me know. I'll just go along for the
ride."

"I want your opinions," Lenora said. "I
just don't want you to be so critical of
everything."

"Fine. I'll shut up."

"Go ahead, Gerald. Be an asshole." Why
was everything always such a challenge with
him? Why couldn't they be in sync the way
couples on television are — rarely arguing
and always understanding of each other?

They walked down the rest of the pathway and climbed into the car in stony silence. Deanna had obviously heard them bickering, although she tried to pretend otherwise. Lenora hated putting her club member through the crap she had going on with Gerald.

"Um, if you want to look in Prince George's County, I'll be happy to take you there," Deanna said as they pulled away from the curb. "I was going to show you a few more properties out here and then closer to Columbia, but I can stop by the office and check what's available in Prince George's County."

Lenora shook her head firmly from the passenger seat. "Stick to the plan."

They managed to get through two other houses that afternoon before Lenora decided to call it quits. Deanna wanted to show them more, but Gerald was being so negative about everything, Lenora wasn't really enjoying the trip the way she should be. She had real money to spend and was looking for her first house. She should be listening to Deanna and taking mental notes. Instead, she was fuming at her boyfriend and he at her. So she decided it would be best to cut the trip short and go house hunting another day without Gerald.

Deanna dropped them off in front of Lenora's building, and she and Gerald walked quietly up to the unit. Lenora fumbled hastily with the lock, marched inside, and tossed her shoulder bag on the couch. She was so annoyed, she thought of canceling their plans to go to a restaurant for dinner.

"What the hell's going on with you?" Gerald asked before Lenora could say what was on her mind.

"You mean what's going on with you," she countered as she turned to face him, arms folded tightly over her waist. "You're trying to take control of me."

"No, I'm not. I was just trying to be helpful."

"How is jumping all over Deanna being helpful? You were finding fault with everything."

He sighed deeply as he removed his suit jacket and draped it over the back of a chair. He sat down on the couch and petted Paws, who hopped up beside him. "You're about to spend a fortune on your first house. It will probably be the biggest investment you ever make. Whether it's going to be my house someday or not, I want you to be smart about the decision. Don't you think you need an agent who has worked extensively at your price level? Deanna hasn't."

"Maybe not. But she's a club member, one of the few I already know before the meetings start in September. This is going to be a big commission for someone, and I'd like to give her a chance to get it."

"Sometimes you have to put your own needs first, Lenora. This is one of those times."

Lenora realized that Gerald had some good points. Buying an expensive house probably was the biggest purchase she would ever make. Yes, Gerald had been extremely annoying during their outing, but he was trying to help her. She had to try to remember that. "You're right. I'll look with Deanna one more time. If it doesn't work out, I'll think about finding another agent."

"Fine," he said. "And I promise to keep my thoughts to myself next time we go out with her."

"I think it might be better if I go alone, Gerald," Lenora said, walking to the kitchen. The heated discussion and all the tension between her and Gerald had left her throat dry.

"You don't think I can behave?" he asked.

"I'm not trying to be difficult, just reasonable," she said as she opened the refrigerator door and reached for a bottle of Poland Spring. "Sometimes you can be a little overbearing."

"Again, only trying to help."

"I know. Maybe once I narrow it down to a few houses, you can go back out with me."

"If that's the way you want it," he said from the main room. "I'm really sorry this trip didn't turn out to be what you expected."

"You should have married me," she said teasingly as she removed the top from the water bottle. "Then you'd have more of a say."

"Well, I thought we were moving toward that," he said.

She took a generous drink of water, then walked back into the main room. Gerald was standing with his back to her and reaching into his suit jacket.

"It's what I've always wanted, but you wanted to wait for . . ."

She paused as Gerald turned to face her, a small navy-colored box in his hand. Lenora stared at the box, then up at Gerald's smiling face. It was the kind of box she had dreamed of seeing Gerald holding out to her. She held her breath as he walked slowly toward her and dropped down to one knee. He popped the box open and Lenora gasped softly. It was a square-cut diamond and platinum ring.

"Oh, my God," she said and placed the water bottle on the coffee table.

Gerald's smile widened at the expression of utter surprise on her face. He took her right hand in his. "We've talked about this long enough," he said. "What do you say? Will you marry me?"

"Oh, my God," Lenora said again. She stared at Gerald. She could barely catch her breath to respond. She had thought that he would never propose to her. She had even told herself that he was right in believing they weren't ready for marriage. Too much bickering, too much disagreement, not enough patience with each other. And now here he was waiting anxiously for her response.

"Well?" he asked. "Will you marry me?"

She giggled nervously. "I . . . I don't know what to say."

"Say yes. Or I'll be crushed."

"Yes, I'll marry you."

"Took you long enough to answer," he said as he slipped the ring on her left hand. "Had me worried for a minute there."

She admired the ring as he stood back up on his feet. He kissed her on the lips. "So, you happy?" he asked. "You're so quiet."

She nodded. "I think I'm in a state of shock." Yes, she thought, that must be it. In her mind she had always pictured this moment as one of joy and excitement. Instead, she felt numb.

"I was going to surprise you later at dinner, but then I thought, What the heck, why wait? Why not give it to her now? Then we can start making some plans at dinner."

She nodded and kissed his lips. "I'm glad you did."

"So, you ready to leave for the restaurant? We can talk about setting a date and all that there."

"Yes. Yes, I'm ready," she said. "Just give me a minute to freshen up." Lenora walked into the bathroom and closed the door. She looked in the mirror. The woman staring back at her did not look like someone who had just gotten engaged to the man she had wanted to marry for three years. The woman in the reflection looked sad, confused.

She was finally getting what she wanted. She should be dancing for joy. Instead she felt like climbing into bed, huddling into a ball, and pulling the sheet up over her head. Why?

She knew why. No point trying to fool herself or pretend. She could sum it up in one word.

Ray.

CHAPTER 30

The first thing Lenora ordered at dinner with Gerald was a big stiff martini. By the time their appetizers arrived, she had finished her first drink and was starting on her second. And she had to admit that she was feeling pretty good — or at least better than she had when she left the condo.

"I've never seen you drink a martini that fast," Gerald said. He reached across the table and covered her hand gently with his. "You don't think you're overdoing it, do you?"

She eased her fingers from his grasp and waved him off. "I'm fine. And we're celebrating, remember?" She bit into a crab-stuffed mushroom and wondered why his hand touching hers irritated the hell out of her. She had always loved his touch before.

"About setting a wedding date," Gerald said. "What are your thoughts?"

She cleared her throat. "So much is going

on with me now, and you're struggling to hold on to your own business. Maybe we should wait a month or two to decide that. By then we should be able to focus on the wedding without so many distractions."

"Sure, makes sense."

"I mean, there's no rush, right?"

"I agree," he said. "We have time."

"Good," she said. "Glad we agree on that."

"So are you settled on staying in Howard County?" he asked. "It's nice out here, but we could get a lot more bang for the buck in other places like Montgomery and Prince George's counties."

"I won't argue with that," she responded.

"And with you striking out on your own, we can buy anywhere."

For some reason, all the "we" stuff was really getting on Lenora's nerves. "Why did you propose to me all of a sudden, Gerald?"

"Huh?" He paused, holding his drink in midair, and stared at her.

"I've been wanting us to get engaged for years now, but you always resisted. Something always held you back. Now all of a sudden you propose."

"Yeah, and I thought you'd be happy about it," he said. "What's the problem?"

"Why now? Why *after* I win the lottery?"

"So you think this is all about the money?"

She shrugged. "What am I supposed to think, given the timing?"

Gerald slapped his napkin on the table and leaned toward her. He spoke softly but pointedly. "I can't believe you're saying this. *To me.* We've been together for three years." He held up three fingers for emphasis and repeated. "Three years. Are you doubting my intentions?"

She quietly took a sip of her drink.

"Since you asked," he continued, "the reason I always said we should wait to get married was that I wanted us to be more secure financially. Naturally, your coming into this money does a lot to alleviate that issue. But if you're trying to say that I proposed only because of the money, that's an insult to me. Why would I stick around for three damn years, even when one or both of us were nearly broke, if it was about money?"

She grimaced and squirmed in her seat. He had a point. If money had been the issue preventing him from moving forward with marriage, her lottery win had eliminated that issue. "I know that you love me, Gerald. It's not that."

"Then what's the problem?" he asked. "Why are you doubting me?"

"Nothing," she said. "I guess I thought

you would never propose after so many years. Maybe I need some time to get used to thinking in terms of 'we' and 'us.' "

He smiled and covered his hand with hers again, and she thought of Ray.

What the hell was wrong with her? Her boyfriend of three years had proposed, just as she had always wanted, and her thoughts were full of another man.

"Isn't that what you always wanted?" Gerald said. "To go forward as 'we' and 'us'?"

She forced a smile and covered his hand with hers. "Yes," she said. Her future was with Gerald, not with someone she barely knew.

CHAPTER 31

Lenora awoke Monday morning knowing exactly what she had to do. She and Gerald had returned to the condo after dinner and stayed up talking until he left at nearly two in the morning. The hours with Gerald were just what she needed. She had come back to her senses. She was going to start her own photography studio and graphic design business. She was going to stop obsessing about Ray, a man she barely knew. And she and Gerald were going to get married in June of next year. It felt so good to have reached these decisions with Gerald and to know that she had his support. It felt like her life was back on track.

By the time Gerald left, he was almost as excited about launching a photography and graphic design business as she was. They even talked about going into business together. He would deal with the finances, and she would handle the creative side of the business.

First, she had to get real live, paying clients. This morning she was going to put finishing touches on the mockups for Ray. He was her first potential client, and Lenora was determined not to mess this up. When they met later this afternoon, she was going to maintain a strict business relationship with him. If he came on to her, she would put him in his place. If she kept things professional and did a good job for him, he might later recommend her to others. That was how you made it in this business.

After working on the project for Ray, she would go into the office before noon, tell Dawna she was leaving for good, and pick up her personal things. She'd had a good ten years at the *Baltimore Scene* magazine. She had learned a lot and developed confidence in her abilities, despite her differences with Dawna. The magazine had helped her to grow as a photographer, and Dawna deserved to hear the news of her departure in person rather than over the telephone.

She tossed the bedcovers aside and stretched leisurely. She was about to start a new life as a wife and independent businesswoman. She came out of the shower with a towel draped around her body and sat on the edge of the bed to apply lotion to her arms and legs just as the telephone rang. She noticed that it was only nine a.m. Gerald was in a big meeting with his partners this morning, so it wasn't him. Lenora figured it was probably Dawna or someone from the office calling to find out what she had decided to do about her job. She leaned over and glanced at caller ID, thinking she wouldn't even bother to answer, since her hands were covered with lotion. But it was Ray. She grabbed the receiver with the tips of her fingers.

"Hey, Ray," she said, holding the phone between her head and shoulders as she continued to put lotion on her legs.

"Hi," he said. "I'm calling about our meeting later today."

She grimaced. Was she about to lose her one and only client before they even got started on any real business? "Something came up?"

"No. Well, yes. We had the office painted over the weekend and ran into some problems. They won't be able to wrap up until tomorrow."

"So you need to postpone the meeting," she said.

"I hate to do that," he said. "Can we meet somewhere else? Maybe your office."

That would have been fine, she thought. Except after she talked to Dawna later this morning, she would have no office. "I'm afraid that's not going to work."

"Okay. Then how about meeting over lunch?"

"Not sure about that, either," she said. "Last time I had one mockup. I have several this time, and I really need a place to spread them out."

"Then it will have to wait," he said.

"Or we could meet here at my place."

"You sure you don't mind?" he asked.

"It's a small condo," she said. "But it's better than a restaurant. We can work on the coffee table."

"I don't mind if you don't," he said.

"Good. I'll see you at noon."

She gave him her address and they hung up. She sat still on the bed. What had she just done? She had invited Ray to her little rinky-dink hole-in-the-wall. She smacked her forehead. What was she thinking?

She looked around the condo in a panic. Then she jumped up, made the bed, and cleaned off the coffee table. She grabbed the vacuum from the closet and ran it over the floor while holding the towel up over her body. She finally got tired of trying to hold the towel up and dropped it.

By the time she was done cleaning in the raw, it was after ten a.m. Ray would be there in less than two hours, and she still needed to put some final touches on the mockups. Then she had to do her hair and makeup. There was no way she could do all that and go into the office to talk to Dawna. She was going to have to quit her job over the phone. She didn't want to end it that way, but getting her new business off the ground was more important than being nice to Dawna. Besides, it wasn't as if Dawna would hear the news cold. She'd had a warning last week.

Lenora slipped into a bathrobe, sat on the edge of the bed, and took a deep breath. Then she dialed Dawna's number. As expected, Dawna uttered a few choice nasty words when Lenora gave her the news. Lenora simply held the receiver away from her ear and waited for Dawna to simmer down.

"You're going to end up regretting this," Dawna said, her voice finally dropping down to a normal tone. "Mark my words. It will take you years to get a freelance photography business off the ground."

"What makes you think that's what I'm going to do?" Lenora asked. Lenora hadn't told Dawna a thing about her plans. In fact,

Dawna was the last person she would ever tell.

"That's what I assumed since you've done some freelance photography in the past," Dawna said.

"You shouldn't assume," Lenora said, irked that Dawna's guess about what she planned to do careerwise was absolutely right. "I do have other options."

"Right," Dawna said. "Good luck!"

Lenora didn't think she'd ever heard the words "good luck" spoken with such venom. It sounded almost like a curse. "Figures," Lenora said under her breath as she hung up the phone. That was a fitting end to a long, tortured relationship. At least it was over.

She had no time to dwell on it now anyway. Ray would be here soon, and she had a thousand things to do to get ready for him. She dressed in a new black pencil skirt and a white cotton blouse that made her look slimmer. She walked Paws, then ran back up to the condo and worked on the mock-ups for about forty minutes. Finally, she went out to pick up some turkey sandwiches and a bottle of wine. She decided against flowers. That might seem too flirtatious for a business meeting, and this *was* a business meeting. But it wouldn't hurt to pamper the client a little, she told herself as she picked out a nice bottle of Chardonnay. If things went well with Ray, it could mean other clients for her down the road.

Back at the condo, she placed the Chardonnay on the table in the kitchen area, along with two of her best wineglasses. She spent several minutes arranging the sandwiches on a platter near the kitchen sink. Once satisfied with how the platter looked, she centered it on the table. By that time, it was almost noon and she led Paws to her bed and gave her a chew toy to keep her occupied.

She checked herself one last time in the full-length mirror near her bed, then reached for the telephone on the nightstand and dialed Gerald's work number. She wanted to make sure he had no plans to drop in for lunch that afternoon.

"Hi, sweetie," she said.

"Hey, what's up? I'm surprised you haven't left for your meeting. Isn't it at noon?"

"Um, we said between twelve and twelve-thirty," she said. "You about to head out for lunch?"

"Nah, I'll be working at my desk all day long," he said. "That is unless you want me to head your way when you get back from your meeting for a little quickie."

"I wish I had time," she said. "Unfortunately, it will probably be after two by the time the meeting ends, and then I want to go by the office to get my things. That could take some time."

"So you don't want to see me?" he asked in a teasing tone. "Is that it?"

"Of course I do, Gerald. But later tonight might be better than this afternoon. I have a full day."

"I'm kidding," he said. "I'll call you this evening. Love you."

"Love you back." They hung up just as the doorbell rang. Perfect timing, Lenora thought. She felt a little guilty for misleading Gerald about where and when she and Ray were working. Gerald thought she was still meeting Ray at his office, and she reasoned that there was no need to tell Gerald she was actually going to be working alongside a man alone in her condo. Gerald would then want to know all sorts of details about Ray. Such as how old he was, what he looked like, whether he was single or married. And he wouldn't like the answers.

At the last second, just before opening the door, she remembered her engagement ring. She stared at it in horror. What should she do? Ray was a client. The ring didn't matter. Still, she yanked the diamond off her finger and placed it at the back of a drawer in the kitchen. Why? She didn't know why, and she didn't have time to figure it out either.

She ran back into the front room and opened the door. Cold shivers ran down her arms. Lenora could not believe that Ray was actually standing at the entrance to her condo.

CHAPTER 32

They greeted each other with smiles, and Lenora noticed everything Ray was wearing, from the neatly pressed blue jeans that fit his cute, tight butt perfectly to the crisp white shirt and stylish brown loafers.

"Have any trouble finding it?" she asked as he stepped in with his briefcase.

"None at all. In my line of work, you have to have a navigation system since I'm always going to new sites all over the state. Looks like my next job will be in Frederick."

She pointed to her couch, and as he sat down, she regretted not having had it reupholstered. She noticed the walls and regretted not having had them repainted. Or the floors redone. But the truth was, until very recently she hadn't been able to afford to redo anything.

"Frederick is beautiful, but it's way out," she said. "Do you ever work outside Maryland?"

"No, haven't needed to. I get plenty of business here. Hope it stays that way."

She nodded. "Would you like some wine before we look over the mockups? I also have sandwiches."

He smiled with appreciation. "Sounds perfect."

She walked toward the kitchen, feeling very much aware that his eyes were likely following her every move until she disappeared around the corner. The minute she was out of his sight, she squeezed her eyes and fists tightly. Damn, he was looking hot. And they both had on white shirts. That was cute.

She picked up the bottle of wine and the glasses from the kitchen table and paused in the doorway just out of his sight to let out a deep gust of air. Get a grip, girl, she thought. Breathe in and out.

She strolled back into the main room and placed the bottle, glasses, and a corkscrew on the coffee table. She went back for the sandwich tray, and when she turned around, Ray was entering the kitchen. She lifted the tray to offer him a sandwich, but he shook his head. Without ever removing his eyes from her face, he took the tray and placed it on the countertop. A tiny voice in Lenora's head said, *No, don't do this.* An even tinier voice said, *Tell him to stop. You know you can't handle it, girl. Put an end to it now before it's too late.*

But it was already too late. It was too late when she agreed to work with him, too late when she allowed him to come to her place, too late when he wandered into the kitchen and hooked her with his eyes. She was hopeless, defenseless, mesmerized. If she had really wanted to avoid this, she should have stopped it way before now.

The next thing she knew, he was bearing down hard on her lips and backing her up against the base cabinets. He was undoing the top buttons to her white shirt, unfastening her bra, and running his lips down her neck.

He removed her top completely, and at first she tried to cover her waistline. But he was having none of that. He spread her arms and flicked his tongue across her nipples and down to her stomach. She ran her hands down his back and shut her eyes. He was rekindling all sorts of feelings that she had long since forgotten.

When he lifted her hips onto the countertop and reached down to remove her underwear, she pushed the sandwich tray out of the way. It fell on the floor with a loud clang. Neither of them paused. She spread her legs wide and he bent over until his tongue met her inner thighs.

Soon — too soon to her liking — he lifted his head and led her to the bed on the opposite side of the room. He lay down beside her and she could hear him panting heavily as he undid his fly and removed his slacks and shirt. He turned onto his back and she lifted herself up over him and guided him inside her. She squeezed the bars on the brass bed until finally she could hold back no longer. Her body shuddered from head to toe. The muscles in Ray's face and arms tightened and he swung her around until he was on top. His mounting desire sent Lenora soaring to new heights until finally they both cried out.

Minutes later, they lay side by side and the only sound was their heavy breathing. She had longed to feel this man next to her almost from the day they met, and she wanted to savor the moment. She hoped his silence meant the same. He sat up against the headboard and smiled down at her. He was already breathing at a normal pace, whereas Gerald would still be trying to catch his breath. Ah, the blessings of youth, she thought, breathing a little heavily herself. Ray's work also kept him in much better shape.

"Whoa," she said.

"Whoa back at you," he said.

They both laughed.

"Don't know where that came from, but I'm glad it did," she said. "I don't remember ever wanting anyone so much."

He placed his hand over her stomach. "I felt sparks flying from our first meeting."

"Really? I had no idea. You didn't let on," she said. "I actually thought you were being real mean."

"I thought *you* were being mean," he said, chuckling. "Showing up late, copping an attitude."

She smiled, lifting his hand and admiring it. She could barely believe she was holding one of his hands so tight. "I was frustrated that I might not get to photograph you."

"But you did. So it all worked out, I'd say."

"Couldn't be better," she said.

"So tell me, you still seeing anyone? You once mentioned a boyfriend."

And with those words he catapulted Lenora into reality. And back to the thought of what she had just done to Gerald, her fiancé. She put Ray's hand down on the bed.

"Sorry to change the mood so abruptly," he said. "But this happened so quickly, and we need to talk about these things."

Lenora nodded. "I'm still with him."

Ray wrinkled his brow in thought. "How serious is it? Not very, I'm assuming."

She didn't know how much she wanted to tell Ray about Gerald. She didn't know how much she would tell Gerald about Ray. She didn't know anything. She was so confused right now. "Um, you assume right."

"You sure?" he asked. " 'Cause I don't like dealing with women who are in serious relationships with other people. Gets too messy."

"It's not serious." How easily she lied, she thought.

"Good," he said.

"I thought you were in a relationship," she said.

"A casual relationship, nothing exclusive. We both see others. I'm not sure where this is going between us, but I'll always be up front with you."

She nodded. "Likewise."

"Good," he said.

Well, she wasn't being *totally* dishonest. At least Ray knew she was seeing someone else. A part of her wanted to tell him the entire truth about Gerald — that she wasn't seeing him casually, that they were engaged. But the truth might scare Ray away before she got a chance to really experience him. Actually, based on what Ray just said, the truth *would* chase him away. And she wasn't prepared to let him run off so soon. She would figure out how to unravel the mess she had created later. For now, she was going to be selfish for a change. She was going to keep both men.

"Too much talk, not enough action," she said as she leaned over and ran her lips across his chest.

He laughed. "Fair enough," he said.

Her lips slid lower and she quickly realized that Ray was a lot faster at something besides catching his breath. Like getting it on a second time.

It was a couple of hours before they got around to the mockups.

When she kissed Ray good-bye at her door, it was almost 9:00 p.m. In between looking at the mockups and her phoning Gerald with excuses to delay his arrival, Lenora and Ray had made love three more times. She lay across the bed after Ray left and petted Paws. She was exhausted. Her head was swirling with emotions. Ray was young, vibrant, sensuous. He aroused in her a burning, insatiable passion, something she had never felt with Gerald or any other man.

The phone rang and she thought her heart would pop out of her chest. She was certain it was Ray. He couldn't get her out of his mind any more than she could him. She grabbed the phone without checking caller ID.

"Hey, you," she said in her most sexy voice.

There was a momentary silence and Lenora panicked as she realized that it might not be Ray on the line.

"Hey, baby," Gerald said. "You sure answered fast. Sounds like you're missing me."

Lenora swallowed. She felt some guilt but more disappointment. She had to work hard to keep that out of her voice.

"Of course I miss you." She got up and dug her engagement ring out of the utensil drawer, sliding it back on her finger.

"You sound different," Gerald said. "Everything okay?"

"Yep, I'm good."

"So should I come by now?" he asked. "Or you still working?"

She sat at the kitchen table. "I'm done but I'm really tired, Gerald."

"You sound tired," he said. "Glad you at least had a good, productive day."

She cleared her throat and tried to perk up. "How did it go for you today?"

"Not good."

"Oh, really?" she asked with genuine concern.

"We can't make the numbers," he said. "Afraid this is the end for us. Or close to it."

"Oh, Gerald. I'm sorry to hear that."

"Them's the breaks sometimes," he said.

"My offer to help is still good," she said.

"No," he said. "The more I thought about that, the less I liked the idea. Didn't even bother to ask the guys about it because I can't be sure we would ever pay you back. I want you to use the money to buy your dream house and start your own business."

"Oh, Gerald, this is sad," she said, her voice breaking. "This was your dream and now it's gone, just like that. What will you all do?"

"Don't worry about us. We'll manage. We're already discussing other ideas. But first we want to take a break, take some time to get our heads together."

"That makes sense. Whatever you need, I'm here for you."

"Thanks," he said. "Are we still on for looking at houses next weekend?"

Lenora frowned. She had completely forgotten that they were supposed to do more house hunting together now that they were engaged. She was so confused. She wasn't sure she was even in the mood to think about buying a house now.

"Uh-huh," was all she could manage in response.

"I spoke to Patrice, a Realtor I told you about who specializes in high-end houses. She's been doing this for thirty years, and she's willing to show us around on Saturday."

"Wait a minute," Lenora said. "What about Deanna?"

"I honestly don't think she's right for us, sweetheart."

She could see that they were headed for an argument about which agent they would use. "Look, Gerald, I don't want to get into this now."

"I'm trying to be helpful. We should at least give Patrice a chance. If it doesn't work out, we can go back to Deanna."

"You can't jerk agents around like that," Lenora protested. "I signed on to work with Deanna for sixty days. Besides, she's a member of The Girlfriends. Some of them could become photography clients of mine in the future. But not if I get on their bad side by dumping one of them as my agent."

"If she's a personal friend, she should understand and let you out of your agreement."

"She's not a personal friend," Lenora explained. "She's a club member."

"It's still a personal relationship."

"What the hell is wrong with you, Gerald? A deal is a deal. You of all people should understand that. You're supposed to be such a savvy businessman. Although sometimes I wonder."

He paused at her sudden abrupt tone. "Damn, what's gotten into you? You've really changed."

"What do you mean?"

"You seem different these past couple of weeks. You used to listen to me and trust my judgment. Now you're distant and testy."

She softened her voice. "I'm sorry if it seems that way."

"Do you still want to get married?" he asked.

"Yes," she said quickly. "Why wouldn't I?"

"Maybe it's my imagination, but the enthusiasm seemed lacking when I proposed. Do you still love me?"

"Yes. Of course. Just because we're disagreeing about something doesn't mean I don't."

"But it seems that we argue much more lately," he said. "We can hardly talk without arguing. Have you noticed?"

"It's just a tense time for both of us. For you because of the business, and for me because I won the lottery."

"You sure that's all?" he asked.

"That's a lot, Gerald."

"I know, but is anything else bothering you? Anything you want to tell me?"

Yes! she wanted to scream. Her whole world had flipped upside down. She didn't know which way was up anymore. She was foolishly lusting over a man she knew she could never have and pushing the one she did have away.

"Nothing else is bothering me," she said simply. "Everything is fine. We're fine."

After they hung up, Lenora moved to the bed and flopped on her back. She stared at the ceiling in frustration. She still loved Gerald. A part of her still wanted to marry him. The question was whether she *should,* given what she had just done with Ray. Again and again.

Lenora realized that she had no real future with Ray. But she also realized that she wasn't going to let him go as long as he wanted her, not even for Gerald. Ray made her feel too good. And it wasn't only the sex, as awesome as that was. It was the thrill of being with a sexy, attractive man. Ray was so hot that he could have any woman he wanted; yet he had chosen to be with her. She was going to enjoy him for as long as she could.

CHAPTER 33

After one more trip with Deanna looking at several houses for sale, Lenora and Gerald finally narrowed the choice down to three that they liked, ranging in size from five to seven thousand square feet. Gerald thought they should go with one of the two smaller homes. Lenora had fallen in love with the largest. It had a huge kitchen with top-of-the-line luxury appliances such as a Viking stove and Sub-Zero refrigerator. If she had the money, she reasoned, why not go all out and get everything she wanted? She had done without all her life. She didn't want to hold back on anything anymore.

Lenora and Gerald were discussing the three houses as they returned to Lenora's condo and she glanced at her watch. She realized with alarm that it was much later than she thought. Instead of the house-hunting trip taking a couple of hours as she had expected, it took nearly four. Ray was supposed to call so they could decide when and where to meet that evening, and she had less than fifteen minutes to get Gerald out of there.

"The fifty-five-hundred-square-foot house is perfect for us," Gerald said as he made himself comfortable on her couch. "There's more than enough room. It's got a pool, gardens, and plenty of land if you should want to expand it someday."

"Why buy something you might have to add on to later when we could have everything we can imagine with the bigger property now?" she said. "It's already got a library, a sunroom, a theater, and five acres of land."

"We obviously need to give this more thought," he said. He glanced at his watch. "Let's go get a bite to eat. We can discuss it over dinner."

Dinner was the last thing on Lenora's mind. She wasn't even hungry, she was so full of anticipation for Ray's visit. "That took longer than I thought it would," she said. "I have a lot of work to do on the freelance job. Maybe another time."

"Then we can grab a sandwich near here. You got to eat."

She shook her head. "I'll just get a salad out of the fridge later. I really want to work on the brochure."

"Fine, you work," Gerald said, standing up from the couch. "I think I'll go pick up a sandwich for myself and come back and watch a bit of tube while you work."

Huh? Lenora swallowed hard. She shifted from one foot to the other. This didn't sound at all like her workaholic boyfriend. She had fully expected him to want to go home and get some work done for his firm. Then she remembered. His firm was winding down. But she decided to go along with Gerald's plans to grab a sandwich. It should at least get him out of the house for twenty minutes or so and give her a chance to talk to Ray in private.

As soon as Gerald left, Lenora decided to call Ray instead of waiting for him to call her. She needed to speak to him in this window of opportunity while Gerald was out.

"So what time do you want me to come by?" he asked after they greeted each other.

"That's why I'm calling," she said. "I was hoping we could meet at your place to-night." She would simply tell Gerald that she had to step out for something if he insisted on hanging around her condo.

"That's not going to work," Ray said.

"Oh," she said with disappointment.

"My folks are visiting from out of town."

Suddenly she realized that she knew very little about this man. "Where are they visiting from?" she asked.

"Chicago. I lived there myself until about eight years ago. They're staying for the week."

She smiled. Interesting, she thought, but irrelevant to the task at hand: finding somewhere to hook up that night. "So your place is obviously out."

"We can always meet another time if your place is a problem," he said.

"I really don't want to have to wait to see you. My boyfriend went to get a sandwich and he's coming back in a few to watch some TV. For some reason, he's decided to hang out here tonight. But I could slip out for a while if we had another place to meet."

"Now I get it," Ray said. "Let's meet at my office," he suggested. "No one is there on Saturdays, and it's not far from your condo."

"Sounds perfect," she said, relieved that they wouldn't have to wait. She hung up and wiped her brow after they finalized the arrangements to meet in fifteen minutes at Ray's office in downtown Columbia. All this scheming and sneaking around was going to make her an old woman before her time.

But it also made things more exciting. She paced the floor, cell phone in hand, trying to figure out what to do about Gerald. Finally an idea came to her. It was kind of weak but would have to do. She dialed Gerald's number and he picked up on the first ring.

"Don't tell me," he said. "You changed your mind and want a sandwich."

"No," she said, ignoring the guilt welling up inside her heart. The desire in her loins was so much stronger. "I have to run out to the printer for something before it closes."

"Huh?" Gerald said with clear surprise in his voice.

"I need to get something printed for one of the brochures I'm working on."

"I heard what you said," he said. "It just seems odd that this came up all of a sudden."

"I just realized I needed it as I was going through my paperwork after you left."

"Uh-huh."

"I called the printer and they close in less than an hour, so I need to get over there now."

"What's wrong with Kinko's?" Gerald asked.

"Huh?"

"Kinko's," he repeated. "They're open all

night, I think. You could go after we eat."

"Right." She smacked her head in frustration. "But they can't do what I need done. I called and asked. That's why I have to go to this other printer. I've used them before and I know they do a good job."

"Uh-huh," he said slowly. "I have my key. I can let myself in while you're gone and wait for you to get back."

"I'm not sure how long I'll be," she said.

"You just said they close in an hour. So you can't be longer than that."

"Right. That should be fine. I'll see you when I get back." She hung up and threw her hands into the air. Bad planning. By the time she allowed for driving to and from Ray's office, she would have far less than an hour to spend with him. Whatever, at least she had an excuse to get out of the condo.

She ran into the bathroom to apply more makeup, just the way Ray liked it. She also tried on a tight-fitting denim skirt that she hadn't worn in a few years. She was actually surprised that she could get it on, even though she had to twist, turn, and tug to get it over her hips. Thank goodness for all the pounds she had shed recently. Satisfied that the skirt would work, she lifted it and changed from her usual bikini underwear to the only thong she owned. She had never learned to feel comfy in them and had stashed this one in the back of her underwear drawer after wearing it just once. Now the little black number felt just right for her rendezvous with Ray.

She lowered the skirt again and checked herself in the mirror one last time. She knew that Ray was likely a bad boy, the kind of man who would discard a woman like yesterday's news the minute he found someone else more intriguing. But she decided not to worry about that as long as she was today's news.

She snatched a pair of baggy jeans from her closet. If Gerald was here when she returned, he would wonder why she had changed into a skimpy skirt he had never seen before. She stuffed the jeans into a tote bag along with her engagement ring and ran to the door. Then she remembered that Gerald thought she was going to the printer. She needed to have something work-related. She grabbed her briefcase from her desk and dashed out.

She and Ray had so little time at his office that they didn't even fully undress. And that was fine with Lenora. She wanted to feel him inside her, and the sooner the better. Ray cleared his desk with one swoop of his arm and unzipped his jeans. She hiked her skirt and he helped her slide her thong down to her ankle. She leaned back on the desk, spread her legs, and bit his bottom lip as he finally enveloped her.

They ground urgently against each other and their movements became frantic. She couldn't remember feeling so much in need of another man's body. Right now, this very moment, was the only thing that mattered. Nothing else came close. She peaked once, then again and again and again.

Back at the parking lot of her building an hour and fifteen minutes after she had gone out, she dug her ring out of the bottom of the tote bag and slipped it on. She would have gotten back sooner if she and Ray had not ended up going for seconds on the floor of his office. Then she had taken a few minutes to freshen up and change into the baggy jeans.

As soon as she opened the door to her condo, she was greeted by Paws, and Gerald's head popped around the corner of the kitchen. He was holding a spatula and had a smile on his face. "It's about time," he said, standing in the doorway of the kitchen. "I was expecting you sooner, since the printer closed thirty minutes ago."

"They still help clients who are already in the shop even after they close," Lenora said as she dropped her briefcase on the couch.

"That's what I figured," he said. "Did you get what you needed?"

"What do you mean?" she asked.

"Did you get whatever it was you went to the printer to have done?" He looked her up and down quizzically, clearly expecting to see a package or something from the printer. That was when Lenora realized that she had nothing that even remotely looked like it had come from a printer. No brochure, no poster, no shopping bag, nothing.

"Oh, um, actually, I left it there," she said, licking her lips. "I wanted some changes made. Should be ready in a day or two." Damn, she thought. She was going to have to get better at this or she would get caught in no time. And as unlikely as it seemed, she did not want to lose Gerald. In fact, this little goof made her realize that even more. Ray wouldn't stick around forever; Gerald would. She smiled broadly in an attempt to take his mind off her flimsy lies and excuses. "So what's cooking?" she said as she approached the kitchen.

"Just some . . ." His voice died down slowly as she put her arms around his neck. The smile that was on his face earlier turned into a frown. Lenora was about to ask him what was wrong when it hit her just before

339

he spoke.

"You have on a ton of makeup," he said, pushing her back to arm's length so he could see her face clearly. "You wear makeup only when we go someplace special, like the theater. And never *that* much."

She felt her face grow hot. While one part of her brain searched for an excuse, no matter how flimsy, another part was telling her that it was hopeless. She should just come out with the truth. How the hell had she thought she could get away with an affair for any length of time? What made her believe that she should be able to hold on to two men? Did she think that because she was now a millionaire she could have any- and everything she desired?

Yes.

"Oh, that," she said, laughing lightly, trying her best not to sound nervous. "I was practicing putting on makeup before I went out."

"For what?" Gerald asked, looking unconvinced.

"I'm going to have a pamphlet designed for my new photography business."

"Yeah?" he said, his voice still full of doubt and confusion. "So?"

"I want to include a portrait of myself. I was trying to see if I could do my own

340

makeup or if I need to hire someone. How did I do?"

"Huh?"

"How does my makeup job look?" she asked.

"Good," Gerald said.

She could see that his accountant mind was turning this over furiously, trying to get to the bottom of her strange behavior.

"Really?" she said. "Then I'll save a bunch by doing it myself."

"Like you need to worry about money," he said sarcastically.

"I still hate to waste it on things I don't need." She turned back toward the main room and away from his probing gaze. She might get away with the lies, excuses, and deception now, but not for long. She had never done this kind of thing before and obviously wasn't very good at it. Sooner or later Gerald was going to catch on if she didn't end this thing with Ray.

She had no intention of stopping.

CHAPTER 34

Over the next few weeks, Lenora spent every moment she could spare with Ray, from midafternoon trysts when he slipped away from his job sites and they got it on in the bed of his pickup truck under a blanket, to late at night when she slipped quietly out of bed as Gerald slept beside her and met Ray at the edge of the parking lot. She was always careful to remove her ring and tuck it somewhere near the front door and then to replace it when she returned.

She did move on in other areas of her life, sometimes making what she thought were difficult but winning choices. "Eliminate the bull, bring on the fun," was her new mantra. When Monica called to arrange the details for a meeting with Alise, Lenora cut her short.

"I've changed my mind," Lenora said. "I don't want to meet with her."

"But why?" Monica asked, clearly

stunned. "You said you would. And Alise has agreed to a meeting."

"I have so much else going on now, what with getting engaged to Gerald." *And screwing Ray.* "Looking for a house." *And Ray.* "I really don't want to deal with her now." *Only Ray.*

"I don't know you anymore," Monica said. "You've changed."

"I haven't changed," Lenora protested. "I just know what I want and I'm in a position to have it."

"All right," Monica said. "Just don't throw the baby out with the bathwater."

Lenora laughed and brushed off the warning. She didn't have time for admonitions from people who frankly weren't in her position. As dear a friend as Monica was to her, she didn't have money to burn or a hunk like Ray to make love to. Only she was in this position. Not Monica, not Alise, not Gerald.

After arguing back and forth with Gerald about which house to choose, she had Deanna make a low offer on her dream house. She and the seller went back and forth for a few days until finally they reached an agreement. Despite his misgivings about her choice, Gerald congratulated her and took her out to celebrate over dinner at the mall. Not surprisingly, they got into an argument in the car on the way and were still bickering as they wove through the crowded parking lot.

"You really don't approve, do you?"

"I don't understand why you had to rush into this," he said. "It's not like that house was going anywhere quickly in this market. You had time to give it more thought or keep looking. But lately it seems you have no patience. You want what you want and you want it right away." He shook his head with exasperation.

"I've waited so long to be able to have the things I want, Gerald. Why should I put it off if I don't have to? And this is a house. It's not like I'm throwing my money away gambling or on something frivolous. A house is still an investment."

"Fine," he said. "I can see you're not going to look at it any other way. You don't feel that you need to consult me anymore or take my thoughts into consideration."

"I mean, I know we're engaged and that you —"

"Oh, so you remembered," he said, his voice dripping with sarcasm.

"Stop being silly," she said. "I listened to what you had to say and I considered it, honestly."

"How? When? It was almost all about what you wanted." He paused. "No, wait. It was *completely* about what you wanted."

"The house that I finally got was one of the three that we both liked," she protested. "And you influenced me to offer a lower price and drive a hard bargain."

"Of course I like the house," he said. "What's not to like? I can see why it's your dream house. But that doesn't mean it was the best choice for us financially." He paused. "Oh, excuse me. That doesn't mean it was the best choice for *you.*"

She smacked her lips. He wasn't being fair at all. She kept him informed from the beginning. He went out with her to look at the houses, together they narrowed it down to three that they liked, he helped her negotiate a good price. What was he complaining about?

"You know, you have really changed," he said as they approached the door to the restaurant.

"No I haven't."

"Oh, yeah. You definitely have. Ever since you won that money."

"You're just saying that because of the house."

"It's not only that," he said. "On weekends when we have plans to go somewhere, you're always canceling at the last minute and running off to do your own thing. You never did that before. Like last Saturday, when we were going to the gallery in Baltimore."

"I canceled to go look at a studio that was for rent. I'm trying to build a business, Gerald. That takes time." She didn't mention that Ray met her at the studio and afterward they drove to a park and made love in the bed of his pickup.

He stopped near the front door and steered her to the side. "Is that also why you wear so much more makeup now and the short skirts?"

She swallowed hard. "Am I not allowed to wear makeup? I have clients now. I want to look nice for them."

"It doesn't seem like you, Lenora. You couldn't have cared less about makeup and clothes before."

"I didn't have my own clients before. I was on salary at a magazine. That's —"

"What clients?" he asked bitterly. "You have one client."

"I'm working hard trying to get more," she snapped. "You are really starting to —"

"Are you having an affair?"

Lenora paused, stunned. She glanced around to see if anyone had heard his question. If they had, they weren't letting on. Everyone seemed to be going about their business. "What?"

"You heard me."

"Of course not. Where did you get that idea?" Lenora racked her brain trying to think of where she might have slipped up, where she had been careless. She did some silly things in the beginning, but she thought she had gotten better at covering her tracks. Maybe not.

"Lots of things," he said.

"Such as?"

"Where did you go when you slipped out of the condo last night?"

Lenora thought her legs would give out. She stared at Gerald. How the hell did he know? And if he knew, why did he wait all this time to mention it?

"I didn't think you heard me," she said.

"Oh, I know you didn't," he said. "I woke up when the bed moved. I thought you were getting up to go to the bathroom and dozed back off. Then I heard the front door open and shut. I got up and you were gone. You came back about thirty or forty minutes later."

"Why didn't you say something before?"

"I figured you would tell me what was going on this morning."

"I see," she said. She shoved her hands into her pockets. "Well, Gerald, I didn't want to have to tell you this."

He watched her closely and waited.

"I smoked a couple of cigarettes."

He jerked his head back. "Are you serious?"

She nodded. "It's all the stress. The money, the house, my job, and looking for a studio. It's too much at once. It's getting to me."

"How long have you been smoking?"

She shrugged. "A few weeks."

"Have you ever smoked before?"

"Years ago, before we met," she said, lying. Unless you counted the occasional puff after sex when she dated a man in college who smoked.

"I didn't know that."

"It's not exactly something I brag about," she said. "I do it to keep the weight off, mainly."

"That's a stupid reason to smoke."

"I agree."

"Why haven't I smelled it on you?" he asked.

"I use a breath freshener," she said. "And last night I slipped into the shower when I came back in to wash the odor away."

"I heard you in the shower," he said.

"That explains a lot. Still, you shouldn't have tried to hide it from me."

"I realize that now."

"And you have to stop," he added. "I don't need to tell you it's dangerous."

She nodded. "Believe me, I know it's dangerous. It's just a really hard craving to kick."

CHAPTER 35

The next few weeks were a flurry of activity. Lenora put her condo on the market at a price she viewed as dirt cheap considering that she still owed more on the unit than the listing price. Unfortunately, that was the nature of the market these days. She just wanted to get it off her hands and move on to her new life, and she was fortunate to be in a position to do that when many others weren't.

She also found a professional photography studio in the neighboring town of Laurel. It was huge, with high ceilings and separate rooms for three offices or workspaces. The sale included furniture, fixtures, counters, lighting, backgrounds, and props. She was extremely excited until she realized that the only way she was going to be able to buy the studio was to make a huge down payment. Since she had little income now and had already taken out a mortgage for the house, no bank would finance the studio at more than fifty percent. She had enough cash, but the purchase would eat up much of the money she had left.

Gerald thought it was out of the question to spend nearly all of her money. Lenora did too, initially. But the more time she spent looking at other cheaper studios, the more she appreciated how nice the first one was.

"If you don't listen to me about anything else for the rest of our lives, hear me on this," Gerald pleaded as they left the new house to walk Paws around the neighborhood. Paws bounded ahead, excitedly exploring every new bush and leaf of grass with her nose, and Gerald extended the leash. "You don't have to buy the most expensive studio in Maryland. Some of the ones we looked at are half the cost of the one in Laurel. One was about a third."

"And they look like crap," Lenora said, turning up her nose. "They either need repairs or a lot of updates to look as good as the one in Laurel. Plus they're smaller."

"Start small and work your way up to something bigger and nicer," he suggested.

"But it would take a lot of time and work to fix them up just so I could use them. I don't want to get involved in painting and updating electrical panels. I want a turnkey situation. Something I can walk straight into and get to work."

"How about renting a studio until you start making some real money?"

"Is that it?" she asked. "Are you worried that I may not be able to pull this off and make money at it?"

"I have all the confidence in the world that you can do it. But there are ways to go about it without spending almost all of your cash. Start slowly and grow as the money is earned. That's one of the hard lessons I just learned."

Lenora shook her head adamantly. "My situation is different from yours. I have the money to start big and get what I want now without borrowing a single dime."

"That's the problem, baby. You want too much."

She would prove Gerald wrong, she thought. She was a damn good photographer and absolutely positive that she would have plenty of clients to pay the mortgages on her new home and studio in no time.

Gerald was trying to get her to allow him to move into the new house with her. He was surprised when Lenora said they should wait until after they were married.

"I don't get it," Gerald had said. "There

was a time when you couldn't wait to get married and you wanted me to move into that tiny condo with you. Now that I've proposed and you have this huge house, you change your mind about us living together."

"We're going to be married soon. Why not wait?"

At least that was what she told him. She still loved Gerald and thought he would make a good husband. He was dependable, smart, and ambitious. But she and Ray were meeting once or twice a week, and her hot young man was a constant reminder of all that was missing in her relationship with Gerald — knees weak with anticipation, loins swollen with excitement, steamy sex that seemed to go on forever. It had become a weekly excursion for them to meet in the far corner of a park. She would drive to the destination and hop into the bed of Ray's truck. They would toss a heavy blanket over them and get busy.

If she and Gerald lived together, she would have to give Ray up. Or it would certainly be a lot harder to keep seeing him. She didn't kid herself for a minute that she could hold on to both men forever. Eventually, she was going to have to let one of them go, and it would likely be Ray. But the time hadn't come yet.

CHAPTER 36

Lenora walked into her new studio on the last Monday in August and it was one of the best days of her life. The studio was everything she had imagined, and thanks to her lottery winnings, it was all hers.

She let her camera bag slide to the floor of the main room, lifted her arms, and twirled around until she was dizzy. She stopped and stood still while her balance came back. Then she picked up her camera bag and entered the largest of the three side offices.

Now for the hard part, she thought as she sat at the desk. She had to get to work if she was going to continue to pay for all of this. Over the weekend, she had put together a list of forty potential clients, culled from previous photo assignments while at the *Baltimore Scene* and earlier jobs as well as freelance assignments.

She spent two hours working the phones

and reached half the names on the list. The result? One potential new assignment shooting portraits for new business cards for a real estate office. She couldn't believe her bad luck.

She stood and looked out the window of her office. For the first time since writing that big check for the down payment on the studio, she felt real anxiety. She was going to have to do way better than this. The money she won gave her a wonderful fresh start on life. But she had spent just about all of it in a matter of months. If she didn't want everything she had put into motion over the past several weeks to collapse, she had to get some clients and get them fast.

But first things first, she thought as she grabbed her shoulder bag from her desk. It was twelve-thirty on a Monday afternoon and that meant a hookup with Ray in the park. Yes, she needed to keep working the phones to drum up clients. But more than that she needed some relief from all the stress, and nothing was better for that than a meeting with Ray.

Before she could get out the door, the phone rang. She stopped and debated whether to ignore it. She didn't want to be late. But this might be a potential client, so she decided to answer. Caller ID told her it wasn't a client but Monica. She picked up.

"Hey there, Miss Entrepreneur," her friend said.

"Hi, Monica. What's up?"

"My shift at the hospital is just ending," Monica said. "Thought you might want to meet for lunch. My treat in honor of your new studio and the new house."

"I appreciate the offer, I really do. But no thanks."

"My money not good enough for you?" Monica joked.

"It's not that. I have other plans."

"Meeting Gerald?" Monica asked.

"Actually, no. Ray."

"You know, between your hot young stud and the new studio and all the other stuff you've got going on, I hardly ever see you anymore."

"Can't help it," Lenora said. "I'm hooked."

"That's what worries me," Monica said. "You got emotionally involved with this guy."

"No, I didn't," Lenora protested. "Okay, maybe a little."

"That's a no-no with a man like him. Don't say I didn't warn you."

"You did warn me."

"You really ought to walk away while you

can," Monica said. "Before it's really too late."

"It already is too late."

"Damn."

"I know."

"Come by tonight and let me talk some sense into you, girl," Monica said. "About this and a whole lot else going on with you lately."

"Okay, I'll call you later."

"No, you won't," Monica said. "We've had this discussion before. You really need a good talking-to, but I can't get you to slow down long enough to listen. You don't even —"

"Look, I have to go," Lenora said, interrupting. "We'll talk."

Lenora hung up before Monica could say another word and ran out the studio door. Ray had canceled the last two meetings due to work, and it had been a couple of weeks since she had seen him. She did not want to miss this meeting for any reason.

She smiled when she entered the lot at the park and saw his pickup truck at the agreed-upon spot. She pulled up alongside and they climbed into the back, pulled a blanket over their heads, and met each other eagerly until they heard several vehicles pull up on both sides of the truck. They froze under the blanket and listened as doors opened and shut in rapid succession.

The first thing Lenora thought of was that the cops were onto them and they were about to be busted. She didn't know if they were breaking any laws, but even if not it would be damned embarrassing to be caught half naked with her legs spread-eagled and a man lying between them. Then she heard the loud voices and laughter of teenagers and she relaxed a bit. When the noises died down more, Ray climbed off her, lifted the blanket, and took a peek.

He came back under the blanket and explained that three cars were parked nearby, and a group of about six or seven teenagers were walking off into the park. Lenora breathed a sigh of relief and reached out to pull him back between her legs. She wanted to continue exactly where they'd left off, before the mood passed, but the incident seemed to have spooked Ray. He pulled his jeans back on and zipped the fly. He waited for her to dress, then tossed the blanket aside.

"You all right?" she asked.

"I'm fine," he said. "The moment was just ruined."

She nodded and rubbed her hand across his hair. "I understand. You want to wait a bit or . . ."

He glanced at his watch and shook his head. "I need to get back to the site."

"Can we hook up later this evening?"

"Maybe. I'll see."

"How will I know?" she asked.

"I'll call you." He let the back of the truck bed down and helped her out.

"About what time?" she asked as he climbed into the driver's seat of his truck.

"Hard to say. As soon as I have some free time, I'll call."

Back at the studio, Lenora tried to focus on the list of potential clients before her and all the calls she needed to make. She tried to concentrate on paperwork that needed to be filled out. But it was hard after the frustrating afternoon with Ray.

She leaned back in her chair. Things had changed dramatically. The hot flame that once burned between them had died down. They used to spend hours together making love, talking about their plans for life, and working on the brochures for his landscaping business. Now they usually spent less than an hour together. He always said he was busy with work, but Lenora sensed that it was more than that. She had always known that he would someday want to move on, but she never expected it to be so

359

soon. Right now she had a hard time imagining her days without Ray. She sat up and tried to push the thought of missing him from her head. But an hour later, she had made only two more calls. Her mind kept drifting to Ray and the steamy sex she missed so much. She would close her eyes until she could see him, smell him, feel him. If she concentrated hard enough, it was almost as if he were there. But he wasn't.

She opened her eyes. If she couldn't be with him now, she wanted to hear his voice. She dialed his cell number and it rang and rang. That was another thing. It seemed to take him much longer to answer her calls these days. He picked up just before it went to the answering machine.

"Hi," he said.

"Hey. Did I catch you at a bad time?"

"I have a few minutes to spare. You back at the new studio?"

"Yes."

"How is it?" he asked.

"It's everything I ever dreamed of," she said. "It's perfect, or almost. It needs only one more thing."

"What's that?"

"Christening. I'm picturing us in the middle of the studio floor with a blanket under us, a bottle of champagne next to us, and you on top of me."

He laughed.

"I'm serious."

"I know you are. When did you have in mind?"

"Today," she said. "Now."

"Mm. As tempting as that sounds, I have to decline. Too much work."

She exhaled with disappointment. "Right."

"Another time," he said. "Gotta run now."

They hung up and Lenora stared into space. Twice in one day he had brushed her off. She wasn't ready for this.

CHAPTER 37

Another day at the office and still almost nothing to show for it. Lenora couldn't stop thinking about Ray long enough to get any meaningful work done. To land new clients she had to work the phones for hours at a time, reaching out to everyone she had ever worked with over the years. She needed to get in her car and drive to businesses that might have an interest in her work and hand them the business cards and flyers that she had yet to design and get printed. She needed to take classes to update her skills with some of the latest technology. The list went on.

Yet other than a few hours on the phone, she had done none of that, and she was beginning to hate herself for it. She knew she was capable of doing better than this, and it was frustrating that she was unable to rein in her thoughts and emotions. Monica was right. Lenora shouldn't have gotten involved with a man like Ray.

He hadn't returned any of her calls since they almost got caught in the truck on Monday, and here it was Friday afternoon. This was the longest they had gone without contact. There was no use denying it any longer. Her relationship with Ray was coming to an end if it wasn't already over. This was really hard to accept, since only weeks ago they were a hot couple who couldn't get enough of each other.

The telephone rang and she grabbed the receiver, hoping that it might be Ray. "Hello?"

"Lenora?"

Lenora frowned deeply. It had been many weeks since she'd heard Dawna's voice. She had almost forgotten what it sounded like. But not quite.

"Hello, Dawna," Lenora said. "Yes, it's me."

"How are you?" Dawna asked.

"Fine." She was struggling to land clients, Ray had all but vanished from her life, and most of her money was gone. But she would never reveal to this woman that she was at a low point.

"I had Jenna dig up your new office number," Dawna said. "Hope you don't mind."

That depends on why you're calling, Lenora thought. "Not a problem," she said.

"I heard that you and Gerald got engaged. True?"

"Yes."

"Then congratulations!"

"Thanks."

"The reason I'm calling is that I have a photography assignment I think you might be interested in," Dawna said. "Are you looking for work? Or are you already swamped with clients?"

Lenora was desperate for assignments, but was she hard up enough to work with Dawna? Yes. "I'm always looking for more work," Lenora said. The word "more" was a joke, she thought. Even the measly job for Ray had dried up.

"I may have just the thing for you," Dawna said. "Ever since you left, I have been struggling to fill your shoes, you know?" Dawna laughed. "This would be a big, multi-month assignment photographing the exteriors and lobbies of various art museums and galleries in Baltimore, including the Walters Art Museum and the Baltimore Museum of Art, for a feature we're doing on the Baltimore art scene. I need someone who can also photograph art pieces from the museums in a studio setting. I've already gotten permission for some of the artwork, and I don't need to tell you that this is a big deal. I need someone who can take this job, run with it, and come up with some glorious, mouthwatering shots. I don't want to trust such an important assignment to any of the amateurs working on my staff now."

Lenora couldn't kid herself. The assignment sounded better and better the longer Dawna spoke. In fact, it sounded like a dream job, almost too good to be true. But it was true. And Dawna seemed to be a lot more pleasant than she ever had before. Maybe Dawna treated her freelancers better than she did her staff. "All right, you got my attention. I'd love to work on this."

"Wonderful!" Dawna said. "We just need to go over the details and sign the contract."

"When do you want to meet?" Lenora asked. "I'm free just about any time that works for you."

"How about this afternoon?" Dawna asked. "Actually, how about right now, before I go to lunch?"

Lenora sat up straight. Dawna was obviously eager to get going on this, and the sooner the better for her. A big smile crossed Lenora's lips for the first time in weeks. She was finally going to land some real photography work. And not only would she get paid well for such a big assignment, but when the feature ran in the *Baltimore Scene* her byline would appear alongside the photographs. That could lead to more assignments from Dawna as well as from others. This could be just the thing to take her mind off Ray and get her life back on track.

"I'll be knocking on your door in thirty minutes tops," Lenora said. "No later than eleven-thirty."

"Good," Dawna said. "I'll be waiting."

CHAPTER 38

Pulling up in front of her old office at the *Baltimore Scene* gave Lenora the chills. It had been a couple of months since she was last here, yet it seemed like yesterday. The parking garage, the building, the elevator — everything flooded her mind with memories, some of them good, many bad. And most of the bad memories had to do with Dawna.

So why was she back here to meet with the dreadful woman and possibly to work with her? Easy to answer, Lenora thought. She was desperate for work, and Dawna had offered her a plum assignment that was simply too good to pass up.

She stepped out of the elevator on the fourth floor and walked into the magazine's lobby. She smiled when she saw Jenna.

"Hello, stranger," Jenna said, looking up from her nail file. She stood and they embraced.

"It's good to see you," Lenora said. "Can

you tell Dawna I'm here for our meeting?"

Jenna nodded toward the hallway. "Go on in. She's expecting you. The door might be closed, since a man went in there about ten minutes ago. But she said to tell you to go right on in."

"Do you know who she's with?" Lenora asked.

Jenna shook her head. "He doesn't work here at the magazine. I've seen him here once or twice, but he always walks into her office without stopping at the desk. He's real cute, so I assumed they were a couple or something."

Lenora nodded and made her way to Dawna's office. This was odd, she thought. Dawna didn't mention anything about anyone else attending the meeting. And Dawna certainly wouldn't have a boyfriend sitting in on a business meeting. Her former boss was too professional for that.

Lenora paused at the door, knocked briefly, and opened it. She froze in the doorway, startled almost senseless by the scene. Dawna sat at her desk, and Raymond Shearer sat opposite her.

"Well, don't just stand there, honey," Dawna said, her tone full of daggers. "Come in and sit down."

Lenora stumbled inside as Ray stood up

from his chair and strolled to the window behind Dawna's desk. He didn't speak to Lenora. He just shoved his hands into his pockets and stood with his back to the room. Although Ray had looked genuinely surprised at seeing Lenora there, his actions revealed a sense of familiarity between Dawna and him that Lenora was unprepared for. The only one who did not look surprised about the strange gathering was Dawna.

Lenora shook her head with confusion. "What's going on, Dawna? I thought we were meeting about an assignment." And what was Ray doing there? And why was he ignoring her?

Dawna gave Lenora a phony smile. "Ray and I got to talking, and I had no idea it was already time for our meeting. Funny how time flies when you're *engaged.*"

Engaged. Dawna lingered on the word and Lenora suddenly remembered the ring on her finger, the one she was always so careful to remove before meeting with Ray. Lenora quickly hid her hands behind her back.

"And you two know each other, obviously," Dawna said.

"Hello, Lenora," Ray said, finally looking directly at her.

Lenora smiled awkwardly and struggled to remove the ring hidden behind her back. "Hello, Ray."

"A few days ago I told Ray that I heard you got engaged," Dawna said. "He's having a hard time believing that."

Lenora stopped trying to remove the ring or hide her hand. Suddenly the weirdness in this whole scenario seemed to have been turned up a notch.

"When's the date?" Dawna asked Lenora.

Lenora hesitated. Dammit! Why was Dawna so fixated on making sure Ray knew about her marriage plans? What the hell was Dawna up to? "June," Lenora said softly. There was no point hiding the date now.

"See, Ray, I told you they would probably be married by next summer," Dawna said. "Lenora has been trying to get Gerald to marry her for years. Have you picked out a dress yet, Lenora?"

"There's really no contract work for me, is there?" Lenora asked, ignoring Dawna's question.

A slow, cocky smile spread across Dawna's face. "You catch on fast."

"So why go to all the trouble to get me here using a lie?" Lenora asked. She looked at Ray. "And are you in on it?"

"I had nothing to do with this," Ray said.

"I had no clue you would be here when Dawna invited me for lunch, just as I had no clue you were engaged to be married. As to why Dawna did this, I'm not sure. I have my suspicions."

"I had to prove to you that she was engaged," Dawna said. She turned to Lenora. "I kept telling him, but he wouldn't believe me. He said you didn't wear a ring and that you would have told him if you were engaged."

"I thought we were being up front about our involvement with other people," Ray said to Lenora. "Especially about anything serious. Seems I was wrong."

Lenora swallowed hard. "Are you two seeing each other?"

"Almost since we met when Ray was working at the Moss Building," Dawna said.

That was even before she got involved with him, Lenora realized. Lenora looked at Ray. "Then you haven't exactly been honest with me."

"I always told you I was seeing others casually," he said.

"Yes, but seeing others and seeing my former boss are two different things."

Ray shrugged. "That's your opinion."

"Ray, I wish you wouldn't keep calling our relationship casual," Dawna interjected.

"You've practically moved in with me these past few weeks."

"That's an exaggeration," Ray said. "I have a few things there."

Dawna smiled. "So far."

Lenora's eyes widened as she listened to the two of them. Why was she standing there arguing about who said what or who lied and who told the truth? The whole thing was bizarre. She was seeing Ray. Dawna was seeing a lot more of Ray. He was seeing them both. Dawna wanted him to herself and she set Lenora up, plain and simple. She had been caught ring-handed, and Ray didn't like it. Lenora backed out of the office and fled down the hallway without even pausing to say good-bye to Jenna. Dawna had lured Lenora into a trap and played her masterfully. Lenora could never hope to compete with her cunning former boss. Dawna already had her beaten in just about every category imaginable — looks, success, smarts. And now Dawna had Ray all to herself.

CHAPTER 39

Lenora had an appointment at three-thirty that Friday afternoon with a wedding planner and a future bride to discuss Lenora doing the photography for the wedding. But after leaving Ray and Dawna, Lenora was too upset to see any potential clients. Wedding photography was not something she enjoyed much anyway. It didn't pay the kind of money she needed to keep her studio afloat. She had agreed to meet with the client only because she was hungry for work, any kind of work. So she sat at her desk and called to postpone the meeting to Monday.

After she hung up, she shook her head at the thought of what had transpired at Dawna's office. Ray and Dawna. Unbelievable. Now that Lenora had gotten past the initial shock, she was racked with jealousy and mostly embarrassment. Jealousy, she was familiar with. She had experienced it often enough before, especially when she learned that Gerald was cheating on her. But that was nothing compared to being made to look like a fool by the other woman, especially when the other woman was Dawna.

Ray had always implied that other women were in the picture casually. There were never signs of other women, and when they were together he turned off his cell phone and focused on her. That was one of the reasons she loved being with him. But she never imagined that she was the only woman he was seeing. No, the problem was that the other woman was Dawna and the nasty trick her former boss had just played on her.

And how could Ray do this to her? He knew how she felt about Dawna. A part of her was furious with him. Still, she wasn't ready to give him up without a fight. Maybe he would understand if she explained to him that she hid the truth about her engagement because she was afraid to lose him. She picked up the desk phone and dialed his number. There was no answer, so she left a message then rested her head on her desk.

The outlandish episode in Dawna's office was such a blur that Lenora could barely remember who said what. But someone mentioned that Ray and Dawna were going to lunch together. Maybe Ray would call after lunch with Dawna. Unless they did more than lunch. Lenora wondered if he had ever taken Dawna to his truck for sex. For all she knew, they might be parked somewhere that very moment, making passionate love to each other.

She couldn't stand it. The truck was *their* special place. Hers and Ray's. She jumped up and paced the floor between the window and her desk, trying to shake the thoughts of Ray and Dawna together. She wondered if Ray had real feelings for Dawna. After all, Dawna was gorgeous, with the kind of good looks that made men salivate. And she could ooze charm when she wanted. Ray might even be in love with Dawna.

Lenora grabbed the phone and dialed Ray's number frantically. The answering service came on again, and she slammed the phone down and flopped into the chair. Why was she being such an ignorant fool? Did she really expect her fat, frumpy ass to be able to hold on to a man like Ray? Of course not. That she had even partly held his attention for a couple of months was amazing.

The phone rang. She snatched it up.

"Hello?"

"You called?" Ray asked coolly.

Lenora gasped. "Um, yes. I . . . I was hoping we could talk about what happened earlier today."

"There's nothing to talk about, Lenora. I don't deal with women who are married or engaged. It can get too messy."

She swallowed hard. "For what it's worth, Ray, I'm really sorry I didn't tell you sooner. I planned to, but —"

"Save it," he said, interrupting. "I probably had no right to expect honesty, given the nature of our relationship."

"Can you ever forgive me?" she asked. Never mind that he was screwing her former boss and didn't bother to mention it. This wasn't the time to bring that up.

"There's nothing to forgive. It's done, it's over. Let's both move on."

"Together, I hope. Please, Ray? I promise to be one hundred percent honest from now on."

"It's best we do it separately."

Lenora's heart sank to the floor. "Are things serious with you and Dawna?"

"Not really."

"Why didn't you tell me about her?"

"There was no need to. We're not serious despite what she implied and what she might want."

"But she's my former boss," Lenora protested. "I told you how I feel about her."

"So? You have a problem with your old boss — you and a zillion others. What did that have to do with us?"

"I can't believe you take that so casually," Lenora said. "And she knew about you and me obviously. Did you tell her?"

"No. You called recently while I was with her. I had put the phone down, and she saw your name on caller ID before I could get to it. That's when she told me you were engaged. She knows I don't deal with women who are in serious relationships with other men. I didn't believe her, though, because I know how determined she can be when she wants something. I thought she was just saying that to get me to stop seeing you."

"And that's what led to the meeting in her office today?"

"Unfortunately, yes," he said. "I'm sorry it all came down that way, but Dawna tricked me into showing up at her office, too. I had no idea you would be there." He chuckled. "That's Dawna for you, though."

Lenora couldn't miss the admiring tone in his voice. He obviously liked Dawna. He had even moved some of his things to her place. So the better woman had won the prize. Or at least the most conniving one. But Lenora still couldn't bring herself to give up on Ray just yet. "I really would like to see you one more time."

"Sorry, I can't."

"You're still out with Dawna? Is that it?"

"Actually, no. I'm on my way to the dealer to take my truck in for service."

"How are you getting home or back to work?" she asked.

"Probably a cab. Dawna was going to follow me and take me back to the job site, but I was so disappointed with what she just pulled, I told her I'd find another way back."

Perhaps Dawna went too far with her scheming this time. "Let me take you back," she offered.

"I'll manage."

"It's not a problem, Ray. I'd love to help out."

He paused for a second. "Okay, it is a long cab ride. Meet me there in about an hour."

Yes! Lenora thought, pumping her fist in the air.

Lenora parked her car and walked into the Ford dealership. She found Ray checking out the new Ford F150 pickups, circling a shiny black one, arms folded across his chest, as a dealer spoke to him. She was so excited to see him. For a while she thought she might never lay eyes on him again. He squeezed her shoulders and introduced her to Tony, the car dealer.

"So is this the fiancée?" Tony asked upon seeing the ring on Lenora's hand. Lenora quickly slipped her hands behind her back.

"No," Ray said. "She's a friend."

The dealer nodded, obviously deciding to zip it up.

"Nice truck," Lenora said.

"Yes, very," Ray said. "Top of the line."

Lenora walked around to the sticker on the window. "Not a bad price," she said.

Ray chuckled. "Not if you can afford it."

Lenora nodded as Ray reached out to shake Tony's hand good-bye. Then they walked toward the parking lot.

"What's wrong with your truck?" she asked.

"I suspect it's the transmission. Probably going to be here a couple of days and set me back a few thousand."

"How many miles does it have on it?" she asked.

"Close to a hundred and fifty thousand."

Lenora stopped and faced him. "Why don't you let me buy you a new one?" She wasn't sure where that suddenly came from. But he needed a new truck. She had the money to buy him one. It would eat seriously into what money she had left, but she would worry about that later. Right now she was all about trying to save her relationship with Ray.

"I can't let you do that," he said.

"Yes, you can. I can afford it." She pushed her dwindling bank account figures to the back of her head.

"Are you serious?" he asked.

"Dead serious," she said. "We can sign the paperwork right now."

He paused and exhaled. "I could always use a new truck for work."

"Then stop fighting me and let me help you. I'll barely miss the money."

"If that's the case, let's do it."

They turned around and searched for Tony.

CHAPTER 40

They left the dealership and he agreed to follow her to the studio in his new truck so they could talk about what had happened earlier that afternoon in Dawna's office. Or at least that was the plan. Lenora was fairly certain it would evolve into more than that. And that was fine with her. She was bursting with eagerness to feel his body next to hers. It had been too long since.

She spent a few minutes giving him a tour of the studio and all the equipment. He was genuinely interested, especially in the extensive lighting system, but once in her office he did what he had done the first time they had sex at his office all those weeks ago. He swept aside everything on the desk except a few photographs sitting on the edge in frames.

She kicked her sandals off, and he watched as she shook her hips and slowly removed her panties. She loved the hungry look on his face as she hiked her skirt farther up and leaned back on the desk. He climbed on top of her and she nibbled on his lips with her tongue, ran her fingers through his hair and down his back, then slipped them up under his white T-shirt. Her fingers roamed down to his tight buttocks and squeezed as he pressed her hard against the desk. Right now, nothing else mattered except the man between her legs.

She closed her eyes tightly and moaned in his ear. "Harder," she said. "Yes, yes!" She yanked his T-shirt off and her fingers clawed his back. They squirmed across the desk until her head dangled over the edge. She could feel her eyes roll to the back of her head. It felt like she was floating in the clouds. She never wanted to come back down to earth.

But she did.

Her descent started with the unexpected sound of footsteps on the hard floor of the outer room. Lenora told herself that it was her imagination and ignored it. She didn't want to stop what she was doing with Ray. She couldn't. He made her feel so good.

Then she heard something she could no longer ignore.

Gerald was calling her name. Ray froze inside her, and Lenora forced her eyes open.

At first she thought the vision of her fiancé standing in the doorway to her office was just that: a vision, a horrible illusion, a nightmare. Her head was dangling over the edge of her desk, and Gerald appeared upside down. It had to be her imagination.

Then she felt Ray climb down off her. He turned his back and pulled up his jeans.

"Oh, God," she muttered and struggled to sit up. Was that really Gerald? She turned and looked as she pulled her skirt down over her hips. The doorway was empty now, but Ray looked like he had seen a spook. She rushed out the office door in her bare feet just in time to see Gerald exiting the large studio through the main entrance.

She brushed aside the nausea welling in her chest and ran in Gerald's direction. Then she remembered Ray in her office. Which way to turn? Ray or Gerald? Without further thought, she walked back into her office to see Ray pulling his T-shirt over his head.

"Ray, I'm sorry," she said as she ran up to him. "He never comes without calling first."

Ray held a hand up and stopped her in her tracks. "I gathered from the photo on your desk that that was your fiancé," he said coldly as he zipped his fly.

She nodded. She had promised to be honest. "Yes."

"Is he still here?"

"I don't know. I saw him walk out the front door."

Ray looked around anxiously. "Is there another exit besides that one?"

She nodded. "Near the back of the outer room. But you don't have to leave. We can talk about —"

"Oh, yes, I do," he said hastily. "It was a mistake to come here. This is exactly why I avoid intimacy with attached women. I don't need the drama."

"But, Ray . . ."

He held a hand up to quiet her. "I'll call you tomorrow so we can work something out about the truck. Right now, your fiancé needs looking after."

"He's probably left by now, and we —"

"There is no we," he said abruptly and strode quickly out of the office.

She watched him leave in silence. Ray was right, of course. She needed to talk to Gerald. She didn't want to admit it because she didn't want to leave Ray, knowing that she might never see him again. And it was likely over with Gerald anyway, after what he just saw. He might not even still be around the studio.

She was startled to find Gerald pacing

hotly up and down the walkway in front of the studio. He saw her exit the building and stormed toward her.

"Who was that?" he snapped.

She didn't say anything. She didn't really know how to answer the question. The name wouldn't mean anything to Gerald.

"Who the hell was it?" This time Gerald yelled so loudly it startled Lenora. She had never seen him so angry.

"A former client," she said.

"The one you were doing the brochure for?"

She nodded silently.

"Oh, man," Gerald said, slamming his fist into his palm. "You been fucking him behind my back all that time?"

"Gerald, please, we should go inside. Someone might hear us."

" 'Scuse me? So you're worried about strangers hearing us argue out here, but you don't give a shit about your fiancé walking in on you with another man."

"I'm not going to stand out here and argue with you," she said. "I'm going back inside. You're welcome to come."

"Is he there?" Gerald asked.

"He left."

She went back in and Gerald followed, hot on her heels. She headed toward her office, but when they reached the middle of the studio floor Gerald grabbed her by the shoulder and flipped her around.

"Does he know you're engaged?" he asked. "Never mind, you have a damn ring. He must know something. What an ass."

"Gerald, I'm sorry you had to walk in and see that. I never meant for things to get so out of hand. I couldn't help myself. Ray is so . . ."

Gerald reached up as if to slap her. She gasped and cringed, and he brought his hand back down. "Save it," he said. "Right now I can't stand the sound of your voice or the sight of your face."

She gritted her teeth.

"I came here to surprise you with good news," he said. "We landed a major client today. All our work finally paid off. But it doesn't matter now." He held his palm out. "Give me the ring."

"Gerald, I know what I did to you was wrong. But can we at least talk before you —"

"There's nothing to talk about," he snapped.

"That's not fair. I forgave you when you did this to me. Yet you won't even talk to me."

"Oh, so that's what this is?" he snarled.

"Payback?"

"No. But —"

"And when I did it, we were a few months into a new relationship. We weren't engaged. Give me the damn ring."

She quickly removed the diamond from her finger, and sadness welled up inside her chest. She placed the ring in Gerald's outstretched palm. "I'm so sorry," she said, fighting back tears.

He ignored her apology and quickly turned and left. That was when it hit her that Gerald, the love of her life for the past three years, had walked away for good. She sank down to the floor. Her shoulders shook violently with her sobs. What had she done? Not long ago she was on top of the world. She had won lots of money in the lottery. She had bought her dream house and opened her own photography studio. She had two men wanting her, one smart and dependable, the other young, sexy, vibrant.

Now she had nothing.

CHAPTER 41

Lenora focused on the reporter sitting at the table in the kitchen of her huge yet nearly empty house and took a sip of black coffee. She had long since stopped buying the flavored liquid Coffee-Mate creamers with names like Italian Sweet Crème, Chocolate Raspberry, and Cinnamon Bun. She had even stopped purchasing sugar when she ran out a couple of weeks ago. Sweetness cost money. And she was nearly broke.

"So after your fiancé walked in on you and Ray at the studio, he called off the engagement?" Donna asked as she glanced up from her notes.

Lenora nodded and frowned at the memory of that fateful day. Of Gerald catching her having sex on the desk with Ray. Of Ray walking out and never speaking to her again. And Dawna and her trickery. Lenora's body flooded with waves of anger whenever she thought about that woman. "I saw Gerald once after that, when he came to the house to get a few things he kept here."

"How long ago was that?" Donna asked.

"It's been several months now."

"So it's officially over with him?"

Lenora nodded. "He wants nothing to do with me."

"What about Ray? Have you spoken to him at all since that day?"

Lenora shook her head silently.

"I see," Donna said. "And the truck? Did he keep it or what?"

"I tried to reach him for weeks after he left the studio. I called. I went by his office. But he never got back to me."

"So you ended up paying for the truck, yet he kept it?" Donna asked.

Lenora sighed with defeat. "When I lost the studio and then was struggling to keep up the house payments, I owed so much that the money I spent on the truck didn't seem important in comparison. I was too depressed to think logically."

"Do you feel he used you?"

Lenora's lips tightened. "Of course, but I asked for it in a way. I acted like a fool over him. I thought Ray was the hottest man to come along in my lifetime, and I could not believe he was interested in *me*. I didn't care why. I saw a chance to have the kind of man who would normally never pay me any attention, so I grabbed it."

"Do you think Ray was ever really interested in you?"

"I think he liked my company. I think he was somewhat attracted to me, but it was mainly the money that got his attention. I'm not stupid, but I wanted the fantasy so badly. I had all this money and thought that meant I could have or buy whatever I wanted. I got greedy and ended up with nothing."

Donna nodded with understanding. Or was it more like pity? Lenora couldn't be sure.

"What do you miss most?" Donna asked. "Or who? Gerald? Ray? The money? The studio?"

"Interesting question." Lenora paused and thought. "The gut response would be Gerald, but I won't even say that. It would never have worked out. All that cheating back and forth by both of us. I was so quick to cheat with Ray because my relationship with Gerald wasn't really right. I need to find a man I wouldn't risk losing for any other man who comes along."

Lenora paused for a moment. "You know

who I really miss," Lenora said finally. "Monica. And Alise somewhat, too. I still talk to Monica now and then, but I poisoned that relationship, probably for good. We're nowhere near as close as we once were. And with Alise, that was all a silly misunderstanding that could probably have been cleared up easily if I had tried. I threw away two good friendships because I became greedy and selfish, and that's painful to think about." She chuckled regretfully.

The reporter nodded and scribbled furiously. "So what's next for Lenora Stone?"

Lenora exhaled deeply. "I honestly have no idea. Taking it one day at a time."

"Would you move back in with your folks?"

Lenora shook her head. "I haven't even told my family half of what happened after I won the money. They don't know I lost the studio and that I'm about to lose the house. I didn't want to burden them." She shrugged. "Maybe I'll take the few thousand dollars I have left and start fresh somewhere else."

"One last question," Donna said. "Would you mind if I interviewed Ray or Gerald for this piece?"

Lenora shook her head. "Not at all. If you can reach them." Lenora gave Donna the last phone numbers she had on record for them, and Donna stood, wished Lenora good luck and thanked her. They made arrangements to meet at Legal Seafood in a couple of hours, and Lenora turned back to her empty house. It felt like a ghost town.

The interview with the reporter had been good for her. She felt better than she had before Donna arrived, when she was foolishly thinking of ending her life. The talk had forced her to think realistically about what had happened over the past several months. The reality was that remembering had not been nearly as tough as what she actually lived through.

She sat at the kitchen table and signaled for Paws to hop into her lap. Lenora ran her hands over the pooch's fur and made plans in her head. It might be nice to start fresh someplace where no one knew her. She could get a simple job like working in a boutique or bookstore. It might do her good to try something that wouldn't take much thought or effort, at least until she got her head together.

She was still sitting and thinking an hour later when the phone on the built-in kitchen desk rang and startled her. She lost the service to her cell phone several days earlier, and the landline rarely rang because few people outside her family had the number. She placed Paws on the floor and walked to the desk. She was so surprised to see the name on the caller ID that she gasped aloud. Raymond Shearer. She shook her head. Why was he calling now? After all these weeks? Should she even bother to answer?

Curiosity got the best of her. "Hello, Ray."

"Lenora? Good to hear your voice. How you been?"

He acted like all was well between them, like nothing had transpired except a little time. "Still breathing," she said curtly.

"I can tell by your tone that you're probably a little upset with me."

"A little?" she said sarcastically.

"I apologize for not getting in touch with you sooner. But I was stunned when your fiancé walked in on us at your studio. That scared the crap out of me."

"We were both shocked, Ray. How'd you get this number?"

"From a reporter doing a feature on you. Donna Blackburn. We just hung up."

Lenora nodded with understanding. "I see."

"So from what she said, you never got married, right? Are you with anyone else now?"

"No to both."

"Sorry to hear that."

"Don't be," she said. "It's probably for the best. You still with Dawna?"

"No, Dawna actually left the magazine a few weeks ago. Moved to Atlanta."

"Sorry to hear that," Lenora said drily.

Ray chuckled at her obvious sarcasm.

"I tried several times to reach you about the truck," she said. "You never returned any of my calls."

"I thought we needed time to cool off. And I honestly didn't have the money to pay you for the truck. Still don't, although I might be able to find a few grand to give you toward it."

"From where? Another woman?"

"What's it to you as long as I pay you?"

What a user this man is, Lenora thought. Why couldn't he buy his own truck? "Never mind," she said. A few thousand wouldn't help her much at this point.

"I know this call is unexpected, but I think about you a lot," Ray said.

Lenora rolled her eyes to the ceiling and let him talk.

"I really would like to see you again," he continued. "I never even got to see your new place, remember?"

That was when Lenora realized that Ray

likely still had no idea she had lost just about everything. Apparently Donna didn't fill him in. "What did Donna tell you?" Lenora asked.

"Said she had just interviewed you at your house for a feature she's writing about people who won big in the Maryland Lottery. Asked what I've been up to since we stopped seeing each other."

"That's it?"

"Pretty much," he said. "It was a short interview. Ten minutes maybe. She also said your house was huge. Beautiful."

"Uh-huh. Tell me, Ray, is this a booty call? Or a leech call?"

"A what?" he asked, sounding genuinely puzzled. "Booty call I know, but what do you mean, 'leech call'?"

"You know what a leech is, don't you? They suck you dry and then move on."

"Wait a minute now," he said. "You were into the sex as much as I was if not more. I told you I might be seeing others. And you volunteered to buy the truck."

"Yes, you're right on all counts. But you could have told me that one of the others you were screwing was my former boss."

"What difference does that make?" he asked.

"It makes a lot of difference, Ray," she said.

"Is that the problem? Or is it that you got emotionally involved?"

Lenora paused. How right he was about that. She made the dangerous mistake of falling for Ray. But his neglecting to tell her that he was sleeping with her former boss was still unethical in Lenora's eyes. Even cheating, in a way.

"You're right," she said, "I got emotionally involved. And if you knew or suspected that and didn't reciprocate, you should never have let me buy the truck for you. Then you disappeared. But forget it. It doesn't matter anymore. I'm past that."

"I'm happy to hear that you're past it. It's been a long time since all that went down. Maybe you think I'm crazy for suggesting we meet again, but you have to admit that we had some good times together. Right?"

Lenora suspected that he was not used to being turned down, especially by someone like her — frumpy, insecure, hard up. But that was the old Lenora. The new one decided to have a little fun with him.

"I have other plans, Ray. Tomorrow I'm flying off to the Caribbean for a month. And since I recently lost thirty pounds, tonight I'm shopping for a couple of new bikinis.

I'm just too busy to see you. Maybe you can drive down to Atlanta and hook up with Dawna. Nice talking to you."

She hung up before he could respond. That was a string of lies, but it felt damn good telling them. She might not be headed for the Caribbean, but right after dinner with Donna tonight she was going to head to the library and do some research on small towns in the South where the living was cheap and easy.

She had no man and no money. But she had something far more precious. She had her new self — a little older, a little thinner, and a whole lot wiser.

READING GROUP GUIDE

1. If you could have only one, which would you prefer: the love of a good man or five million dollars?
2. If you won a million dollars or more, whom would you tell and why? Whom would you not tell?
3. We've all heard the saying "Money changes people." Do you think it would change you? If so, how?
4. And what about the people in your life? Do you think coming into money would change how others, such as your family, girlfriends, or boyfriend would relate to you?
5. What would you do with the money if you won a million dollars or more?
6. Do you think Lenora acted foolishly when she won and if so, why? What would you have done differently?
7. Do you think Lenora blew a good opportunity with her boyfriend Gerald? Why

or why not?

8. What do you think happened between Lenora and Alise?

9. Did you suspect that something was up between Raymond and Dawna? If so, why?

10. What do you think Lenora learned about herself, if anything? Has there ever been a moment in your own life where you or someone close to you learned a similar lesson?

The employees of Thorndike Press hope you have enjoyed this Large Print book. All our Thorndike, Wheeler, and Kennebec Large Print titles are designed for easy reading, and all our books are made to last. Other Thorndike Press Large Print books are available at your library, through selected bookstores, or directly from us.

For information about titles, please call:
  (800) 223-1244

or visit our Web site at:
  http://gale.cengage.com/thorndike

To share your comments, please write:
  Publisher
  Thorndike Press
  10 Water St., Suite 310
  Waterville, ME 04901